AMII LORIN'S ALL-TIME CLASSIC LOVE STORY— BACK IN PRINT AT LAST!

"Amii Lorin always gives her readers something special!"
—*Romantic Times*

COME HOME TO LOVE
Amii Lorin
Author Of Five Million Books In Print!
Winner Of Two *Romantic Times* Reviewers' Choice Awards!

Ruthless, cold, and calculating—those were the words Katherine Acker used to describe wealthy entrepreneur Matthew Martin. So the young widow was stunned when Matt offered to marry her if she would act as a hostess to his business associates. Little did Katherine realize that her new husband had more surprises in store for her—and one of them might be that he loved her....

OUTRAGEOUS PROPOSAL

Matt lifted his head arrogantly, his hard eyes on Katherine. "I'm forty-one years old, I work hard, and I have no time to entertain a woman. In effect, what I require is a woman who will run my home smoothly, be a gracious hostess, a comfortable traveling companion, and of course, share my bed."

Katherine's eyes widened with surprise. "What you're saying is that you want to employ a wife."

A sharp edge entered his voice. "Not at all. What I'm offering you is the legality of marriage with all that entails: a home, security, and anything you want, within reason, for the rest of your life."

"Matt, I don't think—"

"You may take as much or as little time as you like, but at least think it over tonight."

AMII LORIN

COME HOME TO LOVE

LEISURE BOOKS ⬥ NEW YORK CITY

A LEISURE BOOK®

July 1995

Published by

Dorchester Publishing Co., Inc.
276 Fifth Avenue
New York, NY 10001

Printed in the United States of America.

The book is dedicated to:
Marv, Lori and Amy; Sonny and Jan;
Mick and Bill; Bonnie and Norm;
and Marie—who always believed.

1

The wipers slapped hynotically in a vain attempt to clear the windshield of the water that washed diagonally across it. The big car occasionally swayed gently from the slashing wind that drove the rain before it. Long blunt fingers curled easily around the leather-covered steering wheel held firmly, confidently by deeply tanned, broad, strong hands.

The quiet inside the car was broken suddenly by the click of a lighter and the gloom momentarily illuminated as the flame touched the end of a cigarette—then, within seconds, another. The cigarette was placed into the long brown fingers by slim pale ones.

"Matt." Softly, barely a whisper, Katherine wasn't even aware she said it aloud.

"Hmmmm?" His eyes didn't leave the highway, which was barely discernible in the late afternoon cloud-burst.

She raised startled eyes to him as she snubbed out her cigarette, then smiled slighty as the realization hit her that she'd said his name out loud.

"Nothing." Softly, "Just Matt."

Matt glanced at her quickly, noting the soft curve of her lips and the look in her eyes. His hand went to a button on the dashboard and the window beside him slid silently down six inches. His cigarette arched through the opening and he gave a swift, sharp glance into the rear view mirror. Then the window slid back into place. Gently easing an expensively shod foot from the gas pedal he drove the car off the highway across the gravelly shoulders onto the wet spongy grass that bordered the gravel.

A line of trees stood sentinel a few feet back from the edge of the grass, their branches, hanging heavy and sodden, almost touching the ground, giving a tunnel effect. Matt brought the Lincoln to a stop inside this tunnel. The drooping branches formed a screen, not only from the force of the wind and rain, but also the light traffic on the highway.

Katherine watched him quietly, a tingle of excitement beginning to rise, as he switched off the ignition and pulled the hand brake.

He nudged her shoulder with his and said softly, "Move over." She obeyed at once, sliding along the seat until she was almost touching the opposite door. Matt followed, and as soon as his large frame was free of the confining steering wheel, turned and pulled her into his arms.

She was ready for him, face lifted, lips slightly

parted. He lowered his head and covered her mouth with his own.

Her hands went to his shoulders and felt the muscles go taut at her touch and sighing softly she curled her arms around his neck, her body going soft against his hard one. His arms loosened; then his hands gripped her shoulders and turning her, his body pressed hers back against the seat. It was like being engulfed, the sheer size of him overwhelming. Oh Lord, Katherine thought, I want him. And then realized with surprise that she had wanted him, almost continually, for the last forty-eight hours.

His kiss was long, deep and she gave herself completely to it. She forgot where she was, everything. All she wanted to know was this man's arms, his mouth, his hands, one of which now moved slowly from her shoulders to cup and caress her face.

Moaning softly, she arched her back, pressing her body against his as he pulled his mouth from hers. "Damn." He shifted uncomfortably, trying to draw her closer to him and muttered, "I'm too big and too old to make love to my woman in a car, no matter how roomy it is." Then, his lips close to her ear, he whispered, "You're something of a witch, Kate, you know that?"

There was laughter in her reply. "Of course, I've put the Hex on you and you're completely in my power."

"Lo, these many moons," was his strange answer, and she drew back her head to look at him questioningly. But he shook his head, and changing the subject said, "We're never going to reach home at this rate." Disentangling himself he slid back under the wheel and added, "Now stay on your side of the seat and behave yourself."

"Behave myself!" Katherine cried. "I didn't do anything but say your name."

"Well, don't say it anymore, and don't look at me like that either, unless you want to find yourself in the first motel room we happen to come to."

"Yes sir," she replied demurely.

Flashing her a quick grin, Matt drove the car back onto the highway.

Katherine settled back into the soft leather seat. Head resting against the back, she studied Matt through partially closed lids.

He certainly did fill the space behind the steering wheel. There was only one word to describe him, she thought, big, all six feet, five and a half inches of him, from his broad powerful shoulders and back to his long muscular arms and legs. And she knew there was not one ounce of excess flesh on the whole of his frame. His well-shaped head supported a full, thick growth of unruly dark auburn waves, that no amount of brushing could tame. His face was robbed of being handsome by the almost harshly defined features. The straight nose, high cheek bones and firm thrusting jawline were covered with still firm, taut skin, deeply tanned from last summer's sun. Full dark brows arched slightly over the most riveting blue-gray eyes Katherine had ever seen.

Forty-three years had gone into the making of

Matthew Martin. Forty-three years of working, fighting, sweating his way to the top. And he'd made it with a vengeance, by being smarter, faster and gutsier than most. He was hated by some, loved by some, and feared by almost everyone, Katherine included. "Knock it off." The deep rough voice had the sting removed by its soft tone.

Katherine smiled and shifted her gaze to the windshield, watching, as if mesmerized, the wipers fight their valiant battle against the rain.

In a daze or kind of dream, Katherine watched as a picture swirled, then took form, of him twenty-five years before.

Tall, slim to the point of skinny, all gangly arms and legs which never seemed to fit his clothes because of the speed of his growth. Big hands and feet forever sticking out incongruously. Auburn hair a little long, a little shaggy in the current vogue. Hardly the imposing figure of today.

Eyes closed now, Matt thought her asleep, as in her mind Katherine slipped back through the years to when she was a sophomore and he a senior in that Lancaster high school.

It was late winter and she was sitting in the stands at a basketball game. Matt was, without question, the star player of the team. For although he looked awkward and disjointed, when he played he was all smooth, swift, deliberate movement. Katherine had watched him play and had never seen him, for she had eyes for only one.

Time moved forward and she was at a baseball field. Matt was on the mound, arms raised high above his head as his long leg shot out in that

strange wind-up of his, and then the ball went
rifling through the air, across the plate, and the
umpire's voice rang. "Out." Katherine had
cheered and screamed along with everyone else,
but she hadn't seen him, for she had eyes for only
one.

Every high school in the States has at least one
young man, usually a senior, who is the ideal all-
American boy. Kevin Acker was theirs. Kevin
Acker belonged to Katherine. She had eyes only
for him.

Kevin was the All-American boy. Tall, with a
body like the Greek statue that adorned the high
school foyer, short, fair, curly hair and a face
handsome to the point of beautiful. Along with his
high scholastic record he was a fine athlete,
charming and well liked. The heartthrob of every
girl in the school.

Katherine had been fifteen the previous fall, her
first year of high school, and Kevin had tried to
date her within the first week of school's opening.
When she told him she was not allowed to date
until her sixteenth birthday, which would occur
the following spring, Kevin bided his time making
do with phone calls and quick conversations after
school before she had to board the bus for home.

Near the end of that winter he had been allowed
to come to her home to meet her parents and
younger twin brothers, David and Daniel. Her
parents liked him for he was pleasant and well
mannered, and Dave and Dan developed a very bad
case of hero worship.

Katherine had moved through the following

weeks with growing impatience, thinking that May twenty-first would never come. Her sixteenth birthday! Finally it came and Kevin came with it, handing her a bulging birthday card. Her fingers shook as she opened the envelope to find inside a slim square box which held a fine gold neck chain. Lifting her head, her eyes puzzled, she saw Kevin slide his class-ring from his finger; then taking the chain from her fingers he slipped the ring onto it, held it up and said softly: "Will you be my girl, Katherine?" Stunned, unable to answer, she had nodded her head and stood perfectly still while he fastened the chain around her neck. Then he lowered his head and kissed her softly on the lips. Lifting his mouth a mere half inch from hers he then whispered, "And you'll come with me to the prom." It was not a question, but a statement and Katherine had breathed, "Yes! Oh yes."

The next day as she was walking from the school, talking excitedly about the upcoming prom with a group of girlfriends, she heard her name called and turned, eyes widening, to see Matthew Martin loping up to her.

Her friends had kept walking but stopped to wait for her a few feet away, then she heard them grow quiet when they saw who had called to her. And she wondered why.

He came to an abrupt stop in front of her and said in a rush, "Katherine, would you be my date for the prom?" She had been too surprised to answer for a second, he had never seemed to notice her before. Then she'd replied, "I'm sorry, Matthew, but I'm going to the prom with Kevin

Acker." His face had gone oddly still before he startled her even more by saying, "Well, then, may I call you for a date sometime?" And she stammered, "I, no, I'm going steady with Kevin." She felt a flash of irritation at the giggles behind her as the color mounted up his throat and across his cheeks. But he seemed not to even notice her friends. "I see." He started to turn away.

Impulsively, she reached out her hand and touched his arm and as he turned his head to look at her, something, what? had flickered across his face. For the first time she noticed his startling eyes, shuttered now, lids partially lowered as they stared directly into hers. Her voice was a bare whisper. "Thank you for asking me anyway, Matthew."

"Yeah, sure," was his brusque reply as he turned sharply and strode toward his friend waiting a few yards away.

Bemused, wondering at the achey tightness in her throat, she watched him a moment, then shrugging lightly turned to her friends.

"I don't think I've ever heard of him asking a girl for a date." This from Maryann Kline, Katherine's best friend. Cute, petite, Brenda Dodge chimed in, "I've never even heard of him telephoning a girl."

"He doesn't have the time for girls so I've been told!" The amused, throaty voice came from the girl standing next to Katherine and all eyes turned to her. Marsha Drake was the only senior in the group. Of average height, she had a full, rich, woman's body, and a sophistication far beyond her years. "Who told you that?" piped Brenda, seeming to squirm all over with eagerness. "You know I've been dating Mark Hunter," Marsha answered dryly, "he told me."

As if pulled by a single cord all heads swivelled around to the retreating backs of Matthew Martin and his friend Mark Hunter.

"An odd pair," observed Maryann, "Mark barely reaches Matthew's shoulders."

"Big deal," snorted Brenda. "Hardly anyone stands up past Matthew's shoulders. But you're right about them being an odd pair. Who would have thought Mark and Matthew would become friends?"

The girls joined the crush of other students boarding the buses and Katherine found herself sharing a seat with Marsha. A frown creased her smooth white brow, as she turned to the other girl. "I don't understand. Why is it odd that Mark and Matthew should be friends?"

The youngest one of the group and only a sophomore, Katherine had been too involved with her school work and thoughts of Kevin all year to learn much of the senior class.

Marsha regarded her with gentle amusement. Yes, she could see what had attracted Kevin, Matthew too, for that matter. They were both bright boys who saw beneath the surface of things and people.

Right now, at sixteen, thin, and a few inches taller than the rest of their group, Katherine could only be described as young-girl-pretty. Short black hair with an abundance of soft loose curls framed her delicately-boned face. Natural filling out

would save a short straight nose and chin from
being pointed. Well-formed lips with the briefest
touch of fullness gave a hint of future passion. But
what caught the eye was her hair, and black wing
brows that arched over deep violet-blue eyes,
fringed with thick sooty lashes, startling against
her fair skin.

Marsha sighed softly. With a few years and
some maturity the description of Katherine would
be tall, willowy and striking. Yes, she could see
what had attracted both Matt and Kevin.

She voiced her thoughts aloud and watched,
smiling broadly, at the flash of pink that tinged
Katherine's face. Then, waving one hand languidly
she added, "Enough of that. Sit back, infant, and
I'll answer your question. First off, Mark and Matt
do have a few things in common. They are both
intelligent, and I mean really intelligent. Mark
told me last night he'll finish fourth in the class,
Matt'll finish sixth. That's no mean trick in a
graduating class of several hundred. They share a
singleness of purpose. Mark will tell you he's going
to be a doctor. Not that he wants to be a doctor,
but he's *going* to be a doctor. Matt's going into
business." At the slight rise of Katherine's
eyebrows, Marsha shrugged, "I don't know what
kind of business. I don't know if Matt knows. But
you can believe that when he decides there will be
no stopping him."

Marsha paused for breath then added, "They're
both quiet. Too damn quiet sometimes, I think,
and both serious. There the likeness ends."

She lifted an eyebrow at Katherine and asked,

"Did you know Mark's parents are well off?" At Katherine's quick headshake she went on. "Well, they are. In fact they're loaded. And don't look at me that way. Although I have nothing against money, that's not the reason I'm dating him. You must admit he's really good looking and to tell you the truth I'm completely crazy about the guy."

She smiled shyly at Katherine who had quickly agreed that Mark was indeed very good looking.

"As far as finances go Mark's got it made. With Matt it's a different story. Although his folks can't be called poor, there is definitely a struggle most times. You see, Matt's dad owns a small farm and although they have never been able to live high off the hog, they were making it. Then last year Matt's dad had a slight stroke and the burden of the work fell on Matt. He has a brother and sister, but Beth is only eight and Jim ten and too young to be much help. Last fall, his father had improved enough to do some of the chores but I guess by then money was pretty tight and Matt took a job as part-time hired hand on a big farm farther out in the country. It's been rough for him, but it'll probably get a lot rougher. Matt's determined to go to a liberal arts college in Reading and although he's taken a scholarship he is going to have to work like a slave to earn the money it will take to get his degree."

Marsha looked away from Katherine, then with a yelp jumped to her feet. "Good grief! I've been running off at the mouth and nearly missed my stop. I hope I've answered your questions."

"And then some," Katherine laughed. "Thank

you, Marsh, see you tomorrow.''

For a short time afterward Katherine hadn't been able to get the thought of Matthew out of her mind. Wondering at the mild sense of uneasiness it caused her. But she was young and in the bloom of first love with a summer in front of her that promised to be exciting. The incident faded quickly.

The reality of the summer bore out the promise, beginning with the prom and graduating exercises, where Katherine met Kevin's parents. Katherine was sure the Pennsylvania Dutch countryside had never looked more glorious with its rolling hills of patchwork planted crops that would have to be, come fall, one of the best harvests ever.

Katherine and Kevin joined a group of young couples for swim parties, Saturday night dances, afternoon picnics and evening barbeques, where they sat around an open fire, singing popular songs and telling jokes.

That summer had wings on its heels, and by the time the big orange balloon of the harvest moon rose regally in the heat-hazy black sky, Katherine's mind had lost the picture of a tall, too-thin gangly boy named Matthew.

2

The car swerved sharply, rousing Katherine. The past still clinging to the edges of her mind, she lifted her eye lids a fraction to look at Matt. No, there was very little about the man to remind one of the boy. On the surface at any rate. But underneath? Quiet and serious? Singleness of purpose? Determination? —In spades.

Matt was a rich man. A very rich man. But had his drive and ambition lessened with the accumulation of wealth? Not that Katherine could see. He put in longer hours than any other man she knew, and even when he was at home he spent most of his time in his study on the phone or doing paper work. Why? Katherine hadn't a clue. She knew really very little about Matthew Jonathon Martin. Her husband.

The car swerved again and Katherine came fully alert to her surroundings with a start. They were almost to the house. The realization started a

small twinge in her stomach. The house, how she
hated it. But it would be different now, wouldn't
it? It had to have made a difference, she thought
fiercely. Yet the unease swirled into a hard tight
ball and it seemed as if she could feel every muscle
and nerve end in her body begin to tense.

Stop imagining things, she told herself firmly,
but glancing again quickly at Matt, she felt her
throat close. His face had tautened, his lips
formed a straight grim line.

It wasn't her imagination. The relaxed easy
atmosphere of before seemed suddenly to hum
like high tension wires.

Katherine sat up straight, fingers going to her
hair to try and bring some order to the riot of
curls. Glancing around with dull, listless eyes, she
thought, it's beautiful, there's no denying that.
The smooth manicured lawns, the perfectly
clipped shrubs, the tenderly cared for flower beds
surrounded by lacy mimosa, the silvery green
olive and wine red maple trees all set off to
perfection the house they were stopping in front
of.

Colonial style, in warm red brick with white
trim shutters and a huge front door, the house was
not quite large enough to be called a mansion.
Even now, in the gray mist of a late September
afternoon, it stood out like a gem. A beautiful
prison, Katherine thought dejectedly.

"Did you have a nice nap?" Katherine felt her
spine stiffen at the tone of his voice, for even
though it was low, there was a forced casualness
to it. "Yes, thank you." Her own tone sounded

stilted and she winced at the swift, hard look he sent her before he got out of the car and moved to the trunk to get their suitcases.

Katherine moved slowly from the car and across the drive to precede Matt up the four wide steps to the door.

Opening the door she stepped onto the rich, highly glossed hardwood floor of the large entrance hall. Holding the door for Matt, she watched him as he set the cases to one side, then without a word to her, turned toward the hall closet. As he began shrugging out of the light-weight brown raincoat that covered his tan suede jacket, she turned to close the door.

Hand still on the knob, Katherine went taut as a lazy, insolent voice floated across the hall from the doorway to the living room. "Welcome home, Matt. I see you've found the wandering one."

Forcing herself to move slowly, Katherine turned just as Matt, not bothering to reply to his sister's remark, said sharply, "Jonathon?"

"Oh! He's fine. Arrived safe and sound. Still having his afternoon nap, as far as I know."

Beth's voice had changed subtly as she answered her brother. Never, never would insolence tinge her tone when she spoke to him directly.

Divorced from her husband five years ago, she had given up her apartment and moved in with Matt the following year when he had bought this house.

He had bought the house with the idea of persuading his parents, still living in the same small farmhouse, to live with him. They had gently, but firmly, refused. His brother James, still unmarried and working for Matt, had taken up the offer at once.

Beth had run the house and played the role of hostess for both her brothers, on the occasions they required one. She seemed to give way when Matt married Katherine, but both women knew who ruled the roost in this house. It wasn't Katherine.

At thirty-two, Elizabeth Tarrel had life just about the way she wanted it. A beautiful home as a background, an unlimited budget, and a brother who paid the bills, whom she thought she managed very nicely. She had not been about to give it up without a fight.

But the battle had never been joined. Katherine had realized very quickly, on first meeting Beth, that they could never be friends. If she were to assert her rights as Matt's wife it would cause discord, if not an open breach, between brother and sister. She felt she did not have the right to do this and so had abstained.

Beth gave lip service to Katherine as mistress of the house. But everyone knew, with the possible exception of Matt, who seemed forever too busy to notice such things, who actually ran the place.

Now, as Matt turned to finish hanging up his coat, Beth's eyes went over Katherine with disdain. "You're a little too old to be running away from home, aren't you?" Katherine was not fooled by the teasing note in Beth's voice, for her eyes were coldly contemptuous. "I thought one outgrew that sort of thing when one left adolescence.''

Katherine didn't bother to answer but found herself holding her breath, waiting for Matt to silence his sister. The seconds stretched long and as no word of reproof came she had to fight to keep her shoulders straight as a feeling of sick despair washed over her. Nothing had changed. Nothing.

Matt's voice, when it came, was cool, withdrawn. "Any calls of importance?"

"Are you kidding? The phone hasn't stopped ringing. There's a stack of messages on your desk and your secretary called not five minutes before you pulled up." Beth's voice had a triumphant ring that made Katherine feel nauseous. She studied her sister-in-law, wondering why Beth continually played this game of one-up-manship.

Tall, full figured, without being in the least bit heavy, with lovely features and glorious long hair the same deep auburn color as Matt's, Beth was a very attractive woman. She had everything a woman could possibly want, including several nice looking well-off men dancing attendance. So why did she dislike Katherine so? Katherine had asked herself that question a hundred times. The only answer that presented itself was that Beth still considered her a threat in some way to the position she herself held here.

Matt's voice cut across her thoughts. "I'll be in my study until dinner." Whom was he speaking to? Her? His sister? She shrugged slightly and walked quickly across the hall to the magnificent wide curving staircase that seemed to hang suspended in air.

"I'll check on Jonathon," she murmured, hurrying up the stairs. She had to get away from their eyes as she was visibly shaking now.

She didn't pause on the landing at the top of the stairs, but crossed it and went halfway down the hallway which ran the length of the house.

She stopped at the door taking several deep breaths to calm herself, then walked in, closing the door quietly behind her.

Mary Ranzanna looked up from the book she was reading, smiled and said "Hi." A gleam of mischief in her eyes, she added, "Have a nice—rest?"

Katherine felt her cheeks grow warm and Mary laughed softly. "That's one of the things I've always admired about people with fair skin. They never seem to outgrow the blush. I think it's lovely."

Katherine smiled, relaxing a little, and for the thousandth time thanked heaven for Mary. How could she possibly manage without her?

Mary was a practical nurse and had been on duty in maternity when Jonathon was born. Katherine had brought her home with her. Hired officially as Jonathon's nurse, she was also close friend and confidante to Katherine.

Small with a rounded, ample figure, Latin dark hair and skin, and flashing black eyes, she was a bundle of Italian energy. Her friendship and calm counsel helped keep Katherine on an even keel.

"You come to see the boss?" Mary's throaty

voice was warmly compassionate.

Katherine nodded as she walked across the soft carpeting of the small sitting-cum-play room to the door on her left leading to an adjoining room. The door was slightly ajar, so Mary could hear any stirrings, and Katherine pushed it open carefully, then moved to stand beside the crib in the center of the room. She stood gazing down with adoring eyes at the small form sprawled in sleep.

Her son. Matt's son. Obviously Matt's son, for he was a small replica of his father. Mary had laughingly told Matt it was as if he had fed his likeness into one of the copying machines in his office and it had produced an exact copy. Matt had only grunted in reply but Katherine had known the remark had pleased him, as it would any father with his first born.

He's so beautiful, Katherine thought and felt the back of her eyes grow gritty and hot. He'd grown so fast and fleshed out so perfectly, with his skin pink and glowing healthy, that it was hard to believe it was just six months since she had delivered him prematurely, so tiny and scrawny looking. Even then he'd been the image of Matt. She repressed the urge to reach out her hand and smooth the fine auburn hair, and turning quickly went back into the other room.

It was a pleasant room, the walls painted a creamy color, the one fair-sized window hung with dull gold draperies that exactly matched the color of the carpet. In one corner sat a small table and chairs with a mound of toys around it that Jonathon would not be ready for for years. In

another was a large book case which held not only
the latest but also quite a few of the older novels.
Along one wall was a worktable with a sewing
machine on it. Mary had a passion for sewing and
made all her own clothes. Flanking the window
were two comfortable easy chairs between which
stood a table at armrest height. The table held a
lamp, a few of Mary's knickknacks and pictures of
her two grown sons. This room had given comfort
and warmth to Katherine on many of the nights
Matt was not at home—which meant Mary saw
Katherine most evenings, for Matt was seldom
home early, if at all.

Mary waved her hand at the chair opposite to
her own as Katherine reentered the room and,
slipping out of her russet suede jacket, dropped
into it. "You look like you've been through a small
skirmish, so I'll hazard a guess. You met the
general in the front hall, right?" Katherine gave a
small smile and nodded.

Mary's voice took on a slight edge of impatience.
"Why the hell you take it from that bitch I'll
never understand. You're no shy, retiring miss,
Kate, and I know you're certainly not afraid of
her. Why don't you put her in her place?"

Katherine smiled wryly thinking, Mary is the
only one who calls me Kate, and then checked
herself. Matt had called her Kate the last two days.
Her breath seemed to catch in her throat in the
same way it had the first time he'd said it. Her
smile gone now she said, "You know why, Mary."

"Bull!" came the inelegant reply.

Not wanting to jump onto the merry-go-round

with Mary again, Katherine shrugged and said, "I really shouldn't be here, I have to change for dinner. You are joining us?"

"Of course," Mary answered airily, sweeping a hand down the front of her long silky skirt. "As you see, I'm dressed for same."

The remark hit the target it as aimed at. It brought a genuine smile to Katherine's lips. When Katherine was in the house Mary took all her meals downstairs with the family, at Matt's insistence from the first day she'd come to the house. But if Katherine was out, whether for one meal or all of them, Mary ate in this room and didn't bother changing for dinner.

Mary could not abide Beth and made no bones about it from the outset. Perhaps as a result Mary was, with the exception of Matt, the only person in the household that Beth was wary of.

In her forty-five years Mary had worked in a factory, taken her practical nurse's training, raised and helped put through college two fine sons. Two years before she had buried a much loved husband. She had worked hard and seen much and was completely unimpressed with the airs and graces, as she called them, of one Elizabeth Tarrel. And Beth knew it.

Katherine stood and walked to the door saying, "See you downstairs," then retraced her steps to the wide landing at the top of the stairs. A sturdy wrought iron railing ran toward the front of the house at the top of the steps and on either side was a door. Both doors led to Matt and Katherine's rooms, which took up the entire front of the house on the second floor.

She entered the door to the right and paused, as always, remembering her thoughts the first time she'd stepped into this room. At that time she had stood in almost stunned awe. Good grief! you could play basketball in here. The huge corner room had four windows, two overlooking the front lawn and drive and two on the side giving a view of both their own flower garden and the gently rollling Pennsylvania countryside. The ceiling, one wall and the woodwork were white, the other three walls a light brown, her vanity and the double dressers soft beige. The burnt orange of the carpet, draperies and bedspread was picked up in the coverings on the chaise lounge and big easy chair placed near the front windows, but the most imposing thing in the room was the bed. That was what had really stopped Katherine in her tracks that first time. Placed against the white wall, facing the front windows, it was easily ten feet by ten feet.

For some odd reason it was Matt's bed, more than anything else, that brought home to Katherine the extent of his wealth. More than the large penthouse apartment in Philadelphia or this quiet country house, a short twenty-five minute drive from the apartment. More than even the five cars he maintained. No, it was this custom-made bed with its specially ordered sheets and coverings, which she had later found out numbered over two dozen, that had seemed the height of luxury to Katherine.

She moved into the room, walking to the

medium-sized closet set in the wall to her left, used only for the odd items inside. Further along this same wall was another door leading into a large white and gold tiled bathroom. Off the other side of the bath were two smaller rooms, a walk-in closet dressing room where all Matt's and her own clothing and shoes were kept and a small bedroom containing a single bed, a dresser and a straight backed chair. The door from this room led back onto the wide landing.

Katherine went through the bathroom to the dressing room, stripping off her shirt and bra as she walked. Dropping them in the big wicker hamper right inside the door, she kicked off her shoes and slid out of her slacks and pantyhose.

After a quick shower she donned fresh bra and pantyhose, slid her slim feet into soft blue leather sandals and dropped a brilliant peacock-blue caftan over her head. A swift light application of make-up and a vigorous brushing of short black curls and she went slowly down the curving stairs and into the exquisitely furnished, but cold looking, living room.

3

A small sigh whispered past her lips as she walked across the white carpet. Mary was already there, drink in hand, seated on the pale green and gold velvet covered loveseat. She tilted her glass at Katherine in silent salute. "You look terrific in that color, Kate. I don't remember seeing that gown before. Is it new?"

Katherine had stopped at the liquor cabinet set at an angle to the french windows that opened onto a flagstone patio and lower garden. Turning slightly she smiled at Mary. "Thank you. No, it isn't new. As a matter of fact it must be at least five years old."

"The perfect, thrifty house-frau." The drawling voice came from across the room. Katherine turned fully around. Beth sat curled up, yet managing to look elegant, on the matching loveseat that faced Mary.

"How lucky for Matt that he doesn't have to be

in fear of his bank balance."

Not bothering to reply Katherine turned back to the cabinet and poured sherry into a glass, a smile twitching at her lips, as she heard Mary's mock sweet voice. "Yes, isn't Matt lucky. Two extravagant women in the same house could be a bit much."

Beth sat up straight, rigid with anger. "One of these days, Mary, you'll go too far," she snapped. "Then what happens?" came the smooth reply. "Do I get shot at dawn? Or just thrown out, bag and baggage, into the snow?"

"What snow?"

The twitch that Katherine was trying to control vanished at the sound of Matt's voice.

He entered the room with his usual brisk stride, one eyebrow raised in amusement at Mary as he passed her on his way to the liquor cabinet. His expression went cool as Katherine hurriedly moved from the cabinet to sit beside Mary.

How much of the conversation had he heard? she wondered.

Mary played it light. "The snow everyone and his brother have been predicting we are going to get this winter. That's what snow."

His reaction, if any, to this statement went unseen by the three women for he kept his back to them. He poured Chivas over ice in a short squat glass then splashed in a small amount of club soda. His face was bland as he turned around, stirring the drink by moving his hand in a slow circular motion. He lifted the glass and took a long swallow, then slowly lowered it, his eyes going first to Beth, then Katherine and finally Mary before murmuring, "I see."

At that moment his housekeeper, Mrs. Rapp, appeared in the doorway. "Dinner, sir."

Matt nodded briefly. "Thank you." His eyes again went to each of the women before saying coolly, "Ladies."

He moved to Katherine's side as she stood up, his hand cupping her elbow lightly to escort her, as always when he was home for dinner, into the small dining room across the hall.

A larger, stiffly formal dining room adjoined the living room, but Katherine much preferred this small room that was used when the family dined alone.

Katherine was glad to sink onto the chair Matt held for her for his nearness was playing havoc with her breathing and causing a decided weakness in her legs. He paused a moment behind her, then moved around the table to hold a chair for Beth, who was showing signs of growing impatience.

Mary, forever informal, had seated herself, then looked at Matt as he sat down and said, "James not in to dinner this evening?"

Before Matt could reply, James' light, teasing voice preceded him into the room. "James is in to dinner, Mary, love."

He sauntered into the room, tall, and slim and handsome, and sat down next to Beth. The resemblance between the two was almost startling.

"Hello, everyone."

His gaze started with Beth, lingered on Katherine, touched Mary and stopped at Matt. The seconds ticked by silently as Matt's eyes, steady, unreadable, held his.

The only resemblance here was the rich auburn hair, which James wore long, curlilng at the collar. For although James stood over six feet tall, Matt's large, almost rawboned frame dwarfed James' finer one.

Eight years separated the brothers, yet James, with his easy-going, good-natured personality, seemed much younger.

James finally broke the suddenly uneasy silence. "You get all your messages?" Matt nodded, "yes," and turned to smile at Mrs. Rapp who had entered the room to serve dinner.

Conversation was minimal during the meal, being confined mostly to the banter thrown back and forth between James and Mary.

Katherine was feeling nervous and uneasy, as Matt had remained silent throughout the meal. Preoccupied with her unwanted thoughts and longing for dinner to end so she could escape Matt's eyes, she looked up startled when Beth said quietly, "Matt, I hope you don't mind, I've invited a guest to the house for a visit." Before Matt could answer, James said, "Who?" Beth glanced at him quickly but her eyes went back to Matt before she answered. "DeDe."

"Oh God!" James gave a mock groan. "How long must we put up with her?"

"Very funny," snapped Beth, not even bothering to look at him, then her softening voice went on, "You won't mind, will you, Matt? I haven't see DeDe in ages, and she's on her way home from Europe, I'd like to have her stay a while before going on to California."

"Why should I mind?" Matt's voice was indifferent. "You know you may have anyone you wish stay here, as long as you remember my study is off-limits."

"Of course," Beth purred. But something about her self-satisfied expression caused a twinge of apprehension in Katherine. DeDe?

Katherine and Mary exchanged puzzled looks, and seeing the exchange James offered, "DeDe is Miss Diedre Halstead, an old school friend of Beth's. She's all right, I guess, if you can stand giddy females."

"You really are exasperating this evening, James," Beth said coldly. "You know very well DeDe is my best friend and she is not a giddy female. She is, in fact, one of the most sophisticated women I know."

"Heaven protect me from all sophisticated women," he chided.

Beth was about to retort when Matt cut in smoothly. "That's enough, Jim. He's only teasing, Beth. You know we both like DeDe."

Beth subsided against her chair, a small pout on her lips. "I know," came the almost sarcastic reply. Both James and Katherine looked up sharply. He sounded angry with James and Katherine wondered why.

Matt finished his coffee and stood up abruptly. "If you'll excuse me, I have a phone call to make." And as he turned to leave Beth stood also. "I have to leave too, I'm meeting Charles at the Carsons' to play bridge."

The Carsons were their nearest neighbors two

miles further along the black topped road at the end of the driveway. Charles Davis was one of Beth's admirers.

The three sat a few minutes in silence then Katherine rose saying dispiritedly, "I think I'll go up early, I'm tired."

James looked disappointed. "Oh Katherine, don't go up yet. I thought you and I could have a brandy and talk."

"I'm going to take a look at Jon. Good night, you two," Mary inserted as she walked out of the dining room.

"Please, Katherine," James coaxed.

How very nice he is, Katherine thought, his charming gentle personality the complete opposite of Matt's dynamic forceful one.

Smiling gently, she reached out her hand and lightly touched his sleeve. "Not tonight, James, I really am tired. I think I'll have a soak and go to bed."

James' fingers lifted her chin and stared at her closely. "You look tired, something go wrong while you were away?"

She shook her head and his fingers slid along the chin in a light caress. "No, of course not. Don't worry about me, James." Turning, she escaped the room and the tender look that had come into James' eyes. She was becoming concerned with the way James looked at her sometimes.

Back in the bedroom, Katherine stared at her reflection in the mirror that ran the length of the closet door. Her fingers went to the tiny lines at the corner of her eyes. I do look tired. And starting to show my age, she thought wryly. I've lost some more weight, too. She grimaced at her image, remembering how she'd worked to get her figure back into shape after Jon was born. She had gone past her goal and for the first time in over two years was back into a size ten dress.

She had worn a size ten from the time she was in high school, up until the year before she and Matt were married when she'd gone into a size twelve.

She had not been displeased with the added pounds. True, the slim young girl look was gone, but at thirty-nine she had kept that look longer than most. The added weight had given her a softly rounded mature appearance not unbecoming to the mother of two grown children. And now, two years and one baby later, she weighed less than she had twenty years ago. Even the size tens were becoming a little loose.

Katherine peered more closely into the mirror, running her fingers through the soft dark curls. Quite a few gray mixed in with the dark ones. Oh well! Maybe she'd soon have a natural frost.

She shrugged at her reflection and turned away just as the bedroom door opened and Matt stepped inside, closed the door quietly, and leaned back against it. His big frame seemed to take up most of the door and Katherine felt her pulses stir at the deceptively lazy look of him. She knew how lightening fast he could move.

His eyes went over her slowly and the stir that had started at her pulse skittered up her spine. "I like your gown, the color becomes you. Did I pay for it?" His flat, emotionless voice made the compliment left-handed.

Her words were almost an echo of a few hours earlier. "Thank you. No, you didn't pay for it. It's at least five years old."

His eyebrows went up mockingly, and she spun away, walking across the room to the chaise by the window. "It's a perfectly good caftan," she bit out. "I've only worn it a few times. What do you expect me to do? Give it away? Throw it away?"

She had not heard him moving over the soft carpet and was startled to hear his voice so close. "I don't expect anything of you, Katherine."

His voice was low, calm. Too calm. She whirled around expecting to see what? Anger? Frustration? She saw nothing. His face was devoid of expression.

Katherine stared long seconds into eyes the color of gray and blue ice, then blinked as he turned suddenly and walked to the bathroom door saying flatly, "I've got to leave."

"Leave!" She repeated in a hoarse whisper. "Where are you going?" she asked, swallowing hard at the knot of fear in her throat.

"Atlanta. I have an appointment down there at nine in the morning, and I want to see Carl tonight for a briefing. The plane's waiting for me."

He was halfway through the bathroom and she hurried after him, following him into their dressing room.

"How long will you be gone?"

His head jerked around, his eyes seeming to challenge hers. "Two, three days. Why?"

"Would you like me to pack for you?"

The fire left his eyes and he looked suddenly tired.

"Thank you." Again that flat, nothing tone of voice. "That would give me time for a quick shower."

He turned back to the bathroom, only to stop, grow rigid when she called, "Matt."

She wanted to scream at his broad, unyielding back. What's the matter? Why have you changed? But she couldn't, just could not, get the words out. All she said was, "Will you need evening clothes?"

His answer came as a soft sigh. "No Katherine, I will not need evening clothes." He closed the bathroom door behind him.

Blinking against the hot moisture welling into her eyes, Katherine stood staring at the closed door. What must he think? Did he think she was prying? Trying to find out his movements when he was away from home? He'd hate that, she thought miserably. He'd detest the idea of anyone questioning anything he did.

Shaking her head as if to shake away her unpleasant thoughts, she pulled the caftan over her head and hung it in her closet. After shedding her brief undies and dropping them into the clothes hamper, she slipped into a pale lilac satin nightgown and matching long tailored robe, knotting the belt around her almost too-narrow waist.

She packed his soft leather case quickly and neatly and was tugging the zip around the edge when he strode into the room.

She glanced up and froze, breath catching in her throat, eyes clinging as, against her will, they took inventory of his powerful body.

Moving swiftly, missing nothing, her eyes went over him. His usually unruly hair lay wetly slicked against his head, his cheeks and jaw smooth with a fresh shaven sheen. Her bones seemed to go soft, disjointed, as her eyes moved on, running down his strong brown throat to his broad, broad shoulders and chest matted with not quite red hair. The tight curls tapered to a vee at his mid section then formed a half inch trail down his flat belly to disappear under the snug elastic band of the skin-tight briefs that hugged his slim hips. The briefs were the only article of clothing he wore and they left little to her imagination. Katherine swallowed with difficulty, felt her pulse kick in her throat and her eyes shied away, retracing their path until they collided with glittering gray blue ones that were watching her steadily.

She gulped in air, feeling her cheeks go from warm to hot as the realization hit her that for the last few minutes he had stood immobile while he endured her scrutiny. What emotion made his eyes glitter like that? Amusement? Contempt? She didn't wait to find out. Clutching the lapels of her robe together with her left hand, she gave a last vicious tug at the case zipper and fled from the room and his eyes. But not fast enough to miss hearing his muttered, "Oh for Christ's sake!"

She ran into the bedroom, hands brushing impatiently at the moisture blurring her vision. Slowing her pace she walked to the chaise, curling up on it like a small child. Hugging herself tightly, nails digging into the flesh of her upper arms, she fought to control her breathing and wildly chaotic thoughts. He probably thinks I'm an idiot, becoming unglued at the sight of an unclad body. I'm behaving like a silly young girl, and he's probably in there laughing his damned fool head off.

Taking several deep calming breaths she reached for the book lying on the table next to the chaise, but made no attempt to read it. Fingers nervously picking at the book cover, she rested her head against the curving back of the chaise, eyes fastened on the bathroom door. Would he leave through the small bedroom? Not even bother to say goodbye?

He was very quick and within ten minutes came through the door at his usual brisk pace. He paused when he saw her, then went on towards the bedroom door.

He's almost as devasting dressed as undressed, Katherine thought dully, taking in his cream colored sportsjacket, the dark brown and white subtly striped shirt with the top two buttons open, revealing his throat. Then his voice, raw and rough-edged, broke into her confused thoughts as he reached out his hand for the door knob. "I've got to go. Goodbye, Katherine." But he didn't turn the knob, just stood there as if waiting for something.

The word slipped out before she could stop it. A softly whispered plea, "Matt."

His hand dropped to his side as he turned slowly. His eyes went over her, taking in her disheveled hair, her almost white face, her body outlined beneath pale lilac satin.

"Oh hell!" he muttered and dropping his case to the floor was across the room in a few long strides. In one fluid motion he bent, grasped her arms and pulled her up and off the chaise into his arms.

His mouth close to her ear, he growled, "Touch me, Katherine." It was an order. A command. Without hesitation she slid her arms inside his jacket around his waist, spreading her fingers as she moved her hands slowly up his back.

His lips moved across her cheek in tiny, fiery kisses and stopped at the corner of her mouth, his tongue teasing, tantalizing her lower lip.

"Matt, please."

"Please what? Please stop? Please kiss you? What?" His voice, a low, hoarse whisper did strange things to her breathing while his hands, moving slowly sensuously over her spine, set her blood on fire.

"Please kiss me," she managed between gasps for breath.

His mouth covered hers, his lips hard, hungry, his tongue seeking the sweetness within. His hands slid down her spine, drawing her closer, then grasped her hips, moving her in a slow circular motion against him.

Katherine felt lightheaded, her body boneless. She clung to him as the fiery ache grew inside her.

Matt's mouth slid from hers, forced her head back and left a burning trail to the wildly beating pulse in her throat.

"Oh God! I want you," he groaned, "and that damned plane's waiting."

His hands were gentle on her arms as he put her from him. She opened her eyes slowly, reluctantly. "I must go," he said softly.

She nodded dumbly and with a guttural curse he bent his head to kiss her hard. Then he turned and strode across the room, grabbed up his case and left, closing the door quietly behind him.

4

Unconcerned with the tears running down her face, Katherine stood staring at the bedroom door. She had no idea how long she had been standing there. The cold, empty feeling of loss had gripped her when Matt walked out the door.

It couldn't last. Awareness crept back in and, shaking her head like a punchy confused fighter, she sank onto the chaise.

What a fool I am, she thought wiping her wet cheeks with her fingers. It was a pointless exercise as the flow continued unabated.

A stupid fool who should know better. Well, I guess it's true, there is no fool like an old one. Katherine Martin, you should not be allowed out without a keeper, she told herself grimly.

A sound that had been tapping at her subconscious finally penetrated and she turned her head to glance at the window. Tiny rivers of rain ran down the pane, not unlike the ones on her own face.

The slashing rain they had driven through that afternoon, which had tapered off to a fine mist by early evening, had begun again with even more force. She could hear the wind whipping the trees to a frenzied protest. A fore-runner of autumn.

Katherine shivered. Matt was out there. The plane was waiting, he'd said. His plane. One of the four kept by the company for use by the small army of executives forever on the move between the varied and far flung offices of Matt's small empire. The small jet was the one waiting for Matt tonight. This one was kept exclusively, and ever-ready, for the boss.

Autocratic to the soles of his feet, Matt held the reins of his companies firmly in his large strong hands. There were stockholders and the board of directors, of course, but the final word was his. Always. The enormity of the power he held frightened Katherine. He frightened her.

Why had she allowed herself to be drawn into his world? She wondered. This alien world of high gear business and, to her, mind-boggling wealth.

What's the point in wondering why? Katherine asked herself, sighing deeply. I am in it. Now, how the hell do I handle it?

Her tears had stopped and she lay back feeling completely drained. She didn't have the vaguest idea how to handle a situation she had never had control of in the first place.

The first thing she had to do, she decided, was control her own emotions. But how? She had never felt so vulnerable before. His words echoed and reechoed in her mind. I want you. A simple statement, direct and to the point. Never, I love you. Not even I need you. A blunt, I want you.

Well, that had been part of the agreement, hadn't it? The assuagement of his physical wants. He had not asked for her love, nor offered her his. He had stated his requirements clearly, and she had agreed. So what right had she to feel injured now? None whatever. Except if someone had told her, almost sixteen months ago, that by now she would be crazily, frantically in love with her husband, she would have been shocked.

She was forty-one years old. The mother of not only a baby son but two fully grown children, the oldest of which was due, within the next few weeks, to make her a grandmother. She had thought herself mature, settled. If she had thought of love at all, it had been in terms of quiet companionship.

But this! This wildly passionate emotion tearing her apart was beyond belief. She didn't have the beginnings of an idea how to cope with it, let alone handle it.

She was behaving like a young girl in the throes of first love. No! Katherine corrected herself. Not even with Kevin had she experienced anything like this.

Katherine shivered and realized she had been shivering for some time. The air in the bedroom had chilled. Glancing at her watch her eyes widened in surprise. It was past one. Matt was probably in Atlanta by now. She turned to the window. The wind and rain had increased its fury and pounded mercilessly against the house.

Goose-flesh crawling up her arms, Katherine turned a frowning face to the bed. She couldn't face sleeping in that enormous thing alone tonight.

Jumping up she went to the double dresser, slid open the bottom drawer, pulled out a bright orange comforter and went back to the chaise. Stretching out, she drew the cover over her, tucking it in around her feet and legs, then snuggled into the warm folds.

Sleep refused to come. Her mind repeated an earlier thought. Not even with Kevin had she experienced anything like this. Yet she had loved Kevin. So why was the way she felt now different? Her mind puzzled at that difference. When you loved, you loved, didn't you?

Probing now, needing to find some answers, her mind went back, as it had earlier that day, to her time with Kevin Acker.

From the beginning he had been the ideal boyfriend. From that first laughing, sun-filled summer they spent together, to the day she married him, two weeks after she graduated high school, he had been everything a girl could wish for in her first love.

They spent every weekend, holidays and their summers together, as Kevin was going to college in Philadelphia and was able to come home in less than an hour.

The situation had suited Katherine's parents, for she seldom went out during the week, and so did not neglect her school work. By the time they married, her parents had grown very fond of him and her brothers, though now sixteen, still carried the torch of hero worship.

A small smile touched Katherine's lips as she compared that hang-dog adoration the young Dave and Dan had given Kevin to the almost awed respect her two thirty-nine year old brothers gave Matt.

Having a marked talent for drawing, Katherine had considered going to art school, but Kevin had soon put a stop to that idea. He had waited long enough, he'd told her, and had no intentions of waiting any longer. He wanted to get married as soon as her high school days were over. So they had.

The first year they were married they lived with Kevin's parents, in the big old fashioned house where Kevin was born. The first child, Janice, was born while they lived there, eleven months after the wedding and five days after Katherine's nineteenth birthday.

On completion of college, Kevin was offered a well-salaried job with a large advertising firm in Philadelphia. He accepted at once. Though they considered taking an apartment in center city, Kevin's parents, financially comfortable, insisted on supplying the down payment on a home of their own.

Katherine had enjoyed the house hunting, finally deciding on a ranch house in a pleasant Philadelphia suburb.

They moved into the house a few weeks before

Christmas and Katherine should have been content. She wasn't, and she didn't know why.

She had everything a girl could wish for; a devoted husband, a beautiful daughter, a lovely home. Yet something seemed to be missing. But what?

Finally deciding it was the frustration of her artistic ability, Katherine enrolled in an art class in Philadelphia, taking two evening classes a week. She loved it and before long, through Kevin, was doing small illustration jobs for the company he worked for. It suited her perfectly as she didn't have to leave her family and was being paid well for her work.

Yet the vague feeling of dissatisfaction remained. It worried and confused Katherine. If she had someone she could talk to it might help. But she didn't. She had moved away from her close friends and although she was friendly with the wives of some of the men Kevin worked with, she had no close women friends.

Having led a fairly sheltered life at a time when mothers discussed very few of the facts of life with their daughters, Katherine's introduction to the sexual relationship between man and woman came from Kevin, who was himself not overly experienced. And that after the wedding!

Of course they had indulged in light petting, but Kevin had always stopped before it could become too heated, adhering rigidly to his own strict upbringing.

That her feeling of dissatisfaction and unfulfillment stemmed from Kevin's uninspiring, if not downright dull, love-making never occurred to her. If it had she'd have rejected it guiltily. She loved him. He loved her. Sex was the least important part of marriage, wasn't it?

They were in the house a little over a year when Katherine realized she was again pregnant. The baby was due in the fall and both she and Kevin were delighted. Janice would soon be two and Kevin had said she needed a brother to play with.

Kevin wanted a son. He never saw him. Tommy was born four weeks after his father's death.

Even now, twenty years later, the memory of that night caused pain and Katherine stirred uneasily under the brilliantly colored comforter.

Sitting up suddenly, her eyes widened in disbelief. She had thought of the date of that terrible night indelibly imprinted on her mind, and she had just now realized that the anniversary of that date had come and gone while she had been in the mountains with Matt.

She settled back again with a sigh. In all truth, those two days spent in the mountains with Matt had driven thoughts of everything out of her mind.

"Dear God!" Katherine said the words aloud, head swinging to the windows. It had been a night just like this when Kevin died, and Matt was out there.

Stop it, she chided herself silently. It's two o'clock in the morning and Matt is probably sound asleep in his hotel room. If anything had gone wrong on the flight south she'd have been notified by now.

Closing her eyes again, she could almost hear the ringing of the phone that had wakened her that night. Could almost hear the voice, strong yet compassionate, that had informed her of her husband's death in an automobile accident.

There had been four of them in the car. They had been returning home from a bachelor party, given for a young man Kevin worked with. Of course, they had been drinking. Apparently, Kevin had been asleep on the front seat beside the driver. The driver himself must have dozed off and the car skidded across the highway, through a guardrail, and flipping end over end down an embankment, crashed against a tree at the bottom.

Kevin and the driver had been killed instantly, never knowing what hit them. The other two men had died within a few hours of each other the next day.

A shudder rippled through Katherine's body at the memory of those first weeks after Kevin's death. Her mother had come to her to help with what seemed like the hundred and one arrangements that had to be made.

Kevin was to be buried at home, and Katherine was to stay with her parents for a while.

Katherine went through those weeks in a state of numbness. Walking, talking, taking care of Janice, yet not there, as if her feelings had been put on hold.

Until she went into labor. Then the realization hit her. She was going to have Kevin's baby, and he would never see it.

All during labor and delivery she hoped and prayed the child would be a boy and he'd look like Kevin.

Half her prayer was answered. The baby was a boy. But he favored Katherine's side, with dark hair and eyes.

The sudden shrill ringing of the phone brought Katherine off the chaise; head swinging around, eyes wide with fright, to stare at the phone on the night stand next to Matt's side of the bed.

Matt's private phone. Katherine knew the only other phone ringing in the house was the one in Matt's study.

She moved across the room slowly, eyes glued to the noisily insistent intrument, hesitated, then reached out tentively as if the thing would bite .

Drawing a deep breath, she suddenly grasped the receiver and brought it to her ear, her voice a hoarsely whispered, "yes."

"Katherine?" Matt's voice crackled through the wires, vibrant, alive.

Relief washed over Katherine and in a stronger voice answered, "Yes, Matt."

"Sorry to waken you, but in the rush I've come away without some papers I'll need tomorrow— no, this morning. I've sent the plane back and called Jack to pick them up, then deliver them to the airport. He should be at the house shortly. Would you go down to my study and get them for him? You can't miss them; they're in a tan folder on top of my desk."

The request had been rattled off slowly,

consisely, thinking her half asleep. Wanting to hold on to, if only for a few minutes, the warm voice that brought him close over so many miles of wire, she answered, "Yes, of course," then rushed on with, "How was the flight? The weather was so miserable."

"Was it?" He sounded mildly surprised. "I had no idea. The flight must have been smooth for I slept all the way, and it's clear now."

Katherine felt a flash of irritation at his words. She'd been half sick with worry, while he slept peacefully on the damned plane.

His next words banished the irritation.

"I thought I'd better grab what sleep I could, as it looks like this briefing with Carl will take us right up to the time of my appointment, with a full schedule for the rest of the day. Again, I'm sorry I had to disturb you and I hope you have no trouble in getting back to sleep and, Katherine, thank you."

Katherine heard a click and then a buzz; he'd hung up. No good-bye or good-night, just thank you. As if he'd been speaking to his secretary, she thought, annoyed.

She replaced the receiver noting, in a detached sort of way, the damp imprint left on it. Her palms and forehead were moist and she shivered. She had broken out in a cold sweat when the phone had begun ringing, and now she felt chilled.

Giving herself a mental shake she left the room. The papers were exactly where he'd said they'd be and she was just closing the study door, folder in hand, when she heard the car stop on the drive.

Hurrying across the hall, she unlocked the door and pulled it open, before Jack's finger could touch the doorbell and wake someone else.

A grinning Jack came loping up the steps to her, looking wide awake, as if it were the middle of the afternoon and not after three in the morning.

"Sorry to disturb you like this, Mrs. M," he said lightly and then, chidingly, "You know, you should never open a door like that, without checking first who it is. Make the boss very unhappy if he knew."

Katherine's smile was warm. She liked this young man, he was easy going and friendly. Five years older then Tommy, he had taken him under his wing and eased his first summer at the house.

"I promise not to do it again. Will you come in for a cup of coffee?" She stepped back, opening the door wider as she spoke.

Jack shook his head briefly. "No can do, thanks anyway. That little beauty will be landing soon, and I'd better be there with those papers."

Katherine's voice halted him as he started back down the steps. "I may need a car in a day or two to run into Philly."

"Any time, Mrs. M. Just ring the horn in the garage." He went down the steps and pulled the car door open then turned and added, "By the way, how's young Tom doing at school? All settled in?"

"He's doing fine, Jack, thank you. He asked me to say hi to you."

He nodded and slid behind the wheel. "That's a good kid you have there, ma'am." He gave a sketchy salute, then closed the door and the car moved smoothly down the drive.

Katherine closed and relocked the door smiling softly. Yes, Tom was a good kid. She hadn't done a bad job of raising him.

She went up the stairs slowly, her last thoughts leading her mind back into the past again.

Tommy had been a delightful baby. He had given her very few sleepless nights.

They had stayed with her parents until Tom was three months old. Her mother had wanted her to sell the house and move back to Lancaster. She had been tempted, but only for a short time. She loved the ranch house and she was going home.

Kevin had been well insured, including mortgage insurance. The house was paid and free of debt. She'd have a small monthly income which she hoped to supplement with her illustrating work. The checks she'd received from his life insurance policies, she had banked for the childrens' education. It would not be easy, but with careful managing she'd do it.

The first few years had been a little tight. But as her work became known she received more. The company Kevin had worked for offered her a full time job periodically, over the years. She turned it down, not wanting to leave the children all day.

Wrapped in the comforter and curled again on the chaise, Katherine was wide awake. Eyes wide, she saw nothing in the room. She was staring back through those lonely years.

She had few friends since she seldom went out, and she built her life around Janice and Tom. Her days had been full, but for a very long time, her nights had been very bad.

Katherine stirred, remembering the nights she had lain alone. She had lived with a man, slept with him. Her body had all the normal physical urges. Night after night she had fought a silent battle to suppress those urges. She had won.

There had been men over the years. Some lightly, some seriously interested. They all had soon lost that interest when she had made it clear that she would neither sleep with nor marry them.

She had managed to convince all of them, even the most persistent, that she would not change her mind. All that is, until Matt.

Turning her head toward the window, Katherine blinked in surprise. It was morning. She had spent the night in the past, and hadn't solved one of her present problems. I must be getting flaky, she thought wryly, all this reminiscing. I've got to shake myself out of this mood.

Jumping up, she folded the comforter and replaced it in the drawer. She knew what her trouble was. She had too much time on her hands. She was unused to all this idleness.

Casting about in her mind for something to do, she fastened onto an idea.

She had told Jack she might need the car and she would. But instead of going to Philly for an afternoon of shopping she'd wait until closer to Tom's birthday, take Mary and Jon, and go in to the apartment for a week or so.

Her mind raced ahead making plans. She'd plan a small celebration, the weekend of Tom's birthday. Perhaps Janice and Carlos could fly up from Washington. She'd give Carol a call, heavens, she hadn't talked to her in over two weeks. Maybe she could see a few shows, take her time shopping for Tom's birthday present.

Mary would probably love a chance to do some shopping, have a look at the new fall styles.

If they could find someone reliable to stay with Jon, she and Mary could shop together.

A slow impish smile spread over Katherine's face. She had decided to call Matt's secretary and give her the job of finding a babysitter.

On that happy thought she headed for the shower.

5

The following three days were hectic ones. The house was a bee-hive of activity in preparation for Beth's friend DeDe's visit.

Katherine could not enter a room without being confronted with some member of the staff busy polishing, waxing or rearranging something.

Matt had not returned and Katherine silently endorsed Mary's opinion that it was a good thing. "If he walked into his crazy house now," she had stated dryly, "he'd probably blow a fuse."

James had made himself scarce. Like most men he hated the upheaval, promising Beth he'd be on hand to welcome DeDe.

True to his word, he sauntered into the living room the night before her planned arrival. His eyes scanned the gleaming room then settled on Katherine and Mary.

"Good evening, ladies," he said. "Beth not down yet?"

"She had a dinner engagement," Katherine answered, then added, "Welcome home, James."

"Did you miss me?" His voice was teasing, but his eyes studied her face in a way that unnerved her.

Katherine kept her own tone light. "Of course we did. Although I must admit, the house did not seem unduly quiet."

They all laughed, Katherine and Mary out of pure relief that the bustle was finally over.

"Not drinking?" he asked. "Or just too lazy to mix your own?"

"Too lazy," Mary murmured.

"Pampered cats," he teased, going to the cabinet. He mixed the drinks and sat down in the chair opposite Katherine, stretching his legs out and resting his head against the back.

"You look tired, James," Mary observed. "The boss working you too hard?"

"Every chance he can," he drawled. "I'd happily resent it if I didn't know he puts in twice the amount of time and effort as I, or for that matter, any of his employees do."

He sipped his drink slowly, his eyes steady on Katherine's face, then added slowly. "As far as his work is concerned you can't fault Matt."

Meaning what? Katherine wondered. That in other areas you could? She had an unhappy feeling he meant herself, and felt now the familiar twinge of apprehension at the way his eyes seemed lately to caress her.

She felt a wave of relief when Mrs. Rapp announced dinner and hurried in to the dining room, seating herself quickly.

James held Mary's chair then as he sat down, his eyes teasing Mary, said dryly, "How's the carbon?"

The first words James had said on first seeing Jonathon were, "Good grief, he's a carbon copy of Matt."

He had referred to Jon as the carbon ever since.

"Bright eyed and bushy tailed," came Mary's laughing reply. "He's too young to have acquired the male horror of housecleaning."

James cocked an eyebrow at Katherine. "I suppose Beth's planning all sorts of social engagements to entertain the much vaunted DeDe?"

"I don't really know. I do know she's planned a dinner party for Saturday night as she asked me if I knew if Matt would be home."

"And do you?" he asked dryly.

Katherine met his eyes steadily. "No."

"You haven't heard from him?"

She felt a stab of pain though she managed to keep it from showing. It was more a statement than a question and those five small words told her clearly how he, and probably everyone else, regarded her and Matt's relationship.

Pride made her edge around the truth. "He called once but he didn't know exactly how long he'd be gone. He had thought it would be no more than two or three days, but as this is the fourth day perhaps they've hit a snag or something." Shrugging, seeming unconcerned, she turned her attentions to the food on her plate, missing the speculative look that passed between Mary and

James.

The room was quiet for some time, then Katherine went on as if there had been no break in the conversation. "Beth has not told me much of what she's planning, possibly because I told her I would not be here."

James head jerked around. "Where are you going?" he rapped out.

Katherine felt a smile tug at her mouth. Beth's reaction had been the same. Did they suppose she was going to go running away every week or so, she wondered wryly.

Her eyes caught Mary's and saw reflected there the same amusement that lightened her own.

"We're going into the apartment for a few weeks. I have some shopping to do. Also I thought I'd have a small party for Tom's birthday. Will you come?"

James nodded saying, "Of course," then added, "we?"

"Mary and I—and the carbon naturally."

"Matt?" he queried softly, not looking at her.

"Well, that I don't know. It depends on his schedule, doesn't it?"

Again he nodded, but this time his eyes held hers, trying to tell her—what?

Katherine didn't care to speculate. In all truth, she didn't want to know.

"May I call you at your office when I have more details?"

"Certainly. And if I'm not in leave a message and I'll get back to you."

"Fine," she answered, and let the conversation drop.

They spent a pleasant, if short evening together. James was obviously tired, excusing himself early.

Mary sat silent a short time after James had left the room and said quietly, "I guess I cramped his style."

Katherine glanced up startled. "What do you mean?"

"Oh, come on Kate," she chided. "James has gone all soft as mush over you. It was obvious he wanted to be alone with you." She paused a moment then added, "I'd be careful there if I were you."

"Oh Lord," Katherine groaned, resting her head against the back of the chair. "I've been telling myself it's my imagination, but if you see it too." She grimaced at Mary. "You don't think it's just compassion he's feeling?"

"No, Kate, I don't," she replied shaking her head. "I wish I could say I did. But unless I'm reading all the signs incorrectly, I'd say James is definitely smitten."

"Just what I need." Katherine's face was pale, her voice low. "I have no answers to the problems I already have and now I'm handed another one."

She sat very still and quiet for a while, then she cried out, "Mary, what am I going to do?"

It was the first time Katherine had lost her composure in front of Mary, and Mary's eyes grew concerned, almost alarmed.

She put her hand out in a placating motion, and

in a firm voice stated, "Take it easy, Kate. First of all, James has a problem, not you. And if you can avoid being alone with him whatever he feels for you, or thinks he does may wear off."

Katherine opened her mouth, but before she could say anything Mary raised her hand higher, in a stopping movement, adding, "Secondly, I think you should make that move into Philly sooner than you'd planned. As soon as it's possible after Beth's house guest gets here. You're building these problems of yours way out of proportion."

"But Mary—"

"No, Kate, I'm not saying they aren't very real problems. I know they are. What I am saying is, you should get away from this house for a while. You have too damn little to occupy yourself with here. Too much time on your hands. You've been chasing these difficulties around in circles in your mind until they've become bigger than life. What you need is to get out, do things, laugh and talk with other people."

Her gaze became pensive as she finished. "I wonder, Kate, if you have any idea how long its been since you've laughed. I mean really laughed easily, naturally."

Katherine's eyes were wide with surprise. "I don't know. There hasn't seemed to be much to laugh about for sometime now. And somehow, telling myself I walked into this with my eyes open, and so have only myself to blame, doesn't help much."

"It never does," came the sympathetic reply.

"We must stay for the dinner party Saturday night. But as Beth hasn't bothered to inform me of any further plans, I don't know why we couldn't go into town on Monday." Katherine's eyes and voice were steady again as she glanced at Mary.

Mary nodded, then said softly, "And Matt?"

Katherine's sigh was deep. "Yes. Matt. Hell! I don't know, Mary. I haven't the vaguest idea if he'll stay home once he does get here. I guess I'll just have to play it by ear."

Mary nodded again then grinned. "Just give me an hour's notice, and Jon and I will be on the front steps bag and baggage, ready to go."

Katherine, Mary and James were having mid-morning coffee in the living room the next day when Beth entered with DeDe.

Katherine's first reaction was an unaccountable feeling of dismay. From the top of her silvery blonde head to the tip of her hand-made Italian shoes, DeDe was beautiful, in a cool, slightly brittle way. Small, delicate, her skin white and smooth as fine porcelain, wealth seemed to surround her like a cloak.

Introductions were made and Katherine felt her dismay deepening. DeDe's doe soft brown eyes sharpened as they went over her. She felt herself weighed, measured and dismissed in seconds.

The uneasy moment was broken when James places his hand on DeDe's shoulders, kissed her lightly on the cheek and murmured, "You're more beautiful than ever. How many broken hearts have you left behind in Europe?"

DeDe's light laugh rippled through the room and her voice came as a shock, so deep and throaty, from such a small frame. "I'll admit to nothing.

How lovely to see you again, James." Then, eyebrows raised, added, "Don't tell me the boss gave you the day off in honor of my arrival?"

James laughed softly, his face taking on a mock look of craftiness, his voice low, conspiratorial. "You know what they say. When the cat's away."

DeDe's eyes sharpened almost imperceptibly as she turned to Beth, and the beauty of her voice was marred with a slightly raw edge. "Matt's away?"

Katherine felt herself tense and caught the alert look that brought Mary straighter in her chair. What was it? Something in DeDe's tone. But what?

Beth answered smoothly, "You know, Matt, DeDe, about the only time he touches home base is when he has to repack his suitcase. But I do expect him any time now."

The words struck at Katherine. I expect him. I, not we. Nails digging into her palms, feeling almost invisible, Katherine sat quite still and felt the color leave her face as DeDe replied, "You would think *someone* would have instructed him on delegating authority by now. I know I would have."

Katherine went rigid. She knew who that *someone* was. With those few words DeDe had labeled her unimportant. She drew her breath in slowly in an effort to control the flow of anger and dislike that flashed through her. How dare she? she thought. By what right does this china doll make comments like this in my own home? Then she checked her thoughts. It was not, in fact, her home. It was Matt's home. In his absence Beth was its undisputed mistress. Katherine had no doubt at all that DeDe was in full possession of the facts.

"I somehow find it impossible to imagine *anyone* instructing Matt on anything concerning his work." James' words were smooth, even, not matching his eyes which had gone hard.

One delicately penciled brow arched at him as tilting her head DeDe purred, "My dear James, there are ways, and then there are ways."

Beth's smile was one of admiration for her friend as she excused the two of them to show DeDe to her room.

Katherine sat staring at the now empty doorway. What had been the purpose of that conversation? What point?

James' soft voice broke her thoughts. "You must not mind what DeDe says, Katherine. She's been such a familiar figure around here for so long, almost one of the family, that I suppose she feels she has the right to say anything she wishes."

Katherine's head swung around to James, but before she could form an answer, Mary said, dryly, almost too dryly, "I've been told that familiarity breeds contempt." She rose and walked from the room, not even bothering to turn her head as she added, "I see now that it's true."

Katherine stood and moved to follow Mary. James' voice was an urgent plea. "Katherine."

She shook her head. "Not now James, please." And she walked quickly from the room and up the stairs, one urge burning through her. She wanted nothing, at that moment, but to gather her son to her and run. Run as if her very life depended on it.

But she had just learned the pointlessness of doing
that.

She didn't, of course. She had lunch in the
nursery with Mary and by the time she walked
into the living room for pre-dinner drinks she was
completely composed. She had withdrawn into
herself and when she spoke her voice had a cool,
detached sound. She noted the concerned look
James turned to her, but she ignored it.

She sat sipping her drink, feeling strangely
alone, as Mary had decided to have dinner
upstairs declaring one dose a day of DeDe was
about all she could handle, allowing DeDe's
occasional sharp pointed barbs to bounce off her
armor. Only once did DeDe's remarks break
through her defenses and draw blood.

James had asked her if she'd seen the carbon
and she'd laughed delightedly, answering, "Yes,
I've met Matt's son. You're right, he is a carbon
copy of the original. Matt must be extremely
pleased with him."

Not once did she look at Katherine. It was as if
she considered Matt had produced this
phenomenon all by himself with no assistance
from anyone else.

Katherine closed the breach at once, becoming
even more reserved. She tuned them out and so
managed to get through the rest of the evening,
clinging to the thought of Monday as if to a life-
line.

Matt came home Saturday.

Katherine had remained upstairs all morning,

but good manners decreed she join the family for lunch.

They had just seated themselves when he strode into the dining room. He went directly to DeDe, taking into his large hands the very small, perfectly manicured one she held out to him. She had jumped to her feet with a joyous, "Matt, darling, when did you get home?" the minute he'd entered the room, and he answered her now, his voice low, amused. "I just now walked in the door." Then bending as James had done the day before, he kissed her soundly on her white, perfect cheek. Only the words were different. "How are you, DeDe? It's been a long time."

Her hands clung to his a few seconds before sliding away as she answered, "I'm fine, and I don't have to ask how you are; you look fantastic."

His smile was slow, easy, changing his face to almost breath-catching attractiveness. "Flattery isn't necessary, DeDe, you know whatever it is you want, I'll probably say yes."

He had moved to the back of her chair while he spoke and, laughing softly, she sat down again.

Not waiting for her answer, he moved to stand beside Katherine's chair. He said quietly, "How are you, Katherine?" and bending, barely brushed her pale cheek with his lips.

Katherine had assumed the same withdrawn reserve of the night before and with an odd feeling of detachment observed the flash of annoyance that spread across DeDe's face and James' suddenly tightened jawline as Matt bestowed his almost kiss.

"I'm fine, Matt. Welcome home." Her voice sounded too cool and slightly far away, even to her own ears.

His eyes flickered over her face in what she was sure was anger for her extreme reserve, then he went to his own place at the head of the table. He nodded to Beth and James as he seated himself then his eyes paused an instant at the empty place. Eyebrows raised, he looked at Katherine. "Where's Mary?"

Beth answered for her, her voice acidly. "She must be having a fit of sulks. She didn't choose to join us for dinner last night, either."

Katherine opened her mouth to protest, but not fast enough. Matt's eyes were cold as he regarded his sister, although his voice was silky. "Mary doesn't sulk. If she chooses not to join us at the table, it's entirely up to her." A mild reproach and yet it was the same as if he'd snapped out an order. "Lay off Mary."

Color tinged Beth's cheeks and the silence stretched until, his eyes again on Katherine, he broke it himself. "How is Jon?"

It seemed she was not to be allowed to answer his questions, for DeDe gushed, "Oh, Matt, he's beautiful. How pleased you must be with him."

One eyebrow arched over eyes that had gone the color of a winter sky, and his tone conveyed displeasure at the interference. "Thank you. Yes, we have grown fond of him." His voice dry, he added, "I suppose we'll keep him."

Katherine's lips twitched and she bent her head

to her salad. Would she ever understand this man? For it was obvious that at times he mystified his brother and sister as well as herself.

DeDe did not enjoy being in Matt's disfavor apparently, for she said in a cooing sweet voice that set Katherine's teeth on edge. "You said I could probably have whatever it was I wanted, Matt. It's a simple request really—I'd like your company for a while."

Katherine stiffened. This woman was not to be believed. It would be a different story if he were still a free agent. But to make a request like that of a married man! Her eyes flew to Matt's face and she felt a twinge of pain in her chest. That slow devastating smile touched his mouth as he answered indulgently. "You may have my undivided attention through today and most of tomorrow, up until I have to leave tomorrow night."

"Leave!" Beth wailed. "You're not going away again so soon? Matt, you just came home."

"I have no choice. There's some labor trouble at the Pittsburgh mill and I must fly out."

James head turned sharply to his brother, and he spoke for the first time since Matt had entered the room.

"It's not contract time at that mill, Matt."

"I know," Matt answered grimly. "That's why I have to go."

"But Matt," DeDe coaxed, "I've just arrived. Surely you can send someone else this time."

"No, I can't. The negotiators have informed management they'll talk to no one but me. I don't relish trying to settle a wildcat. These men work for me. I'm going."

There was finality in his tone. He would listen to no more arguments.

There are ways, and then there are ways, Katherine thought wryly. But this way had not panned out for DeDe, who sat pouting prettily. James' face wore a concerned look and surprisingly, Beth had tears in her eyes.

Katherine sat quite still, hands clasped tightly in her lap, returning Matt's gaze. The effort it took to maintain that cool had caused her to tremble inside. But at least he would never know that.

6

The engine purred like a big contented cat. Katherine's sigh was not unlike a purr as she settled back comfortably against the deep red plush seat. The Thunderbird was show-room new, its sleek lines covered with sparkling white paint, and it had an untouched, virginal look. The interior even smelled new.

Matt, as usual, had been driven to the airport the day before, in the Continental. Like the small jet, the big black car was labeled "Matt's." It had nothing to do with ostentation. The roomy back seat afforded him space for both his large frame and for the business papers he invariably spread around himself.

She had voiced her surprise to Mary when they had come out of the house a short while ago. Not only at the sight of the unfamiliar car, but at Jack's father as well. She studied him as he helped

Mary and Jon into the back seat and stowed their cases in the trunk.

John Kline was of the same average height and burly build as his son. There the resemblance ended.

The father was weatherbeaten and craggy as opposed to the boyishly handsome countenance of the son. John wore his steel gray, tightly curly hair clipped close to his head whereas Jack wore his dark curls in the current vogue, full and bushy.

A deceptively slow moving, taciturn man, Katherine had seen John move with lightning speed. He had been driving her and Matt at the time and in avoiding a highway accident had reacted with such quickness and daring she had gasped out loud. Matt had barely glanced up from the papers he was reading.

She had heard the story of both father and son from Tom, who had heard it from Jack.

John Kline had gone to sea at the age of sixteen. He spent twenty years as a merchant seaman, retiring when his wife became ill. He had drifted from one job to another, trying to find his feet, when he met Matt. That had been fifteen years ago. The first five years he'd worked as general legman for Matt. The last ten, he'd been Matt's driver.

A short time after becoming Matt's driver John's wife succumbed to her illness. Within six months, on questioning from Matt, John reluctantly admitted he was having trouble with Jack. The boy, not yet sixteen, was running wild, becoming uncontrollable. Matt had said quietly, "I'll see what I can do."

Jack had told Tom frankly that at the time he was in all probability headed for the slammer.

Somehow Matt had known all about Jack. From his grades in school, to the names of everyone of the gang of boys he traveled around with and the fact that he had a passion for cars and their engines. Jack was, in his own words, a "motor head."

Matt had made Jack a proposition. If he stayed in school, going half day to academic classes, the other half to mechanics trade classes, on graduation he would be given complete charge of the care and maintenance of Matt's growing fleet of cars.

Jack had jumped at the chance. For not only, he explained to Tom, did this mean Matt's personal cars, but also the several he kept for his executives' use as well. A few years ago, as a bonus, Matt had allowed him to take instructions from his mechanics in the maintenance of plane engines.

Only on rare occasions had Jack been called on to do any chauffeuring until Matt married Katherine. Then he'd been told to keep himself available for her. So, wherever Katherine was, whether at the house or the apartment, Jack was usually there, too.

Surprisingly, Jack had not seemed to resent this, Tom had told Katherine. To the contrary, he seemed delighted with the added duty.

Tom had remained quiet for some time after relating all this to Katherine. He had just recently met Matt himself and, Katherine knew, was feeling somewhat jealous and usurped. Then he had said seriously, "You know, Mother, Jack said both he and John would gladly lay their lives on the line for Matt, and he meant it. What kind of a man is he, to get that sort of loyalty and respect?"

What kind of man indeed? Katherine had asked herself that question more than once since then.

"Jack's at the apartment now," had been John's first words on seeing the surprised look on her face as she left the house a short while ago. Before she could reply, he had tacked on, "They were planning to do some work on the Cessna's engine last night. That's why Jack drove the boss to the airport. But I've phoned him and he'll be in town by the time we get there."

Katherine was speechless for a moment. Was this man apologizing to her? She managed a small laugh as she said, "That's perfectly all right, John, what really surprised me is the car. It's very new, isn't it?"

"Yes, ma'am, delivered a half hour ago. This run to Philly will give me a chance to see how she handles." He paused then added, again his tone apologetic, "I'll have to bring it right back again, Matt left orders it was to be here for use by his sister and her guest. But the LTD is in the apartment garage and of course Jack had the Lincoln, so you won't be without transport."

This statement was tantamount to a speech for the usually silent John, and for the second time in ten minutes she found herself without words.

Katherine smiled now as the car sped along the highway towards the city, still amused and mildly amazed at John's attitude. Whatever gave the man the idea he had to explain anything to her?

She had wakened that morning with a small bud of pleasure inside her and had felt it growing as she prepared to leave the house. Now it was in full bloom and she recognized it for what it was. A deliciously exciting feeling of freedom. She had told herself she was being silly, but it hadn't stopped the growing feeling. After the weekend she had just gone through, if anything had happened to delay her plans, she'd have wanted to cry like a child denied a promised treat.

The dinner party Saturday evening had grown into a full scale bash. There had been twenty-four at the formal dinner table, but they had no sooner left the dining room than their ranks had swelled to at least fifty.

True to his word, Matt had spent almost the entire evening by DeDe's side, leaving Katherine with an empty ache inside. The fact that James, trying to compensate for his brother's lack of attention, spent far too much time by her side only caused her more discomfort. She would have had to be blind to miss the arch, curious glances that were leveled first on Matt then on herself, by most of the guests.

Mary had declared herself fed up not long after dinner and had escaped to her room. Katherine longed to do the same but knew somehow that to do so would incur Matt's anger, for although he barely spoke to her all evening, she had not missed the times he'd glanced around until he saw her. She hadn't the vaguest idea why he wanted her there, except to deliberately humiliate her, and that thought made the ache much, much worse.

By two in the morning the smile she had pasted onto her face had faded and she felt incapable of any more pleasant conversation with people she didn't know. Except for a few, she had never met any of the guests before. She had had it and noting Matt was nowhere in sight at the moment, thought, the hell with it. She slipped up the stairs into her room, and a few minutes later into bed.

She woke Sunday morning with a headache, a feeling of weariness, and a definite urge to roll over and go back to sleep, until she looked at the small clock on her night stand. Ten-thirty! She groaned aloud and dragged herself off the bed. She had no idea what time Matt had come to bed or if, in fact, he had been in bed at all for there was no sign of him now.

She was partially dressed, putting the finishing touches to her make-up, when Matt's voice called through the bathroom door. "Are you almost ready, Katherine? It's almost time to leave."

Violet eyes regarded their reflection in total blankness. Ready for what? Leave for where? She repeated the last thought out loud. "Leave for where?"

"Don't you remember?" Did his voice have an edge of impatience?

"We've been invited to the Carsons' for lunch."

No, she did not remember, she was tempted to

retort, simply because she had not personally been invited. But all she said was, "I'll be ready in a few minutes."

She had slipped into the mauve jersey dress that seemed to make her eyes look an even darker violet, and was brushing her hair when he strode into the bedroom.

"All set?" His voice, though brisk, was pleasant, and he looked disgustingly rested and attractive in a tan suede sports jacket. He didn't wait for an answer but went on, "Everyone else is ready to go. You'll need a coat, it's been raining and the air is raw. Which one do you want? I'll get it for you."

Katherine glanced out the window for the first time since wakening. She was not surprised to find the weather matched her mood.

"It doesn't matter. The gray raincoat, I suppose," she answered dully, her eyes still on the window.

She felt his eyes on her and turned, giving him a weak smile as she brought the brush back to her hair.

His eyes went over her slowly, then, apparently, satisfied with her appearance, turned on his heels and headed for the dressing room. She dropped the brush on the dressing table and hurried across the room calling out as she went through the door. "Matt, I'm going to take a peek at Jon. I'll only be a minute."

She was standing by the crib, thinking ruefully that the only times she'd seen her son the last few days was when he slept, when she felt Matt behind her. He stood very close, without touching, and she had the almost overpowering urge to turn, rest her head against his chest, draw strength from that large, vital frame. She turned the other way instead and walked to the door and whispered, "We'd better go."

The lunch had been an almost instant replay of the night before. The only difference being their numbers had been cut in half. Katherine ate very little and her headache grew steadily worse. It was late afternoon when they finally got home and Katherine went straight to her room.

It was over an hour later when Matt entered the room, paused a moment, then said quietly, "Katherine?"

"Yes?" She was lying on the chaise, head back, eyes closed. "I had a headache, but it's much better now," Katherine lied.

"Maybe if you ate something. Mrs. Rapp is putting out a cold supper."

"No," she interrupted him. "I'm not hungry. I'll just rest here a while longer then I'm going in to Jon. You go and have your supper." Then she caught her lip in her teeth as she saw his jaw harden. Her tone had held a note of dismissal, and she was quite sure it had been a very long time since anyone had used that tone with him. Her teeth dug more deeply into her lip as she braced herself for his anger but oddly it didn't come. He was quiet for some time and when he finally did speak his voice was calm, controlled. "I don't have time for supper, Jack's waiting now. You do remember I said I had to go to Pittsburgh tonight?"

"Yes, of course I remember, but I thought you

meant later tonight." She didn't add that on Friday he had merely said Sunday night and had barely spoken to her since then.

He was shaking his head before she'd finished speaking. "No, my case is already in the car. I'm leaving now." He hesitated then moved to stand beside the chaise, bend and brush his lips across her forehead.

"Matt wait! I must talk to you before you go." Fully awake now, Katherine realized she hadn't told him her plans for the next few weeks. He had turned and was halfway across the room when she spoke. He paused then shook his head again. "Not now, Katherine, I've told you I must go. Jack's waiting." Hardly breaking stride, he continued to the door.

"But . . ."

"Not now, Katherine, it'll have to wait. I have no idea how long I'll be gone. We'll talk when I get back. Goodbye, Katherine."

He was gone. What good would it be to talk when he got back? For all she knew she would be back by then. Katherine shrugged, oh well, if he was that uninterested she certainly wasn't going to worry about it.

Now, as the car ate up the miles into town, she thought about it again. Matt had seemed almost anxious in his haste to leave before she could speak. Had he been afraid she'd be difficult about the amount of time he'd spent with DeDe? No. The very idea of Matt being afraid of anything she had to say was ludicrous.

Katherine sighed, then, pushing all thoughts of

Matt away, felt again the surge of freedom bubble inside. She was going to enjoy the next two weeks.

The car slowed then turned onto the ramp that led to the underground garage of the large apartment block on the fringes of the city. A grinning Jack ambled up to the car as John slid from behind the wheel.

"Morning Mrs. M., Mary. Hi Dad, you heading right back to the house?"

John gave a brief nod of his head and seeing Katherine step from the car, went to the back seat to help Mary with Jon.

Jack removed their cases from the trunk, then walked slowly around the car, his eyes missing nothing. "I guess there's no time for me to take a quick look under the hood?" he asked his father, a faint tinge of hope in his voice.

"That's right," came the flat reply, but then relenting a little added, "you can play with the engine later."

"Okay," he answered cheerfully, and his grin broadened at the understanding smile that passed between Katherine and John.

"Goodbye John, and thank you." Katherine said as she walked toward the elevator.

"See you, Dad. Buzz me if there's anything."

Again John nodded briefly, then slid behind the wheel.

Jack watched as his father backed, then turned the car. Picking up the cases, he followed Katherine and Mary into the elevator.

Jack talked playfully to Jon as the elevator rose swiftly, silently, then halted and stopped at the penthouse floor. They stepped onto the deep pile carpeting of the wide hall just as the black painted door of the apartment directly opposite opened.

The man waiting by the door was large for a Filipino. Not quite six feet tall, he had a muscular frame, straight black hair and expressionless black eyes in a round, bland face completely devoid of any sign of age. From a distance he looked like a young man. Katherine knew him to be seven years older than Matt.

He had sole charge of the apartment, doing all the housework and cooking himself. The six months Katherine had lived there he had moved about the rooms silently, competently. The place was always spotlessly clean, and food perfectly prepared.

The only emotion Katherine had ever seen him display was one of almost dogged devotion to Matt. In all other respect he was quietly independent. How he and Matt met or the circumstances surrounding their relationship of almost master and slave, Matt had never told her and she'd been too timid to ask.

Smiling slightly now as he held the door wide he said, "Welcome Mrs. Martin. Hello Mary, Jack. How is young Jonathon today?"

'Fine, thank you, Clyde." Katherine answered as she stepped into the wide foyer landing. The smile inside was wider than the one on her lips. The incongruity of the man's name never failed to amuse her. She had decided, on first meeting him, that his mother must have been in a very humorous frame of mind when naming him.

Jack sat the cases on the floor and with a wave of his hand left the apartment saying, "I'll be in the garage if you need me, Mrs. M."

Clyde picked up the cases and stood back waiting for Katherine and Mary to precede him down the three shallow steps that led from the landing to the short hall leading to the bedrooms.

He set Katherine's case inside Matt's bedroom and said softly, "I'll serve lunch whenever you're ready, Mrs. Martin."

"Give us an hour to get settled, Clyde. Will it keep 'til then?"

He nodded, then walked down the hall to the rooms kept ready for Mary and Jonathon.

Less than an hour later Katherine and Mary entered the dining room and seated themselves at the table placed close to the large picture window. The tall buildings of the city were visible from this height and Katherine felt a small curl of anticipation just looking at them.

Clyde moved about the room silently as Katherine and Mary sat discussing plans for the next two weeks as they ate lunch. He had cleared the table and was serving coffee when Katherine mentioned her idea of calling Matt's secretary about a babysitter, to allow the two of them to shop together. "That won't be necessary, Mrs. Martin," he offered softly. "I'll be here with Jonathon."

Katherine looked up startled. "But I can't let you take care of an infant besides all your other duties," she protested.

"I assure you, he'll be no trouble for me at all.

I'm really very good with youngsters. I had six younger sisters and brothers."

"Well," she faltered. "I insist, Mrs. Martin." His voice though still soft was firm. Katherine capitulated with a laugh. "All right, Clyde, but I hope you fully realize what you're letting yourself in for."

"I do. And now, shall I leave the coffee pot and can I get you anything else?"

"Yes, leave the pot and would you bring the phone to the table, please?"

He did as she asked and left the room. Mary followed soon after, telling Katherine she'd leave her to her phone calls.

She lit a cigarette, then picked up the receiver and punched out Carol's number on the push buttons.

Carol's phone rang a long time before she answered it. With a sigh of relief Katherine said, "Hello Carol, how are you?"

"Katherine!" Carol cried joyfully. "How wonderful to hear from you. I was beginning to think you'd died or something. How are you?"

Katherine laughed. "I'm fine. I'm at the apartment, staying about two weeks. When can we get together?"

"How about coming for lunch tomorrow?" Carol asked, then added, "I'm on the last chapter of my latest masterpiece and then my time's my own for a while. Why don't you come early and stay late? We have a lot of catching up to do."

"Just what I had in mind," Katherine answered. "How does eleven o'clock sound?"

"Sounds great. I'll roll out the red carpet," Carol enthused.

"I'll be there. Now I'll leave you to get on with your labor pains. See you tomorrow."

Katherine was still smiling as she cradled the receiver. It would be good to see and talk to Carol again. She was a good friend and could always get her to laugh. And as Mary had said, it was a long time since she'd really laughed. Then her smile turned pensive. It had been through Carol that she'd met Matt.

7

The last thought plunged Katherine back into the past again. Without consciously thinking about it, she refilled her coffee cup and lit another cigarette. It had been Carol who had brought her to the city that first time.

Carol wrote books for children and Katherine had been commissioned to illustrate one of them. She had been enchanted with the story and pleased with her own finished product when she sent it back. Then she'd forgotten about it. At the time her mind had still been reeling from Janice's wedding.

Janice! Katherine shook her head drawing deeply on her cigarette. She had never understood her. Even as a child she had shown a singleness of purpose that had amazed Katherine.

She had grown from a quiet, pretty, fair-haired little girl into a cool, composed, golden-haired beauty. It seemed she had always known what she wanted and exactly how to get it.

Not long after Christmas, while in her first year
of college near Washington, she called Katherine
to tell her she would not be home for the weekend
as planned. She had accepted an invitation to a
house party at a school friend's home in Virginia.
Katherine had told her to have a good time, and
had thought no more about it.

The following Monday she had called again,
completely stunning Katherine with her first
words. "Mother, I've met the man I'm going to
marry."

It was a few seconds before Katherine could
ask, "Marry? Janice what are you talking about?"

"I've just told you, Mother," Janice answered
coolly. "Now don't interrupt and I'll tell you about
him. He's from Argentina." At Katherine's soft
gasp, she went on quickly. "Don't get upset,
Mother. He is very handsome and very aristo-
cratic. His name is Carlos Varga Ramirez, he is
twenty-six, the second son of an old, respected
family, and he is an aide with the diplomatic
corps. Of course, as you've guessed, I met him at
the house party. I mean it, Mother, I'm going to
marry him."

"But good heavens, Janice!" Katherine exclaimed, "you don't mean to tell me the man has
already proposed?"

Janice's cool, sweet laugh rang along the wire.
"Mother, really, of course he hasn't. But he will.
Oh, yes, he will. And very soon, too."

"Janice." Katherine's voice had taken on an
edge of impatience. "Aren't you being just a little

premature? You're only eighteen, you've just started college. I don't think—"

"Mother," Janice interrupted, "I mean what I say, so there is no point in arguing about it. Besides which this phone call will cost a fortune. I've invited him home next weekend; then maybe you'll understand."

Maybe she'd understand? Did Janice think she was an idiot? These were Katherine's thoughts as she cradled the receiver. To her way of thinking, her daughter had become infatuated with a man's good looks and demeanor. A teenage crush, which would soon pass.

It hadn't. Katherine told herself later that she should have known better. Janice was not like other girls her age. Had never been. Everything had gone as Janice had said it would, from beginning to end.

The following weekend had brought Janice and Carlos. Katherine had not known what to expect, but by Sunday evening, she was completely charmed with him. As Janice had informed her, he was extremely handsome, dark with classic features. Added to that he was sophisticated and urbane with a dry, sharp wit. To put the icing on the cake he was charmingly warm and friendly. Katherine found herself won over.

Their engagement was announced in March and for the next twelve weeks Katherine found herself in a frenzy of wedding preparations. Nothing would do for Janice but a June wedding. A lavish June wedding.

Katherine still paled at the thought. She had

fought a rising panic as the bills mounted during those weeks. Janice would not be dissuaded from the smallest trifle. She was marrying into a very old, very wealthy family, she had explained to Katherine. Everything had to be perfect.

Everything had been. The wedding was solemn and beautiful, the reception a smashing success. By the time the bride and groom left on their wedding trip to Europe and Katherine could go home and relax, she was depleted, both physically and financially.

When the last of the bills were finally paid, Katherine was appalled. Her bank balance, so carefully guarded over the past sixteen years, was practically wiped out. In another year Tom would be ready for college and she had barely enough to cover his expenses for one term.

The fact that the sixteen year old Tom didn't seem very concerned over her financial state didn't fool Katherine for one minute. She knew how much he had looked forward to college.

Tom had never given Katherine any trouble. He and Janice were as different as day and night. Where Janice was cool and disdainful, Tom was easy-going and calm. With a nature not unlike her own, he and Katherine had always been close. As he grew, his attitude had changed from one of dependence on her to protection of her.

It was Tom, more than anyone else, who had kept her stable during those frantic weeks before the wedding, laughingly telling her to "Keep it cool, Mom, you can handle it," every time she groaned over another expense.

His attitude to Carlos surprised her. She had expected him to be overwhelmed by the sophisticated Argentinian. He wasn't. Though he obviously liked him, he was in no way impressed. When she had gently probed his reason he had answered bluntly. "What's the big deal? Carlos is an aide with the corps and what money he has comes from his family. He'll very probably have a briliant political career, but up to now he's done nothing spectacular, so like I said, what's the big deal?" She had been too stunned to find an answer.

He had even gone as far, in the weeks before the wedding, to stop teasing his sister. Giving up, he told Katherine in mock seriousness, his mission in life, that of deflating his sister's overinflated ego. Then, when it was finally all over, he had given Katherine's own ego a boost by telling her that next to the bride, she was the most beautiful woman there.

Katherine had been determined to get the money for Tom's education. How to get it together was the problem that gave her many sleepless nights. Tom would be ready to enter college in a little over a year. Not nearly enough time to save the money, and the idea of taking a loan, going into debt, gave Katherine the horrors.

This was her state of affairs when Carol Benington came on the scene. Some three weeks after Katherine had submitted her illustrations of Carol's story she had answered her door chimes to an unfamiliar woman.

"Katherine Acker?" the woman had asked.

"Yes, I'm Katherine Acker," she had replied.

"I'm Carol Benington, may I come in?" Katherine had been delighted to meet the author of that enchanting story and told her so as soon as they had seated themselves in Katherine's living room.

Carol had laughed lightly, assuring Katherine the feeling was mutual. "Your illustrations are beautiful. I'd like you to do all my stories."

They saw quite a bit of each other after that. Not only because Carol was very prolific, but also because they became fast, firm friends.

Carol was a human dynamo. Of average height with a thin, wiry frame, a mass of fiery red hair around a vibrantly alive, pretty face, she was seldom still for more than a few minutes and seemed to charge the very air around herself.

They had been friends for months before Katherine confided her monetary problems to Carol. Carol had said at once, "That's no problem."

"What do you mean, no problem?" Katherine had asked, mystified. "Well, of course it's a problem, but easily solved," came the prompt reply.

"How?"

"Sell the house."

"Sell the—I can't do that!" Katherine had blurted.

"Why not? Doesn't it belong to you?" Carol had asked bluntly.

"Yes, of course it belongs to me." Katherine's voice had become defensive. "But it's my home.

Tom and Janice's too. I can't give it up."

"Katherine, I can give you a number of reasons why you not only could but should. Would you listen?" At Katherine's nod, she went on. "In the first place, you no longer have to make a home for Janice, that's Carlos' job now. As for Tom, once he starts college all he'll require is a place to touch home base every so often. That scamp would be happy anywhere you are. Now you, Katherine, have you any idea how empty this house is going to be after Tom goes away to college? The time is going to hang very heavily on your hands. Besides which, it's time you thought of yourself. You're a damned good illustrator, and you should be closer to where the action is. Sell the place, get an apartment in the city. Believe me, in no time you'll have more work than you'll know what to do with, and no time at all to feel homesick." Then she sat back, regarding Katherine steadily.

Katherine's thoughts were visible on her face. She had lived in this house seventeen years, had raised her children here. It was her home. But by the same token she knew Carol was right. Once Tom was no longer in and out every day, the house would be empty, too full of memories, both good and bad. She returned Carol's steady gaze. "I suppose you're right, but I must think about it."

"Of course you must," Carol had answered. "A decision like this is not easy to make. But it is a way out."

Katherine thought of little else the following weeks and finally decided Carol was right. Her mind made up, she wasted little time in placing the house on the market.

Tom took the proposed change in living accom-
modations in stride, surprising Katherine more
than a little when he said candidly, "It's the best
thing for you to do, Mom, and my going to college
or not has nothing to do with it. You're too young
and much too talented to bury yourself in the
suburbs."

Janice's reaction to the move was the direct
opposite. She was shocked and upset at the idea,
claiming that as long as Katherine had the house it
gave her (Janice) some sort of background.

Katherine wavered, not wanting to cause Janice
any unhappiness, until Carlos ended the
discussion telling Janice quietly but firmly not to
interfere with her mother's plans.

The house sold quickly, bringing almost double
the amount they had paid for it. With Carol's help,
Katherine found and rented a small two bedroom
apartment in center city. She and Tom made the
move and were settled in just two weeks before he
started college in New Jersey.

Even with the capital gains tax she had to pay on
the profit made from the house, Katherine again
had enough money in the bank to cover the cost of
Tom's schooling.

As the weeks went by, Katherine found she had
little time to miss either Tom or the house very
much. She was working in the office now, putting
in regular hours as well as many hours overtime.
She was swamped with work, and she loved it.

She was leaving the apartment on Friday
morning in October, on her way to work, when the

phone rang stopping her in mid-stride toward the door. She hesitated a moment, not wanting to miss her bus, then, thinking it might be one of the kids, ran back across the room and lifted the receiver. Carol's voice greeted her with, "I don't want to make you late, Katherine, so I'll make it quick. Do you have any plans for the weekend?"

"No."

"Good. How would you like to come out to the homestead with me? It will give you a chance to see the gorgeous horse who is the hero of my new book, plus give the two of us a chance to discuss the illustrative end of it before you get started. What do you say?"

"It sounds fine," Katherine laughed, "what time?"

"Well, if you can cut out of the office a bit early, I'll pick you up at the apartment about six-thirty. Can do?"

"Can do."

"Good, see you then. Bye." And the line went dead.

Katherine laughed softly to herself as she hurried out the door. How like Carol to save her from a quiet weekend. Tom had already informed her he was not coming that weekend as he had too much to do. Katherine was sure the real reason was that at the advanced age of eighteen, Tom was feeling his independence. At last, she thought, I'll finally get to see Carol's family home. She had heard all about it, in installments over the last year, and was looking forward to seeing it. Carol and her brother Richard had been born in the house and although Richard and his family were now in residence, Carol's parents having retired to Florida, Carol had been granted the right to come and go as she pleased.

Katherine stowed her case in the back seat of Carol's small car then herself in the front seat and said, "My coming along is all right with your brother, isn't it?"

"Of course, silly, as a matter of fact when I called to tell him we were coming he said they'd been wondering when they were going to meet you."

Katherine's brows rose in question and Carol grinned at her, adding, "You know I'm a blabbermouth. I've told them all about you, and of course they've seen your work. They were both very impressed."

Their progress was slow due to the heavy early evening traffic. Katherine saw little of the surrounding countryside as darkness had closed in before they had left the city behind.

The house was old and large. The kind of place that used to be referred to as belonging to a gentleman farmer. Katherine caught just a glimpse of the paddocks, looking ghostly white in the moonlight.

They were given a warm welcome by Richard and his wife Anne and within a half hour were sitting down to dinner, which Anne had kept waiting for them. By the time they had finished dinner and were having drinks in front of the fire in the living room Katherine felt as if she'd known them for years.

The next morning, after breakfast, Katherine was given a tour of the house and grounds and introduced to the prototype of Mister Midnight, the hero of Carol's story. An enormous stallion, his shiny coat as black as coal, he was a beautiful sight in the morning sunshine.

She set about at once making rough sketches of hm as he danced around the corral, tossing his head and snorting, performing for the delighted group watching at the rails.

"He's a magnificent animal," she said later to Carol, as they walked back to the house.

"Yes," Carol smiled, then she laughed out right and added, "just like the man who gave him to me. About as independent too; very few people can handle him."

"Who, Richard?"

"Richard! Heavens no. Richard's a pussycat. Matt gave him to me for my last birthday." Carol's mouth twisted in a mock grimace. "My thirty-fifth." Then she laughed again adding, "He said we deserve each other."

Who? Katherine wondered, Carol and this man Matt, whoever he was, or she and the horse?

She was about to ask who Matt was when Carol offered. "You'll meet Matt at dinner tonight and I hope you'll be suitably impressed."

Katherine had opened her mouth to ask who this Matt was when again Carol spoke first. "Richard and Anne are having a few close friends in for dinner this evening and Matt's Richard's closest friend besides being his most important client."

Katherine knew, from things Carol had told her

about her family, that beneath Richard's charming indolent facade lay a personality as dynamic and energetic as Carol's own. She also knew that he headed one of the fastest growing firms of corporation lawyers in the Philly area. So it would seem this Matt whoever was a business man.

Carol had barely paused for breath before plunging Katherine into a discussion on her ideas as to illustrating the story of Mister Midnight and with a mental shrug, Katherine decided she'd surely learn the man's name that night.

It was not to be, for he didn't show up. Dinner had been for eight o'clock and it was now a few minutes after eight. Katherine had met the five other guests and was sipping her pre-dinner drink listening to the conversation and observing her host and hostess when the phone rang. She smiled softly as she watched Richard saunter from the room to answer it. He reminded her of Carlos. Tall, slim and almost beautifully handsome with a natural elegance enhanced by his perfectly cut clothes. Anne matched him perfectly. She was also tall and slim and although not pretty in the accepted way, her face was animated and vivacious. She had a charming manner which at once was endearing. Katherine had spent the afternoon getting to know them better and was looking forward to meeting their two teenage daughters who were in Switzerland in school.

Richard strolled back into the room, a wry grin on his lips. When the room had become quiet he laughed softly and said, "I have just received a telegram," as he waved a small piece of paper in front of him. Then, steadying the paper, he read aloud, "Sorry. Stop. Last minute conference prevents my making dinner. Stop. Look forward to seeing you all over the holidays. Stop. My apologies to Anne. Stop. Kiss the wild one for me. Stop. Matt." And still laughing, Richard added, "We may as well go in to dinner."

As they walked into the dining room Carol grinned and said impishly to Katherine, "I'm the wild one."

Katherine's eyes widened and she said chidingly, "Carol, you've never mentioned a special man before, I had no idea there was one in your life."

Carol's face sobered and her smile was somehow sad. "Oh, there is one. Oh yes! But it isn't Matt. Matt is an old and very dear friend. Someday, when I'm in one of my feeling-sorry-for-myself moods, I'll tell you about *the man.*"

Katherine could do nothing but stare at her. Never had she heard that bitter tone from Carol. She looked at her friend in consternation, sensing a deep hurt inside her, and felt a strong urge of compassion. She wanted to say something to Carol, offer her help, if only a shoulder to cry on, yet she hesitated, not wanting to pry.

She was pulled out of her own thoughts by the sound of Richard's voice and she glanced up to see him lift his wine glass. He waited until the others at the table had lifted theirs then said, "Wherever he is, at whatever conference table, to Matt."

The voices around Katherine were strong as they echoed, "To Matt."

8

Matt.

Katherine's sigh was just short of being a moan. Oh Matt. A wave of pure misery swept over her, leaving her feeling empty, drained, as blinking her eyes she emerged from her reverie.

She stared a moment at her still half full coffee cup and made a face at the now unappealing contents. Then her eyes shifted to the ashtray which held the remains of four cigarettes she didn't even remember lighting. A look of self-derision crossed her face as she told herself, well, you silly woman, you've done it again. You seem to spend more time in the past lately than in the present.

Why? Why had she accepted his offer of marriage? Up to that time she had known what it was to be lonely, and had dealt with it, but never before had she experienced this racking sense of desolation or, worse yet, this greedy yearning to

be close to a man, both physically and mentally.
Why had she said yes to his offer? She hadn't been
in love with him then. Had she? And yet the questions that tormented her even more were, what
were his reasons? Why had he made the offer?

Dragging her thoughts from the labyringth of
her own mind, which had produced no answers
anyway, she again picked up the phone's receiver
and punched out a long distance number. As she
listened to the connection being made and then
the phone ringing she lit a cigarette and drew
deeply. She was smoking too much. She knew it.
Most times they didn't even taste good anymore.
Then giving a small shrug, she thought, what the
hell does it matter, just as a voice said "Hello" at
the other end of the line.

"Janice? Hello darling, how are you feeling?"
Katherine congratulated herself for the normal
tone of voice.

"I'm fine, Mother, becoming a little impatient to
have it all over with. But of course you understand
that feeling."

"Yes, I do." Katherine laughed. "And how's
Carlos bearing up?"

Janice's answering laughter sang along the
wire. "You know Carlos by now. His breeding and
upbringing forbid any emotional display, but he is
starting to look a little strained around the edges."

Katherine's voice deepened with warmth. "Poor
Carlos. I suppose the first baby is always harder
on the father."

"It didn't seem to affect Matt." Janice's voice
had sobered.

Katherine winced and felt glad Janice could not see her face at that moment. With effort she kept her tone normal. "Yes, well, Matt's quite good at keeping his thoughts and feelings to himself. I believe he's an excellent poker player."

"I don't doubt it," Janice's voice again held laughter. "How is he, by the way?"

"He's fine. Working very hard. He had to go to Pittsburgh last night, some sort of labor problem." Katherine heard the tightness beginning to edge her tone and she hurried on, "Has the doctor limited your traveling, Janice?"

"Only as far as long distances are concerned, why?"

"I thought of having a small celebration for Tom's birthday next weekend and I was hoping you and Carlos could come up." Katherine's voice had steadied and she went on firmly, "Nothing very eleborate, just family and a few close friends."

"Unless I'm actually in the hospital, of course we'll come. I wouldn't miss Tommy's birthday party. I can hardly believe he's going to be twenty years old next week."

"Neither can I." Katherine smiled. What was even harder for her to believe was the change in attitude, to each other, that her offspring had shown since Janice's marriage. Gone was the disdain Janice had always accorded her brother. And although Tom still teased his sister, it was in a different manner, one she seemed to enjoy.

The only discord they had shown was in their reaction to Matt. Janice, social climber that

Katherine ruefully admitted she was, was stunned and then thrilled when Katherine had told them she had accepted Matt's proposal. Matt was an important man and Janice was delighted at the idea of having him as a stepfather. Tom, on the other hand, had grown sullen and withdrawn, confusing and hurting her with his uncharacteristic behavior until a chance remark of his made her realize he was jealous of Matt.

For the first few months after their marriage, Tom had treated Matt with cold civility and Katherine had worked unceasingly to assure him of his continued place in her life and affections. She did not to this day know whether it was her efforts or Matt's that had finally won Tom over. In all fairness to him, she had to admit that Matt had shown exceptional patience with her son. Tom's behavior at times had been downright rude. Katherine had found it hard to believe that Matt would take that kind of treatment from anyone, let alone an eighteen year old boy. But he had not only taken it, he had somehow used it to his own advantage, bringing Tom to a complete about face. There existed between them now an easy comaraderie that she sometimes envied.

Janice's voice broke her thoughts. "Mother did you hear me? I asked when you wanted us at the house?"

"Not the house, dear. I'm at the apartment in town. I thought Tom might like a night out so I'm considering one of the restaurants here in town. And I came in early to make the arrangements and do some shopping. Do you think you could come up in the afternoon a week from Friday? That way you'd be here when Tom gets here Friday night."

"I'm sure that can be arranged, unless as I said, I'm otherwise occupied with producing the heir. And if there is anything I can do from here let me know."

"I will," Katherine answered, "but I doubt if there will be anything. I want to keep this party small, you know how Tom hates any fussing. At any rate I'll call you again at the beginning of next week to see how you're feeling. So, bye for now and take care."

After replacing the receiver, she wandered into the living room, glancing around with satisfaction. She liked the room, felt comfortable in it, which was odd, for it was definitely Matt's room. It seemed to speak his name out loud to her. Functional, almost stark, yet she could relax in it.

Katherine smiled, remembering how she'd caught her breath the first time she'd seen it. A large room, two of the walls were of glass, giving a panoramic view of the city beyond. The ceiling and two other walls were painted flat white, the carpeting was salt and pepper shag. An extra long sofa and several occasional chairs were upholstered in white ultra suede and four end tables and a coffee table were of ebony. The only splashes of color in the room were the crimson of the draperies, which could be drawn completely across the glass walls, the six toss pillows on the sofa and a large painting on the one wall, which depicted a fiery sunset behind mountains shaded from purple to black. The lamps and ashtrays which were the room's only ornaments were in the same flat white and ebony.

Black and white. Functional and businesslike. As is the man himself, Katherine thought, with now and then splashes of emotional color. Shaking her head at her own whimsey, she went to the bedroom to unpack.

Lunch with Carol the following day was a small celebration in itself. Carol was getting married. Katherine had no sooner stepped into the apartment when Carol hugged her and whirled her around the room. Eyes glowing with happiness she nearly sang her news. "I could hardly wait for you to get here, and I didn't want to tell you over the phone yesterday. Paul's wife has finally agreed to a divorce. It's already been started and it will take a few months but, oh Katherine, he'll be free and then we'll be able to get married and I'm so happy it almost scares me." Laughing and crying at the same time, she stopped in the middle of the room and let go of Katherine's hands. Murmuring, "Sit down," she sank onto the sofa, covered her face with her hands and cried unashamedly for a few minutes.

Katherine pressed her handkerchief into Carol's hand then sat quietly, waiting for the storm to abate. She knew what this meant to Carol, and that she needed the release of tears after the long wait.

Carol had told her, almost exactly two years ago, that someday when she was depressed, she'd tell her about the man in her life. That day had come two months later. It had been a gray, blustery day in mid-December and Katherine had not been home from work too long and was thinking about getting herself some supper, when Carol had shown up at the apartment. She had seemed strangely subdued and when Katherine had commented on it, she'd shrugged and said she had the pre-Christmas blues and Katherine had made no further comment on it. They had finished a light soup and sandwich supper and were having their second cup of coffee, when Carol started to talk.

She had met Paul Collins at an afternoon cocktail party at the home of her publisher three years before and had liked him at once. After the party broke up she had gone out to dinner with him, and over dinner he'd told her he was married and that he and his wife were legally separated. It had not seemed too important at the time, but she had continued to see him and before long it was the most important thing in the world. For the first time in her life she was deeply in love. She had been in love before, of course, she had told Katherine, three or four times in fact. But there was no comparison whatever in the way she had felt about those other men and the feeling she had for Paul.

Carol had been seeing Paul for several weeks when one evening over a nightcap in her apartment, he told her he thought they had better stop seeing each other. She had been so sure that he returned her feelings that his words had left her speechless for a few seconds. She had just stared at him, then blurted, "Why?" He had stared back at her, then answered quietly, "Because I'm in love with you and I don't want you hurt." She started to speak and he interrupted. "Carol, you know my daughter will be thirteen next month?" She nodded, feeling confused. What had his daughter to do with it?

"My wife won't give me a divorce," he'd gone on, "and if I start the action she'll turn it into a dog fight. Carol, honey, I can't have Sue in the middle of that. She's just beginning to accept the separation. She's at such a difficult age, and an ugly divorce fight would tear her apart. Do you understand that?"

She'd nodded again dumbly, still not sure what his point was, then she'd whispered, "But what has it got to do with you and I seeing each other?"

The control he'd shown up to this point, Carol had gone on to Katherine, seemed to crack, and with a muffled curse, he'd grabbed her shoulders and given her a shake. "It has everything to do with us. I can't make any plans for the future. I can't offer you anything. I've just told you, I love you and I don't want you hurt and if we go on seeing each other you will be."

"But I haven't asked you for any promises," she'd objected. With that his control had shattered completely. He'd groaned and pulled her against him. "I know you haven't. But don't you see, I want to love you, damn it, I want to sleep with you, and I have nothing to give you."

"You have yourself," she'd answered.

He stayed that night and he'd stay many nights since.

Carol had been staring at the carpet during her narrative and then she'd glanced up to study Katherine's face. "You're not shocked?"

"Shocked?" Katherine's eyes widened in surprise. "Did you think I would be?" Then, her voice dry, she added, "I do know people sleep together, Carol."

"Yes, of course you do," Carol's smile was wan, "but you always seem so cool, so self-contained. The more earthy things seemed beneath your notice."

Then Katherine had been shocked. Was that how Carol saw her? Was that how everyone saw her. "You consider me frigid and unfeeling?" she asked in a low tight voice.

"No. No. Not unfeeling." Carol shook her head, her voice contrite. "But, oh, I don't know, you never seem to notice men or anything about them. I'm putting this badly, and Lord, Katherine, the last thing in the world I want to do is hurt your feelings. Please forget I said anything. I'm in a blue funk and not expressing myself well."

At the look of unhappiness on Carol's face Katherine's thoughts went from herself back to Carol. They had talked the night away and Katherine's personality was not referred to again. But she was to remember Carol's words many times over the next two years.

Now, Carol wiped her face, blew her nose and grinned at Katherine. "I'm really an idiot. Do you know, I've not given into tears once over the last five years. Now here I am blubbering like a fool because the impossible has happened." Although her words were self-mocking, the glow was back in her eyes.

"You amaze me," Katherine said warmly. "I don't see how you got through those years without the release of a good cry regularly. I know I wouldn't have." And she didn't know whether to feel amused or concerned at the look of disbelief on Carol's face.

She thought of that look, and Carol's words of two years ago, while she changed clothes after returning to the apartment. First cool and self-contained. Now tearless. She didn't know if she wanted to laugh or cry. If they only knew, she thought.

There were more lunch dates and shopping trips with Carol over the next eight days and Katherine and Mary went shopping twice together, thanks to the ever-surprising Clyde's capabilities as a sitter for Jon.

The following Thursday morning Katherine woke late, and stretching her arms high over head, lay there planning her day. She still had shopping to do, for although she had added quite a few things to her own and Jon's wardrobe, she had not been able to suit herself as to a gift for Tom.

She yawned, still feeling sleepy. James had asked her to have dinner with him soon after her arrival in town and she had hedged uncertainly until finally giving in and agreeing to go with him last night. She had been uneasy with him at first but her reserve soon melted under the warmth of his charm. She'd had a lovely time and it had been after two that morning before she'd slipped into bed.

Even sleepy, she felt good. Better than she had in weeks. Most of the tension which had had her in its grip, when she'd left the house almost two weeks ago, had drained away. She was much more relaxed, the only sour note being that she had not heard a word from Matt.

Thinking his name brought his image to mind and with a soft sigh she rolled across the bed and buried her face in his pillow. A wave of longing swept over her, so intense it left her feeling weak in its wake. Did he care so little for her and Jon, that he couldn't bother to phone? The question that had stabbed her for months jabbed again. Why had he asked her to marry him? Why her? Not wanting to think of him or the past she closed her eyes hoping for sleep to claim her and blot out memories. Her action had the opposite effect.

It was the Monday between Christmas and New Year and Carol had called her in the office during the morning asking her to meet her at Bookbinder's for lunch. Katherine had been a few minutes late and Carol had a Margarita waiting for her. Barely giving her time to slip into her seat, say "hi" and sip from her drink, she said, " What are you doing New Year's Eve?" Then she laughed and added, "I should put that to music, I'd make a fortune."

"I think you're just a few years too late." Katherine laughed. "I'm not doing anything. Why?"

"I have an invitation for you from Anne and Richard. They'd like you to join their gathering. They'd have invited you sooner but they somehow got the idea you and Tom were spending the holidays in Washington. I spoke to Richard on the phone this morning and when he asked if I'd heard anything from you I mentioned the fact that Tom had been invited to spend New Year's Eve and Day with a friend. He insisted I call you at once and not take no for an answer."

"How big a gathering will it be?" Katherine asked.

"Well, it won't be a crush. Thank heavens they don't go in for that kind of bash. But it will be quite a few. More New Year's Eve than Day. You've probably met most of them by now and I'm sure you'll like the ones you haven't met yet. With New Year's Day falling on Thursday, Richard suggested you drive out late Wednesday afternoon and stay through Sunday. What do you think?"

Katherine had thought it sounded wonderful. She had not been looking forward to spending what was left of the holidays alone. Janice and Carlos had flown to Argenina to spend the holidays with his parents and Tom had left two days after Christmas for some skiing at Camelback and from there to a New Year's Eve party at a friend's house outside of Reading.

They had a change in plans at the last minute. Richard decided it would be foolish for Carol to drive to the house as he was leaving the city soon after a business luncheon and could pick the two women up and take them with him. He would be driving back into the city Monday morning in plenty of time for Katherine to get to her office, so why waste the gas using both cars?

The house was gloriously decked in shiny, deep green holly with dark red velvet bows strategically placed. A live blue spruce tree stood in the center of the bowed front window, shimmering in white and silver from its base to its tip, which touched the ceiling twelve feet above.

After greetings and hugs were exchanged with Anne, Katherine was introduced to a couple, about the same age as Richard and Anne, who were also guests for the weekend. Dr. Charles, called Chuck, and Corrine Kearney were from Boston and as this was the first time in years they were all together, the general atmosphere was one of festive anticipation.

They spent the following few hours in relaxed conversation and Katherine learned that Chuck, who had taken his pre-med at the same small college that Richard had done his pre-law, and Richard were two of the trio known, in their college days, as the terrible trio. The third member being the oft mentioned, but still never met, Matt. She also learned she would not meet him that night either, as he always played host to his family New Year's Eve. "The one ritual he induges Beth in," Carol had remarked, laughingly. Katherine had assumed Beth was his wife.

The party had been fun and although there were easily forty guests the large house accommodated them without crowding. Katherine had moved from one group to the other talking and laughing, sometimes wondering, for much of the conversation seemed centered on the elusive Matt.

9

Lying on her back on Matt's side of the bed, Katherine stared at the ceiling as if at a large T.V. screen. Uncaring of the passage of time, no longer trying to blot out the images rushing across her mind, she allowed the web of memories to close around her like a cocoon.

She could see the New Year's morning breakfast table. Could hear the laughing voices around it. They had all been in high spirits that morning and they had done more laughing than eating as they held a post-mortem on the party.

Katherine had finished eating and was starting on her second cup of coffee and first cigarette of the day, when Corrine sighed, "I wish Matt could have been here." Chuck squeezed her hand murmuring, "We all do, honey."

"Yes," Richard's smile was cynical, "But you know Beth when she sets her mind on something.

And these law few years this New Year's Eve bash of hers has become her pet project."

"It's ridiculous really." Carol's tone held impatience. "Most of Matt's friends were here last night. I doubt if he even likes the people she has to her parties. Excluding James, of course. The way he has spoiled that sister of his amazes me."

His sister? No one had offered any comment on Carol's statement, but Richard had nodded in agreement, then said, "Well, barring a major catastrophe or any minor business problems, he'll be here today. And, believe it or not, he assured me he'll stay until Sunday morning."

"I'll believe it when I see it," Carol had snorted. "I can't remember the last time that man had a vacation. He works too hard."

"He loves it. He always has, and you know it," Chuck chided her, then turning to smile at Richard he said, " 'The terrible trio,' together again."

Glancing from one to the other, Katherine had asked curiously, "How did you acquire the title 'terrible trio'? I can't imagine two less terrible men." Both the men had grinned at her, and Chuck supplied the answer. "The terrible part pertained to our grades. We all had the highest levels, in our courses, and we were informed by quite a few of our fellow students that we were setting a terrible example." Here Richard had taken up the explanation. "We seemed to gravitate to each other from the beginning and could be found together whenever we had free time. Even though free time was already a luxury for Matt even then. Thus, the trio." He had paused, then added thoughtfully, "I suppose, to others, it seemed an unlikely combination. Not so much with Chuck and me, as with the two of us and Matt, who was, I might add, even then the undisputed boss." Chuck, laughing softly, had nodded his head in emphatic agreement.

At the look of confusion on her face, Carol had supplemented, "both Richard and Chuck came from what was generally referred to as well-to-do people. The fact that the two of them not only liked Matt but deferred to his opinion seemed to bewilder some people."

"He came from a different background?" Katherine had asked. "Entirely," was Chuck's prompt reply. "And he had to work his tail off just to stay in school. While Richard and I were making trips to the bank to cash checks from home, Matt was scouting around doing all kinds of work he could find. From busing tables in one of the bigger restaurants in town, to selling men's wear in a department store at Christmas. The summers were even worse. I know for a fact that for three summers he held down two full time jobs in different factories. One first shift, the other third shift. I believe he owns one of the places now. Doesn't he, Richard?"

"Both of them," Richard answered. "He bought the second one a few years ago."

Corrine entered the conversation then as, turning to her husband, she asked, "Do you remember that Christmas you finally managed to drag him to your parents' home?" At his nod, she turned to Katherine and explained. "It was the last year they were in school together and Chuck's parents had invited Richard and Matt for the holidays. On first meeting him I was stunned. I couldn't believe that this ill-dressed young man could be the person Chuck thought so highly of. Yet, within a very short time his clothes didn't seem to matter at all. When I think of the way he looked then and the way he looked the last time I saw him, I can hardly believe it. Yet he is exactly the same. Compelling, exciting. I don't know why but I feel more alive, somehow, when Matt's around."

At this last remark, Katherine glanced around the table noting the three others nodding their agreement. "Seems to make things hum, Matt does," Richard said laconically, then glancing at his watch, added, "Do you ladies realize that in about forty-five minutes our guests will be ringing our chimes, so to speak?"

In unison, the four women had jumped to their feet and, the men's laughter following them, made for their respective rooms to change.

It had been well over an hour before Katherine left her room, the majority of that time being spent in indecision over whether to wear the jumpsuit she had bought with this day in mind. In deep amethyst velvet, it was cut beautifully, with a two inch wide belted waist and oversized shoulder pads. The plunging neckline was trimmed in rhinestones and silver as was the edge of the long sleeves which hung wide and full from the shoulders and tapered triangularly to fit snugly an inch above her wrist. She was wondering if perhaps it wasn't a bit too much when she remembered Carol's stated intentions of wearing white silk lounging pyjamas and with a tiny shrug, left the room.

There were already quite a few guests in the living room. Six or seven of them, all female, sat with Carol and Corrine in a loose circle directly across the room from the large double doorway, in which Katherine had paused to glance around. On seeing her, Carol waved to her to join them and moved a high wing-backed chair into the only open space in the circle.

She made her way slowly across the room, stopping to exchange New Year's greetings as she went and on reaching the circle faced a grinning Carol. "We thought you'd never get here. We're in the middle of a good gossip and we're waiting with bated breath for Helen to continue."

Katherine had not met several of the women and after introductions were made she sat down, accepted a cup of coffee Carol poured from a large glass pot which sat on a low table in the center of the circle, shook her head at the tray of cookies and sliced fruit cake Carol offered her and sat back comfortably as one of the women said, "I don't believe it."

"I tell you he's left her." The speaker was Helen, a tall, buxom woman in her fifties, who was seated

two chairs away on Katherine's right. "I had lunch
with her yesterday, and I can assure you that I'm
giving away no confidences as I was having lunch
with Opal and Tina Franklin and she spoke freely
in front of them."

At the assorted gasps and groans when the
Franklins were mentioned Carol glanced at
Katherine and stated, "Tina Franklin is the worst
gossip on the Eastern Seaboard."

"Exactly," Helen snorted. "I tried to give Peggy
the high sign to caution her tongue, but she was
already on her third double Martini and she just
kept on."

Katherine was sitting across the low table from
Carol and she saw the brief look of pain that
crossed her face as she sighed. "You may as well
tell us what Peg said as we'll probably hear it from
Tina before too long anyway."

"Well, she was more than a little depressed."
Helen smiled. "But of course, after three double
Martinis, I'd be more than a little unconscious.
She told us he had been very kind, he had been
very considerate, he had been very definite. And I
don't know anyone who can be as definite as Matt
can."

Matt! Again? Katherine was beginning to think
cynically, that this man was the only topic of
conversation these people knew. It seemed she
had heard very little of anything except Matt since
she arrived. She was getting pretty weary of the
name.

A small, thin woman, whose name Katherine

couldn't remember, sighed wistfully, "I really thought this time we'd be going to Matt's wedding. This one lasted longer than most of the others."

"Good Lord, she's only twenty-two," Carol snapped. "Nineteen years younger than he is."

He's only forty-one! The same age as Richard, Katherine thought. That fact surprised her. Somehow with all the talk of his success and the way everyone seemed to look up to him, even in his college years, she had gotten the impression he was much older.

"Well, the question of ages really doesn't matter now because for him, at any rate, the affair is finished." With this Helen again gained control of the conversation, adding with brows raised, "Peg is really wracked out about it and she went into some detail."

Was it her imagination, Katherine wondered, or did some of the women actually lean forward in their chairs, as a chorus of "go on's" followed Helen's last words. She knew she didn't imagine Carol's wince.

"Well, it seems he's not only one of the most attractive men she's ever met," Helen smiled, then chuckled, "or any of us has ever met, but also, the most exciting ever, in bed."

"Helen," Carol warned, frowning.

"Oh for heaven's sake, Carol," Helen frowned back. "It isn't something we haven't heard before. At least from the ones who'd talk after he'd finished with them. How many has it been now since he and Sherry divorced? He even manages to inspire loyalty in the ones who do talk. I wonder how many times I've heard, either first or second hand, how wonderful, how attractive, how generous, how down right excitingly sexy he is."

Katherine leaned foward to hand her cup to Carol for refilling. As she poured the coffee Carol said quietly, "It's ten years since Matt and Sherry were divorced and you know it, Helen. And there really have not been all that many women. But I do wish he'd get married again. I think he needs a wife." Then, smiling at Katherine over the coffee pot, added, "As an innocent bystander, what do you think, Katherine?"

"Me?" Katherine asked in surprise and, at Carol's nod, lowered her eyes to her cup considering her answer carefully as she stirred cream into her coffee. In so doing, she missed the look of happy welcome that transformed Carol's face and was unaware of the total silence in the circle around her. She decided to be totally honest and answered slowly. "I think he needs a keeper, and I'd feel sorry for any woman who found herself married to this rich man's Don Juan."

"Happy New Year, Matt." Carol's happy voice brought Katherine up straight in her chair. The sentiment echoed round the circle and Katherine wished fervently to shrivel up and die. Had he heard? As Carol moved around Katherine's chair, hands outstretched, she thought, oh damn, he must have heard, he's standing right behind my chair.

"Happy New Year, Outlaw." The deep, faintly

raspy voice was incredibly masculine causing Katherine's spine to go rigid. There was a muffled sound that told her Carol was being kissed, then Carol's voice saying softly, "Katherine."

She stood up slowly, willing herself to be calm. By the time she turned and moved around the chair, she was the picture of Carol's description of her, cool, self-contained, uncaring.

Her composure was tested at the first sight of him, for without being, in any way, brawny or bulky, he looked enormous. In fact he was almost slim, but the breadth of his chest, the width of his shoulders on a large, angular frame which easily stood six feet five or six inches, gave the impression of sheer size.

As if the look of him hadn't been enough, she was tested even further when, tilting her head back to look up at him, she encountered the most unnerving pair of blue eyes she had ever seen. That the eyes now held more than a touch of amusement only served to annoy her.

"I finally get to introduce you two," Carol's voice held satisfaction as she went on. "Katherine Acker, Matt Martin."

Something stirred inside Katherine as she thought, he reminds me of someone. But who? The thought was quickly forgotten as she repeated his "How do you do" and felt her hand swallowed up in his long fingered, broad one.

"I've seen some of your work. I'm impressed." The statement was delivered in a low tone that seemed to laugh with mockery. She felt herself bristle and before she could stop the words, replied acidly, "I've only just heard about yours. I'm not."

Turning on her heel she walked across the room to where Richard was standing, Carol's gasp and Matt's soft laughter burning her ears.

What in the world had come over her? To speak to a guest like that in Richard's home was unthinkable and not at all like her. These thoughts, plus the nagging idea that he reminded her of someone, plagued her for the rest of the afternoon.

It seemed, as the room grew steadily more crowded and her own thoughts continued to torment her, the velvet suit became heavier and heavier and she became more and more warm, until finally she felt she had to get some fresh air or she'd scream. She made her way slowly out of the room, down the wide central hallway and out through the door at the back of the staircase.

The flagstone path she followed led around the house to the rear. She stopped midway along the path where she had an unobstructed view of the paddocks and the meadows beyond. The cold January air was a shock as well as a relief and sliding her hands into the deep slash pockets in the narrow pants, she lifted her eyes to the sky. The morning sun had been a spring daffodil yellow but sometime during the day, unnoticed by Katherine, clouds had overcast the bright blue. Now, at the time of day when the fiery gold fingers of sunset should be blazing on the horizon, everywhere overhead looked like dirty cotton wadding.

Intent on her observation of nature, Katherine didn't hear the footsteps until just before they stopped next to her. Somehow she knew who it was and her fingers curled into her palms inside the pockets.

There was no sound for some minutes, then his deep voice confirmed her intuition. "My mother would say that's a mackerel sky and that it looks like snow." A small smile tugged at the corner of her mouth as she felt the tension ease out of her. "My mother would too. As a matter of fact I used the expression myself as my children were growing up. I've even heard my daughter refer to a snow gray sky as mackerel."

Then turning, she looked up at him and said quickly, "Mr. Martin, I want to apologize for what I said to you earlier."

"Accepted." His deep voice grated. "But why apologize for something you believe to be true?"

"I don't know if it is true," she murmured. "And I have no right to speak like that to a guest in Richard's home." As she finished speaking Katherine slid her hand from her pocket and touched his arm impulsively. Again the feeling of familiarity stirred through her, leaving her confused, wondering why. As if her thoughts were printed on her forehead, he laughed and said softly, "You haven't figured it out yet, have you?"

"What?" she asked, more bewildered than ever.

But he shook his head and turned his eyes back to the sky. "I'm afraid my mother's prediction would be correct. We'll have snow before too long." Her own eyes followed his. "Yes."

He turned abruptly to her, his eyes intent on her face, then stated firmly, "We'd better go back to the house. Although I'm sure that lovely jumpsuit is warm, I don't think it's much protection against the teeth in this air. Come along before you catch a chill." She couldn't help smiling as she asked mildly. "Are you always this bossy?"

"Always." His reply was equally mild, yet firm.

The next two days passed uneventfully. Katherine saw very little of Matt or the other two men as they were off somewhere together. Being the "terrible trio" once again, she supposed. She and Carol went for short walks after lunch but the days were so damp and chill they soon sought the warmth of the living room fire place and the company of Anne and Corrine. The weather left Katherine feeling lethargic and she went to bed early. She woke Sunday morning to the quiet of a snow white world outside and Richard and Anne's exuberant teenagers inside.

The girls, Lisa and Gayle, had been sent to spend part of the holidays with Anne's parents and now, happy to be home, they were noisily taking possession of their parents again.

Katherine entered the dining room to the sound

of young voices recounting in detail everything that had happened since they'd left. They paused in their narration long enough to acknowledge her, then plunged, head-long, back into it until Matt entered the room. With squeals of delight they jumped away from the table in unison and flung themselves against him.

"Good Lord," his raspy voice growled at them. "Don't you brats have any consideration for a man just out of his bed?" And catching them up in his long muscular arms, he pulled them off their feet against his chest in a fierce bear hug.

Laughing, trying to catch her breath and speak at the same time, the thirteen-year-old Gayle gasped, "Uncle Matt, how long are you staying?"

"I'm leaving right after lunch."

"No, please," the girls begged.

"Right after lunch." His tone was adamant and although they both gave him pouty looks they ceased to beg. He seated himself at the table before adding teasingly, "Now if you'll both let me have my breakfast in peace and comparative quiet, for this place has sounded like a mad house for the last half hour, I'll give you your Christmas gifts. A little late I know, but I somehow think you won't be disappointed."

The room became blissfully quiet and Katherine had finished her breakfast and was sipping her coffee when the phone rang and Lisa went to answer it. She was gone only a few seconds and as she reentered the room said, "It's for you, Mrs. Acker."

"Thank you," she replied quietly as she hurried from the room, the thought springing to her mind of Janice and Carlos flying back to Washington from Argentina. She said "Hello" breathlessly and heard Tommy's voice saying gaily over the wire "Hi, Mom, Happy New Year, I'm home." Katherine had called his friend's home before leaving town, leaving a message for him where she'd be but she had not thought to mention when she'd be home as he'd planned to go on to school from his friend's home. Letting her breath out now in mixed relief and consternation she cried "Tommy, honey, I thought you were driving straight to school from Curt's home."

"I was going to, but last night I decided to spend today with you so I left early this morning."

"Oh dear, and I'd made arrangements to drive into town early tomorrow morning with Richard."

"It's okay, Mom, I'll see you next weekend."

"No, wait Tommy, hold on a minute." With that she laid the receiver down on the desk and went back to the dining room. She waited until Richard had finished speaking then said, "Excuse me Richard, but is there any sort of bus or train close by that I could get into the city? Tommy's home and I would like to spend some of the day with him."

Before Richard could answer, Matt said quietly, "I'm driving into town, you can go with me."

"Oh, are you are sure it would be no trouble—"

"Of course not," he cut across her impatiently. "Can you be ready to leave after lunch?"

"Yes, certainly."

"Good." He nodded and turned back to Richard.

10

A light tapping brought her abruptly awake and into a sitting position. Blinking her eyes in confusion she glanced around wondering what in the world she was doing on Matt's side of the bed. A second series of taps and Clyde quietly called, "Mrs. Martin, are you alright?" brought her fully awake and aware. Brushing her hand through soft black curls, she answered, "Yes, Clyde, of course. What is it?"

"There's a phone call for you from Washington, on line one."

"Thank you, Clyde," she replied as she swung her legs over the side of the bed. She reached for the phone, pressed down the blinking button and said quickly, "Hello, Janice?"

"Yes, Mother." Janice's voice held a smile. "You sound sleepy. Surely you weren't still in bed? It's after noon."

"Yes dear, I was still asleep. I didn't get to bed

133

until very late and although I was awake earlier I dozed off again. How are you feeling?"

"I feel fine. I've just come from seeing the doctor and he's given me the okay to come up to Philly as long as I don't overdo. So I'll see you tomorrow. I don't know what time we'll arrive as Carlos is playing it cagey and waiting until I'd seen the doctor before making flight reservations." Janice laughed softly as she finished speaking and Katherine joined her. "Very clever of him. I hope you told your doctor that I have no intentions of letting you overdo anything. And Janice, please call me when you know your arrival time, I'll come and pick you up."

"All right, I will, but it probably won't be until sometime this evening. Carlos has a full afternoon and I won't be talking to him until dinner."

"Anytime dear. If I'm not here give the time to Clyde."

"Will do. Bye for now, see you tomorrow."

Katherine had no sooner replaced the receiver and was sliding her arms into the sleeves of her robe when the light tapping sounded on her door followed by Clyde's voice. "I have coffee for you, Mrs. Martin. May I come in?"

"Yes Clyde," she answered, pulling the belt tight on the severely tailored satin wrap.

He entered carrying a tray which held, beside a pot of coffee, a glass of juice and a plate of toast. He set the tray on the small table in front of the window and as she sat down Katherine murmured, "Thank you, Clyde, I believe you are trying to spoil me." She looked up in surprise when he answered, seriously, "I don't think that's possible, even though you could do with some spoiling." Before she could think of a reply he added, "Will there be anything else?"

"Yes, ask Mary to bring Jon in, please. And Clyde, thank you again." Nodding briefly he left the room, a smile playing at the corner of his mouth.

Katherine had finished her juice and was munching a piece of toast when, after one short rap, Mary walked into the room carrying Jon.

"There's my angel," Katherine cooed, stretching her arms out to him. The baby wriggled excitedly as he reached for her and she held him close in a gentle hug before laughing up at Mary, "I'm glad he remembers me. I was afraid, after the little he's seen of me the last few days, he'd forget who I am."

"Never worry about that, Kate," Mary replied complacently. "This one knows who his mother is. Strangely enough, he knows who is father is too. The minute his daddy walks through the door he gets all kinds of excited."

So does his mother, Katherine thought wryly. For some reason the word daddy in reference to Matt caused odd sensations inside her and she quickly changed the subject.

She talked to Mary and played with Jon until it was time for his nap. After Mary had taken him off to his crib, she had a quick shower.

In nothing but lacy bra and sheer pantyhose, Katherine stood, one hand braced against the closet door, as she slid one foot then the other into low heeled shoes and looked up with a startled, "Oh!" when the door opened suddenly. She felt a thrill of pleasure run through her as Matt stepped into the room closing the door quietly behind him and in an expelled breath she exclaimed, "Matt, it's you."

He stood just inside the door looking sophisticated and urbane in a light brown suit, beige silk shirt and brown necktie. With expensively clad shoulders looking almost as wide as the door they leaned on, he raised one eyebrow fractionally and asked in a soft rasp, "Who were you expecting?"

Flustered, her cheeks tinged pink, she shook her head sharply. "No one. That's why you startled me. When did you get back?"

He didn't answer, but stood negligently, letting his eyes roam over her slim, scantily clad form. With an abruptness that unnerved her he rapped out, "You've lost more weight, Katherine. Did you see Mark for your six month's check-up?"

"Yes, of course. He said I'm as healthy as a race horse." She answered defensively, feeling the color deepen in her face. "Hmmmm," he murmured, then just as abruptly answered her question. "I flew in a short time ago. Needless to say, I was surprised to find Jack waiting for me. He's the one informed me 'my lady' was at the apartment and not the house. Why hadn't you told me you were planning to come into town?" He had moved slowly into the room as he spoke, his voice growing hard and more raspy. He stopped in front of her, blue gray eyes cool, questioning.

Still on the defensive, she turned, plunging her

hand into the closet for the suit she'd planned to wear. She muttered, "I tried to tell you before you left. You told me you didn't have time to talk, we'd talk when you got back. I couldn't wait." Then she froze as she felt his lips on the curve from neck to shoulder.

"You smell good." The hardness had left his voice and the soft rasp made her flesh tingle. "What is that scent?"

"I—" For the first time she couldn't remember, but it didn't seem to matter. He appeared unconcerned with her lack of answer and more concerned with slipping his long fingers under her bra strap and tugging it over and off her shoulder, his mouth following its passage.

"Matt, I must get dressed." She caught her breath on the last word as Matt's hand slid around her waist and drew her back against him. His mouth now at her ear, he rasped, "Not for what I have in mind. Katherine, it's been over a month since I've touched you."

What was he telling her? she wondered vaguely. That he'd been without a woman for that length of time or that it had been that long since he'd felt any desire to be with her? Then all coherent thought vanished for he turned her around sharply, enclosing her against his chest with hard, muscular arms. Bending his head, his mouth crushed hers in a deep, mind shattering, completely demoralizing kiss.

Without thinking she slid her hands inside his jacket and slowly up over his silk covered chest. Her fingertips felt the shiver that went through him and lifting his head his words were a hoarse echo of a month ago. "Oh God, Kate, I want you."

Katherine was lost. Lost in the warmth that surged through her. Lost in the aching need within that yearned toward him. Lost in the passion in him which overwhelmed her.

For the second time that day she was startled awake by a light tapping on the door. Three questions sprang into her fuzzy mind: What was she doing in bed? What time was it? Why was the room so dark? The next moment the first question was answered as beside her Matt's voice growled, "What is it?"

"Sorry to disturb you, Matt." Clyde's bland, expressionless voice came through the door. "There's a call from New Jersey for Mrs. Martin. Line one."

Matt had reached for the phone before Clyde had finished speaking. Placing the instrument on his chest he replied, "Thanks, Clyde." He punched the number one button and handed the receiver to Katherine.

Fully awake now, the room no longer seemed quite so dark, yet she was now glad of its dimness, for as he placed the receiver in her hand her fingers brushed his and she felt a tingle snake its way up her arm, felt her face grow warm. This is ridiculous, she thought impatiently, a woman my age blushing, going warm and excited at the slightest touch of a man's hand. Clapping the receiver to her ear·she murmured, breathlessly, "Hello, Tom?"

"Yes, Mother. Did I drag you away from the

dinner table?" Tom asked contritely. Dinner table? What time was it, for heaven's sake? Tom, not yet as astute as his sister, had not noticed the hazy, not quite awake sound of his mother's voice.

"No, honey, you didn't. And if you had it wouldn't matter. Is something wrong?" Katherine's warm tone was tinged with anxiety.

"No, Mom, nothing wrong. I just called to tell you I probably won't get into Philly before noon Saturday. Okay?" He didn't wait for an answer before asking, "Is Matt home yet?"

"Yes, he arrived a short time ago." Again warmth touched her cheeks. "Great." His voice seemed to shout over the wire and she held the receiver away from her ear. "Then he'll be at my birthday dinner."

"Well—I don't know, Tom." Katherine hedged. "You know how busy he is. But I'm sure he'll be there if he can." She had barely finished speaking when Matt's voice rumbled irritably, "Tell him I'll definitely be there."

Katherine swallowed quickly. Why was he angry? Did he feel she'd placed him in the position of having to agree to go? Or was it her ambiguousness with Tom?

"Tom, Matt just said he will definitely be there." There, she thought peevishly, if he's going to be angry, I may as well give him cause. Then she ground her teeth as his soft laughter floated into the dim room. Damn the man.

"Good." Katherine's eyes widened at the note of satisfaction in Tom's vioce. She had long ago faced the fact that her young Tom was a cynic who rarely bestowed his respect and approval. Now, it seemed, he had capitulated unconditionally to Matt. Somehow this knowledge both shocked and pleased her. "Look, Mom, I have to get on the move. I've got two mind bending tests tomorrow and I must hit the books. Say hi to Matt for me. I'll see you Saturday. Oh yeah, I hope you got me something really bad for my birthday. Bye now." With that he hung up.

Shaking her head and smiling, Katherine turned to replace the receiver. Then she gave a sudden yelp, practically threw it onto the cradle, tossed back the bed covers and began scrambling out of bed.

"What the hell!" Matt exclaimed, replacing the instrument on the bedside table. "Katherine, have you flipped out?"

"Don't be silly," she snapped. "Tom said he hoped I'd bought him something terrific for his birthday." Here her voice sank to a wail. "Oh, Matt, I haven't bought his gift yet. I was dressing to go shopping when you came in and I won't have much time tomorrow, Janice and Carlos are flying up and I'll have to meet them." She stopped, having run out of breath. As she moved to get off the bed he sat up swiftly, curling an arm around her waist, holding her firmly still.

"Calm down." His voice held deep amusement, his breath tickled her ear. "I've taken care of it."

"You've—but, Matt, I must have something for him from me."

"Katherine." A definite warning note had replaced the amusement. "I said I've taken care of it. The gift is from both of us. To Tom, from Mother and Matt." The emphasis on the last word was final. "Believe me, the one gift will be sufficient. Now, if you will go and dress, I'll show it to you."

She pondered his attitude while standing under the shower. It had been the same over Tom's tuition for school. He had wanted to pay it. That time she'd won. But not without a bitter argument which ended with her saying sharply, "I sold my home for the money to send Tom to school, and I'm damned well going to pay his fee myself." Matt had gone rigid with anger, his eyes looking as cold and stormy as the Atlantic Ocean in January. Without another word he had turned from her and left the room. This time he'd won simply because she'd not been able to satisfy herself over a gift in her earlier shopping trips.

Some thirty minutes later Katherine stood in front of the bathroom mirror, a displeased frown on her face. She had dressed in purple suede slacks and a pale pink cowl necked pullover, that, combined with the matte lilac eye shadow she'd applied to her lids, gave her face a soft glowing look. She didn't notice it. The frown deepened as she gazed in dismay at the mass of black, riotous curls that framed her face and lay tangled at the back of her neck.

Sighing softly she wondered how it was possible she'd not noticed before how long and unmanageable her hair had become.

Hair brush in hand, she swiped frustratedly at a wayward curl that refused to stay in place, bouncing back each time to lay against her cheek. "Damn it," she muttered, then, at the sound of soft laughter, turned startled eyes to the bathroom doorway.

Matt leaned against the frame, freshly showered and shaved, casually dressed in plaid slacks, turtlenecked pull-on and sport coat, looking relaxed and far too attractive.

"I wish you'd tell me what's so damn funny," she snapped in irritation. "My hair's too long and it's a mess."

Still grinning, shaking his head slowly, he walked into the room and stopped in front of her. Reaching out his hand he lifted the curl from her cheek and smoothed it neatly into place, saying quietly, "I don't know what you're so upset about, I like it." Leaning back he studied her a moment before adding, "Not unlike Elizabeth Taylor's hair."

Katherine stared at him in astonishment then began to laugh. "Of course," she said, when she could finally talk. "But if now I'm supposed to say you look like Richard Burton, I'm afraid you're in for a disappointment. Even though I must admit, there is a slight similarity in the deepness of the voice."

The smile still pulled at the corners of his mouth and blue gray eyes gleamed at her, but his voice was quite serious as he replied, "The same dulcet tone, eh? But surely you know that Burton's out? It's that guy from Virginia now. Handsome devil. Perhaps you think I resemble him more?"

As he had finished speaking one eyebrow had

inched up, slowly, deliberately.

Still laughing she walked past him and out of the bathroom feeling buoyant and strangely excited. Never before had they exchanged this kind of nonsensical banter and she decided she liked it, very much.

She reached the bedroom door before she felt him behind her. As his arm reached around her and opened the door she turned her head, gave him an arch look and said laughingly, "At a party one evening, I heard you referred to as a giant-sized, rich man's Clint Eastwood. I must admit I'd silently agreed, with one reservation."

"And that is?"

"Generally, you look even more ruthless than he."

Matt threw back his head and roared with laughter, completely startling her. She watched him wide eyed, enchanted. Never had she heard him laugh like this, the sound was one of pure joy.

When he could finally speak he reached out a hand, drew one long finger down her cheek and said softly, "You better believe it, baby, and flattery will get you just about anything. Do I hear any requests?"

"Dinner," she answered promptly. "I'm starving."

"You got it, even though that would have been my second choice." He gave her a wicked grin before adding, "Better get a coat, we're going out."

"But—"

"No buts," he gave her a gentle shove in the

direction of her closet. "Get your coat and let's go."

They were in the elevator before, remembering, Katherine blurted, "Matt, I can't go out tonight. Janice is going to call to let me know what arrangements she made." Her hand had jerked out and touched the button that brought the car to a halt but as her fingers moved to touch the button marked penthouse his hand caught her wrist.

"Relax, everything's been taken care of."

"What do you mean, everything's been taken care of?"

Releasing her wrist, he leaned back against the wall of the car, seemingly unconcerned with the fact that they were at a stop between floors.

She waited a few seconds for him to continue, then sighed in exasperation. Getting information out of this man was like pulling teeth.

"Matt." Try as she would she could not keep the irritation she felt from showing. "Will you please explain?"

"I spoke to Janice while you were in the shower." He drawled lazily, "everything's arranged."

Voice heavily laced with sarcasm, she snapped. "Do you think you could force yourself to tell me what the arrangements are? I told Janice I'd meet their plane."

His eyes had narrowed as she spoke, but his voice was still a soft drawl. "I'm having the Lear pick them up at nine-thirty tomorrow morning. Jack will be waiting at this end. What I don't understand is why you didn't."

Katherine stared at him in confusion before asking, "Why I didn't do what? Have the Lear pick them up? Matt, you've just returned with it."

"All you had to do was lift the phone and talk to my secretary," Matt explained patiently. "You know there are three other planes."

"But they are business planes," she objected.

"They are my planes."

It wasn't so much his words as the hard arrogance of his tone that shook her. Her own voice not quite steady she explained, "I wouldn't have dreamed of asking for the use of one of the planes. I don't consider I have the right to do so."

Quietly, slowly, the words evenly measured, he replied. "The day I married you I gave you that right. I think, Katherine, you choose not to use it."

Uncertain, more confused than ever, Katherine searched his face, his eyes. What was he accusing her of? Or trying to tell her? She found no answers with her search for his face was now expressionless, his eyes cool. Then even eye contact was broken as he straightened suddenly, stretched one long arm past her and touched the button marked "Garage."

Tom's birthday present was the first thing she saw when she stepped from the elevator. The flame colored Trans-Am seemed to shout youth and fun, and boisterous spirit. It seemed to draw her like a magnet and she walked up to it slowly, smiling gently at a grinning Jack, standing to one side, but watching closely, like a new father. Silently she stood in front of it studying first the wing-spread eagle, painted in gleaming black and gold, on the hood then the enormous gold bow above the windshield with an out size card attached which read: From Mother and Matt.

She heard Matt and Jack discussing the merits of the car vaguely as she walked around it, and admitted to herself it was a beautiful piece of machinery. She stopped when she reached the door on the driver's side, opened it and leaned in to touch the supple black leather of the upholstery, the soft pile of the carpet in the all black interior. She felt Matt move to stand beside her as she straightened and closed the door, heard his quiet voice ask, "Do you think he'll like it?"

"Like it?" Katherine gasped. "He'll go out of his mind. But, Matt, I don't think—"

"Good, keep it that way. Let me do the thinking," he cut in sharply. "Now let's go have dinner." Taking her elbow he turned her around and half walked, half dragged her toward the Lincoln.

"But, Matt, you don't understand!" she murmured, not wanting to make a scene in front of Jack.

"I understand one helluva lot more than you think," Matt ground out. He jerked open the car door, then added, "Stop arguing, Katherine, and get in the car."

They drove in silence for close to half an hour until Matt, in a tone of suppressed fury, asked, "Are you going to sulk all through dinner?"

The words stung like salt on an exposed nerve. In a voice gone cold and flat Katherine replied, "I'm not sulking and I'm no longer hungry. I'd just as soon go back."

"Tough," he said curtly. "I am hungry and we're having dinner, together. And you'll eat or I'll force feed you. So put a smile on that lovely face of yours and make up your mind to enjoy it."

His voice dripped acid and Katherine turned amazed eyes to him. She had seen many sides of him; from cold and emotionless, to urbane and charming, to the passionate lover of fiery expertise. But never had she seen this tough, deliberately cruel side. A small shiver snaked down her back and she decided that being Matt's enemy would not be a pleasant experience.

11

With Matt's eyes watching her warily, Katherine managed to eat most of her dinner. At any other time she'd have enjoyed the lovely old Inn, where he'd finally parked the car after what seemed like an endless drive.

Colonial in decor, it had open beamed ceilings and pewter pieces placed on a shelf that ran along the wall a foot from the ceiling. They had been seated at a small table not far from the large fire place above which, in vivid colors, was a blazon of the Pennsylvania State Seal, the eagle above the shield which bore a ship, a plow and bundles of wheat and behind and alongside the shield, the olive branch.

The orangish fingers flicking into the room from the fire added a warm glow to the subdued lighting. The early American costumes of the waiters and waitresses added local color to the atmosphere.

Katherine refused dessert and sat staring at her
wine glass, unaware of her fingers smoothing and
resmoothing the gleaming white tablecloth. The
wine Matt had ordered was white, light and dry
and as delicious as the food he had also ordered
for her.

The charm of the room, the quality of the food
and service had registered superficially, but she
felt no pleasure in it. There was no room inside for
any emotion other than the anger and contrition
that were at war within her. Now, with Matt's last
scathing remark, anger was getting the upper
hand.

He had said little during the meal, but the few
remarks he had directed at her were heavily laced
with sarcasm and now, as she glanced up at his
dark saturnine face, she felt her anger flare into
fury.

He finished his coffee then casually flipped his
napkin onto the table. Cool eyes raked her face,
paused a moment on her hand clenching the stem
of her glass.

"If you're quite ready, we'll go."

Her own napkin flew onto the table and using
every ounce of willpower she possessed she kept
from flinging her glass at his mocking face. His
tone and manner implied he had been waiting
patiently for her to finish, when in truth he had
dawdled a good twenty-five minutes over his
coffee.

Biting her lip to keep herself from lashing out at
him she got jerkily to her feet then, back rigid,
preceeded him from the room.

Silence. It filled the inside of the car, stretching her already taut nerves. In self-protection she withdrew into herself, drawing a curtain of cold composure about her like an invisible shield.

His words dropped into the silence like a heavy stone. "You're not angry and upset because you didn't get to choose Tom's gift yourself. No, you resent the fact that I paid for that damned car. Also, that I arranged to bring Janice and Carlos to town. You're annoyed anytime I involve myself in any way concerning your precious children. Or should I say Kevin's precious children?"

She spun her head around to him, her face white with shock, hot denial on her lips. "That's not true. I—"

"I'm not finished," he snapped savagely. "And it is true. In fact, you even resent any interference from me as far as Jonathon is concerned. I'll go even further and suggest you resent me entirely and would like to forget that I even exist."

Cold, icy eyes in a face gone hard and unyielding held hers, for although he had started the engine the car sat motionless in the parking lot next to the Inn.

"The truth hurt, Katherine?" The hoarse sound of her own voice shocked her. "It's not the truth."

"Yes, it is. You want no support from me of any kind, be it physical, moral or financial. You accept it only when I insist, and most times not very gracefully. When we married, I was fully prepared to accept responsibility for Tom. Don't interrupt. He needed the guidance of a man, a father figure, if you will. Believe it or not I enjoy the role. I've become very fond of Tom and I think the feeling is returned. Regardless of what you think, Katherine, it has never been my intention to usurp your place in his affections. I couldn't if I wanted to since he adores you. Now I'm afraid I must make you even more angry then you already are by telling you I've picked up the tab for his birthday dinner."

Katherine had stared into his eyes the whole time he spoke unable to break their hold. His last words startled her into breaking that hold. Blinking in surprise she exclaimed, "But that's not possible! I've paid a deposit on the bill and expressly asked to have the balance bill sent to me. Besides which, you've only been home a few hours. I haven't even mentioned where we're having the party. How did you know?"

"Katherine," he said softly, almost pityingly, "there is very little that goes on around me that I don't know. I make it my business to know. Do you think I'd be where I am today if I didn't? Your deposit will be returned to you."

"I don't want it returned," she cried, "I want—"

"Katherine, stop it." His sharp words cut across hers, silencing her. "Why is it so important to you who pays the bills?" Not giving her a chance to answer, he continued. "The main thing is Tom will have his party. What I'd like you to answer for me is; why the hell I wasn't informed as to where the dinner is being held, or what day, or for that matter, that you were even planning the thing?" Then his tone softened, but dangerously so. "Not that it surprises me, you understand, considering you didn't even bother to let me know when you went into labor with Jonathon."

"I didn't know where you were," she flared defensively.

"Bull." The crude reply was issued from between lips that were pulled back, in anger, against his teeth. "My secretary knows where I am practically every minute of the day. Or is it too much of a bother for you to lift the phone?"

His voice had turned nasty, the rasp heavy, no longer attractive.

Katherine sat perfectly still feeling battered by his lashing voice. She turned her head to stare, unseeing, out the windshield, unable to bear looking at him any longer. His face looked older, almost harshly ugly. She shuddered, she did not know this man. Did not understand him.

When she turned her head away without speaking, he cursed viciously and with barely controlled violence, set the big car in motion. It seemed to leap forward pressing her against the back of the seat and her breath caught in her throat more from his cursing then the sudden movement.

As soon as he turned the car onto the macadam road his foot pressed down on the gas pedal and the car shot ahead, picking up speed at an alarming rate. Katherine felt real fear crawl through her mid section and fighting panic said, "Matt, please slow down." Cold. Contemptuous. The sound of her voice was like a slap on the face. How in the world had she managed that? she thought in amazement, then realized that in trying to control the rising fear inside herself she had reacted like a frightened parent on the arrival of a child hours over due. Completely opposite the way she felt. She had no way of knowing that that same opposite effect worked on her appearance. For while the strain was beginning to tie her in knots inside, what Matt saw, when he gave her a glance after slowing the car's speed, was a woman apparently cool, composed, seemingly above the normal irritations of the every day.

Fully under control now, his calm voice cut into her, "You're unbelievable, you know that, Katherine? Does anything touch you?"

Touch her! God if he knew. Slowly she closed her eyes against the hot, gritty aching behind her lids. Lashes wet, she directed all her determination into one thought. She would not cry. Could not let this man see her reduced to tears.

She had turned her head even further away from him. Now, tears under control, she opened her eyes to stare at her shadowy reflection in the side window.

It was not true. She did not resent him. But how to tell him without giving her true feelings away? She was used to making all the decisions concerning her children. She had had to. She had continued to do so after her marriage, even in respect to Jonathon, simply because he worked so hard, was always so busy, on the go, that she felt she had no right to bother him.

If there had been any affection in their union she would have gladly transferred the cloak of responsibility from her own to his shoulders. But, he situation being what it was between them, she could not.

She felt herself in some sort of limbo. She was legally his wife, with all the rights and privileges that went with that title, and yet she felt she could not make use of them. She knew that many women would think she was out of her mind. Matt was a wealthy man, apparently ready to assume all her responsibilities, financially or otherwise, and she could not let him. How could she explain to anyone, least of all Matt, her feeling that the scale was already way out of balance? To allow him to take complete control would put the scale at full tilt. He giving everything, she giving nothing.

Once again the questions rose to torment her. Why had he asked her to marry him? Why her? More important still, why had she agreed?

The darkened countryside flashed by the window unseen by the haunted eyes staring through it. In trying to find answers, she was looking inward, not out.

The car she was riding in was the same make, only newer, as the one he had driven her home from Richard and Anne's party in.

"Can you be ready to leave after lunch?" he had asked. She had been ready long before lunch time. She had gone to her room at once, exchanged the slacks she was wearing for the matching skirt to her suit, packed her case then wondered what to do with the rest of the morning.

The sound of delighted laughter drew her to the window facing the paddocks. She stood observing Richard, Anne, Carol and Matt as they talked and laughed with Lisa and Gayle who were patting and caressing two fillies inside the rail. The horses obviously Matt's Christmas gifts, were sleek and beautiful and even from this distance Katherine could tell the girls were in near delirium over them.

She sighed softly, wondering what it felt like to be able to afford to give such costly gifts to people you cared for. She had seen Matt's gift to Carol the night before when Carol had seemed to dance into her room, as she was getting ready for bed proudly displaying her arm. Katherine had gasped at the exquisite diamond encrusted watchband encircling Carol's fragile wrist.

Now, standing at the windows, Katherine saw a brief rainbow flash as the mid-morning sun struck the watch exposed from Carol's jacket sleeve as she gestured with her hand. Again she wondered about the relationship between Carol and Matt. Although Carol claimed there was nothing beyond a deep friendship, Katherine had some doubt, for Carol had seemed to bloom from the moment Matt arrived, and they had gone off alone together more than once. But, if there was more than friendship between them, why had Carol been so upset over Paul just a month ago? Then with a mental shake, Katherine told herself to mind her own business and turned away from the window.

As soon as they had finished eating lunch Matt stood up, told Katherine he'd bring the car around to the front of the house and strode from the room. Katherine barely had time to thank Richard and Anne for the weekend, say good-bye to Lisa and Gayle and give Carol a quick hug, when he came in the front door, picked up their cases and said, "Are you ready?"

The car, black and gleaming in the sunlight, appeared to Katherine to be at least a block and a half long, and the words custom made sprang to mind as she slid into the soft crushed leather of the front seat. She had time for a brief wave, then the car was rolling along the drive and turning onto the road.

They drove in silence for some minutes, Katherine's thoughts already ahead with Tom, and the sound of his voice, although quiet, startled her.

"This Tom that's waiting for you, your husband?"

"No, my son. My husband's dead."

"I'm sorry."

"Thank you, but there's no need."

He shot a sharp, questioning look at her, and sighing she explained. "My husband has been dead for eighteen years."

"How old is your son?"

Katherine shifted in her seat, turning to face him, resigned to the inquisition. "Eighteen."

Again the qustioning look. Katherine took her time, lighting a cigarette, before explaining. "My husband was killed in a car crash a month before Tom was born."

Matt was quiet a few minutes, lighting his own cigarette. Then his voice impersonal, he asked, "You never married again?"

"No," she replied quietly.

"That couldn't have been very easy, raising a child by yourself."

"Two children. I have a daughter two years older."

Matt's eyebrows inched up. "Your husband left you well provided for?"

Katherine felt a flash of irritation. Did this man think that giving her a ride into the city entitled him to ask her this kind of question?

"I managed." She answered shortly, turning her head away.

That put an end to conversation until he stopped the car in front of her apartment house. As she moved to open the car door his hand closed over her arm, his voice quiet he said, "I'm sorry if I annoyed you with my questions. I was genuinely interested, not prying."

She had looked pointedly at his hand, which was instantly removed, then his face, before answering. "That's all right, I suppose I'm too touchy about it."

She was standing on the sidewalk, waiting for Matt to get her case from the trunk of the car, when Tom came bounding down the stairs from their second floor apartment, through the front door and off the small porch calling, "Hi Mom, I saw you from the window."

Fairly tall and still growing, slim as a reed in tight faded jeans and beat up sweatshirt, Katherine thought him the most attractive young person she knew.

A grin on his good looking face revealed perfect white teeth and as he gave her a quick, fierce hug she reached up her hand and ruffled his wavy dark hair and said, "You need a haircut, young man."

"Nag, nag," he murmured, the grin widening, before turning to Matt, who now stood to one side, patiently waiting.

Maybe it was the way he stood there, silent, unsmiling, that made Katherine feel oddly flushed as she turned to Tom and hurried through the introductions.

"Tom, this is Mr. Martin, a good friend of the Benningtons, who was kind enough to offer me a ride into town. Mr. Martin, my son, Tom."

As Matt proffered his hand to Tom, she saw one brow twist slightly in question at her. She had very nearly stammered the words and now she rushed on, one thought upper-most in her mind, to have him go.

"We mustn't keep Mr. Martin, Tom," she broke in on whatever it was Tom was saying to him. In surprise at her own rude behavior she noted the startled look Tom gave her. Almost breathlessly she finished, turning to Matt, "I know you have an appointment and I don't want to make you late, thank you very much for the lift in."

She had offered her own hand before she finished speaking and as he took it in his she glanced into a face devoid of expression, withdrawn.

"Anytime," he answered shortly, then nodding briefly to Tom, he strode around the car, slid behind the wheel and within seconds had driven away.

Tom eyed the car appreciatively until it turned

the corner then, his confusion mirrored on his face, turned to Katherine. "What the devil was that all about, Mom? You really gave that guy the bum's rush."

She had laughed somewhat shakily. "Is that how it seemed? I assure you, honey, I did not. Bringing me home probably took him out of his way and I didn't want to take up any more of his time. He is a very important and busy man."

Tom had been quiet as they walked up the stairs to their apartment but as they reached the door he turned to her suddenly and asked, "He's not *the* Matthew Martin is he?"

"Yes, he is," she'd answered quietly. "He was also a guest of the Benningtons this weekend and before you start asking all kinds of questions, I'll tell you this; I know very little about him and in all honesty, I don't care to know as I can't imagine having anything in common with his type. So could we speak about something else, please?"

Tom had given her a curious look, but the subject of Matt was dropped.

The following weeks had seemed to fly by. Katherine was loaded down with work, hardly noticing winter's passing until one early April morning on her way to work. The breeze no longer bit at her nose with sharp little teeth, but seemed instead to kiss her cheeks softly and there was that indescribable scent on the air that only comes in early spring.

The brilliant blue sky and sparkling butter yellow sunshine combined with the feel and scent of spring caused a ripple of feeling through Katherine that was almost painful.

The first thing she'd done on entering her office was phone Carol and suggest they play hooky that afternoon and do some spring shopping. Carol had been delighted with the idea and they set a time and place to meet.

They shopped happily until late in the afternoon then, pleasantly tired, strolled along discussing the pros and cons of the different restaurants in the area where they could have dinner.

Suddenly Carol's face lit up, "I've got an idea." She smile impishly, heading for a small coffee shop. "Come on, we'll have a cup of coffee and I'll make a phone call." As they entered the shop Carol murmured, "You sit down and order, I'll be right back," and she walked toward a public phone in the corner of the shop.

The waitress had just set the coffees on the table of the tiny booth when Carol slipped onto the seat across from Katherine, a look of satisfaction on her face.

Katherine finished lighting her cigarette, arched delicate black brows at her and asked, "What are you up to?"

Carol had the look of a well fed kitten. "Not only do we no longer have to lug these packages around, but we're getting a free meal." Katherine's brows arched higher.

"We, my friend, are being taken to dinner by a very charming and handsome man."

"You're incorrigible," Katherine laughed, "and who is this so charming and handsome saver of foot-weary females?''

"You'll see." Carol softly sang the words, refusing to say anymore.

She had seen, not much more than ten minutes later as glancing up, Katherine went cold. Striding through the door was one Matthew Martin, looking big and confident and far too attractive.

12

The evening had gone smoothly enough. Katherine managed, with some effort, to conceal the uneasiness she felt in his presence. Her emotions baffled her. She had never felt uncomfortable in the company of any man before. Matt was simply too masculine, too attractive, too successful, too rich.

Carol, unknowingly, acted as a buffer, which helped some. At one point during the evening, after Katherine had answered him with a Mr. Martin, Carol had cried, "For heaven's sake, surely you two know each other well enough by now to use first names?"

Matt had agreed quietly; Katherine had no option but to go along.

She didn't see him again until late in May. She and Carol were having a working lunch, discussing the illustrations for Carol's latest "baby," when Carol had stopped speaking in mid-

sentence and stared across the room, her face
paling.

"What is it?" Katherine asked concernedly, her
eyes following the direction of Carol's stare. Her
eyes encountered a strikingly beautiful auburn
haired young woman, who had obviously been
drinking her lunch.

"Peggy Darren, Matt's ex-paramour," Carol said
softly, "and she's bombed out of her mind. I'd
heard she was drinking rather heavily. The man
with her is her husband. She married him less
than a month after Matt broke off their—ah—
friendship. I can't decide whether I feel pity or
disgust for her."

"I should think compassion would be my
reaction," Katherine stated tartly. "She's been ill-
used surely."

"No way," Carol said sharply. "She knew what
the outcome of the affair would be from the start.
They all did, for that matter. As I understand it
Matt leaves no chance of doubt of that from the
beginning. But I suppose they all hold out some
hope of snaring him someway." Then she added
chidingly, "No, Katherine, she has no right to feel
ill-used."

Katherine opened her mouth to protest what she
considered an obviously biased opinion when
Carol groaned, "Oh no!"

Glancing around to find the cause of Carol's
dismay she saw the man in question just coming to
a stop at Peggy's table.

Bending slightly over the table Matt spoke
quietly a few minutes then, at the young woman's

agitated reply, placed his hand on the table to brace himself and bending closer to her, spoke even more quietly.

Fascinated, Katherine watched the look of annoyance that flashed across Peggy's husband's face as her hand fluttered then came to rest on top of Matt's. Matt spoke a few more words to her then turned to say something to her husband who nodded, seemingly in agreement. The light that had been turned on in Peggy's face at the sight of Matt was as suddenly extinguished as Matt slid his hand from beneath hers and moved away from the table. Katherine felt a shaft of pity go through her at the look of pain on Peggy's lovely face as she watched him walk away.

Unable to look at that unhappy young face any longer, Katherine shifted her gaze to Matt and caught her breath, thinking, this man's inhuman. As he walked away from the table his bearing was one of supreme confidence, his visage ruthless unconcern. He had taken just a few long strides when turning his head arrogantly his gaze clashed with Katherine's and held.

Making a sharp angled turn smoothly he made for their table, his eyes still locked on Katherine's.

Carol had sat through the small drama as quietly as Katherine but now, as Matt stopped in front of them, she smiled and said softly, "Hi, Matt."

"Hi, sweetheart, how have you been?" The smile he bestowed on Carol did strange things to Katherine's spinal column. A devastating flash of white that transformed his face. But not for her, for it disappeared as turning to her he gave a brief nod and murmured, "Katherine."

She returned his nod, a tight small smile on her lips, then looked down to study her pre-lunch drink as if its contents held the secret of the universe.

Carol and Matt exchanged pleasantries and Katherine paid little attention until she heard Carol ask with genuine concern in her voice, "Is Peg all right, Matt?"

"She will be, her husband will take care of her. Seems like a nice guy." He paused, then went on even more quietly. "I blame myself in this, Carol. I shouldn't have become involved in the first place."

"Matt!" Carol objected. "You have nothing to reproach yourself for. She made the run at you, you know that, and now if she's found she fell and scraped her knees, she has no one to blame but herself."

Katherine had looked up in surprise at the vehemence in Carol's voice and was struck by the almost tender expression on Matt's face.

"Maybe so," he replied softly, "but she is hurt and I don't like it. The hard part was convincing her it would have been much worse if I hadn't ended it."

Well, perhaps he wasn't completely ruthless and inhuman, Katherine admitted to herself grudgingly.

He shot his cuff to glance at his watch, then said ruefully, "I have to go, business lunch, take care of yourself, outlaw. Katherine. Oh, yes, don't worry about the check, I'll get it." The words had come out strung together and on the last one he turned and strode away.

Carol laughed softly while Katherine watched his retreating back thinking, what a strange man.

Spring sprang into summer with a vengeance. Most of the month of June had been hot and humid and by the last week of June she had been feeling tired and edgy.

On the Monday the week before July Fourth Katherine practically had to drag herself to work. She could not remember ever being at such a low ebb, either physically or mentally.

She had been working nine and ten hours a day plus keeping the apartment tidy. And if that wasn't enough Janice and Carlos were in the Bahamas and Tom had come home at the close of school term only to leave again two days later for Wildwood, New Jersey. Of course they'd be home for the fourth but they'd be off again a few days later, Janice and Carlos for Argentina, Tom for a camping trip in Canada. The prospect of spending the lion's share of the hot, sticky summer alone did absolutely nothing for Katherine's flagging spirits.

That Monday had been a loser from the beginning. The sky had hung oppressive and gray until late afternoon when it grew steadily darker. By five-thirty it was a blackish-green with jagged streaks of lightning tearing through it like a crooked sword through rotten cloth. Minutes later it seemed as if all the water in the world was pouring from those rents onto center city.

A six o'clock Katherine threw in the towel,

pushed her high stool back from her drawing board and drew the back of her hand across her forehead. The office air conditioner had not been able to keep up with the mugginess of the outside air and the room was close, airless. Reaching for the phone she decided to give Carol a call and ask her to dinner. Her hand lifted the receiver then replaced it remembering Carol was at Richard's until after the Fourth.

Picking up her umbrella and handbag she left the office slowly. The elevator was empty as most of the employees had gone home at five. Standing in the middle of the car Katherine suddenly felt old and alone and very weary and, for the first time ever, defeated. She gave herself a mental shake; as the door slid back she hurried toward the wide glass door facing the street.

The rain still poured down like a solid wall of water and Katherine stepped through the door, paused under the narrow overhang, head bent, fingers working at her umbrella catch, not noticing the long black car at the curb.

Glancing up as she opened her umbrella, the movement of the car's rear door swinging open caught her attention at the same time as a familiar low, raspy voice called, "Katherine."

She stood, blinking through the rain in surprise that quickly changed to astonishment as Matt stepped from the car, strode across the pavement unmindful of the rain, gripped her arm and said impatiently, "Come on, get in the car before you're soaking wet." Apparently unaware or uncaring of the fact that by now he was getting wet, he practically dragged her to the car and shoved her inside.

The car moved smoothly into the sparse flow of traffic as Katherine blurted, "What are you doing here?"

"Taking you to dinner," he replied casually.

Leaning back against the seat with a deep sigh, Katherine closed her eyes murmuring, "Oh, Matt, not tonight, I'm too hot and tired to go out and eat. Please, I'd just as soon go home, have a shower and a light supper."

His voice was very low. "All right, I accept."

Eyes wide, she straightened. "Oh, but . . ."

"That was an invitation to join you, wasn't it? Not in the shower, of course, but the light supper?" His voice had gone even lower and held a slightly coaxing quality.

Too tired to argue, Katherine gave in with a small laugh. "Yes, Matt, that was an invitation."

Two hours later, in a deliciously cool living room, Katherine sat on her small loveseat, legs curled underneath her, sipping at a glass of white wine. Lifting her eyes from her glass she let them rest on Matt standing at her window, back to her. He had shed his damp jacket on entering the apartment and his white silk shirt stood out like a beacon in the dimly lit room.

Idly she watched the play of muscles in his back as he lifted his glass to his mouth and drank deeply of his wine. Again she felt that odd sense of recognition. Seconds later a picture swam into her mind. A picture of a tall, skinny boy who was all gangling awkwardness on the sidewalk and poetry in motion on the baseball field and basketball court.

"Oh God," she whispered.

Matt turned, a frown creasing his brow. "Something wrong?"

"Oh God," she repeated, voice still low. "You're *that* Matt Martin."

The frown was replaced by a wry grin. "The dawn finally broke."

"You knew," she accused. "You knew all the time."

"Yes, all the time." His face had sobered as had his tone.

"But why didn't you say something?" she asked in confusion.

He shrugged turning back to the window. "Guess I was curious to see how long it would take for the penny to drop."

"Well really, you could have—"

"Forget it," he cut in none too gently. "It's not important."

Silence, not quite as comfortable as before, settled on the room. Katherine drank her wine, eyes once again on Matt's back. Much to her surprise it had been a quiet, pleasant evening.

Matt had sat reading the paper while she showered and dressed, then he had competently set the table, opened the wine and poured, while she tossed a salad and cooked a western omelet for their supper. The meal was eaten in comparative quiet and yet it was a restful quiet. And the last hour had been much the same, one or the other of them making an occasional remark.

Matt turned suddenly, catching her eyes on him, and said abruptly, "Will you marry me, Katherine?"

Stunned, she had stared at him some minutes before asking dumbly, "What?"

He repeated his question softly, adding, "Don't give me a flat out no. Let me explain, then think it over. Okay?"

She nodded numbly, eyes following him as he walked to the table holding the wine bottle, picked it up, then seated himself at the other end of the loveseat.

"I need a wife." He stated flatly as he filled first her glass then his own. Lifting his glass, he took a long swallow before continuing. "A hostess, companion for the long weekend invitations that include the wife, the working holiday sort of thing."

"But I understand your sister—" Katherine began.

"Yes," he interrupted her, "Beth has been acting as my hostess and has occasionally accompanied me when the invitation included a wife. But a sister is not the same as a wife. You would be amazed at the business deals that have soured because the wives didn't jell. Besides, Beth is still a young woman with a life of her own, and I can't expect her to devote it to me."

"But why me?" she asked blankly. "I would think a younger woman would—'"

Again he interrupted her. "No, a younger woman would not. A younger woman would make demands. Demands I'd have no inclinations to fulfill." He lifted his head arrogantly, eyes hard on hers. "I'm forty-one years old, I work hard and I have no time to entertain a woman. Most of the men I do business with are the same age or older, with wives not much younger. In effect what I require is a woman who will run my home smoothly, be a gracious hostess, a comfortable traveling companion and, of course, share my bed."

Katherine's brows went up over eyes that had widened with surprise.

"Yes, of course." He answered her questioning look flatly. "I'm a normal healthy man with all the natural drives. I am not a fool and to propose some sort of platonic relationship would be foolish. It couldn't possibly work. I'm away on business a lot, often weeks at a time. Your free time would be just that, your time, to do whatever you wish."

"What you're saying is you want to employ a wife."

An edge of sharpness entered his voice. "Not at all. I can hire a housekeeper-hostess. I can engage a traveling companion, I can pay a woman to sleep with me at X number of dollars for so many days or weeks or months. What I'm offering you in return for fullfilling my requirements is the legality of marriage with all that entails; a home and security along with anything you want, within reason, for the rest of your life."

What if he later met someone and fell in love? She hadn't even bothered to put the thought into words. From what she'd heard about his dealings with women and from his own words of a few minutes ago that contingency seemed unlikely.

"Matt, I don't think—" she began softly, when his sharp, raspy voice cut in. "Katherine, you agreed to think it over. You may take as much or as little time as you like, but at least give it your consideration overnight."

While he was speaking he walked across the room to her small desk where her phone sat, a note pad beside it. Picking up the pencil alongside, he wrote on the pad, continuing, "This is my office number. When you've reached a decision call me. No explanations will be necessary either way. A simple yes or no will do."

Lifting the receiver he punched out a number, waited, then said, "I'm ready." He turned from the desk, slinging the jacket that had hung on the back of the desk chair over his shoulder, and walked toward the door. "I'm going. You're tired and have some thinking to do. If I were you I'd think it over very carefully, Katherine. Don't get up, I'll see myself out."

He was gone, just like that, no good night or good-bye. He just went.

Katherine sat staring at the door, lips slightly parted, stunned. The arrogance of the man was overwhelming. Think about it indeed. She had no need to think about it. The answer was no, period. He had been right about one thing, she was tired.

She tidied the apartment, washed and changed quickly, then dropped onto her bed to lie wide-eyed, thinking. Hours later, beginning to feel as if her rumpled bed was smothering her, she went into the living room, pacing back and forth in the darkness. She smoked one cigarette after the other, made a pot of coffee and drank it, cup cradled in her hands, still pacing.

At dawn she stood at her window watching as life slowly came back to the city. Her mind had circled and dodged around his words all night, and now, finally, she faced the cold, hard facts.

He had said she was tired and that was true. What he hadn't known was how tired, both physically and mentally. The reason was not, as he had probably assumed, over-work. She had suddenly realized she was facing her fortieth year. Her children were grown, no longer needing her. In a few more years Tom would be out of school and gone. She would be alone except for the now and then visits. The prospects terrified her. She had been on her own, of course, a long time but with two children to raise her life had had purpose. Now it stretched in bleak emptiness in front of her.

She had her work, true, but she could not spend twenty-four or even sixteen hours a day in her office. And what else was there?'

She had no doubt as to her ability to fulfill Matt's requirements, except one. On her hesitation about that she chided herself gently. She had been a wife. Had performed that particular act without any great discomfort. And even though it had been over eighteen years, surely she could manage to share a man's bed with composure. Couldn't she?

Around and around her thoughts flew, always to

come back to the same fact. Almost anything was better than living the rest of her life alone.

At nine-thirty she moved from the window to her desk, back straightening unconsciously. Glancing at the boldly scrawled numbers on the otherwise pure white paper, she lifted the phone and punched out the numbers. A bright, alert voice answered on the second ring, "Good morning, Martin Corporation. May I help you?"

Katherine drew a deep breath before replying calmly, "Yes, may I speak to Mr. Martin please?"

"I'm sorry," the bright voice said. "Mr. Martin is in conference. Who's calling and is there a message?"

Fighting down the urge to say no thank you and hang up, she answered. "This is Katherine Acker, and there is no—"

The voice breaking in had become somehow even more alert. "Oh! Mrs. Acker, just a minute please." A click, a pause, then another click and Matt quietly rasped, "Yes, Katherine?"

He had said no explanations needed, so she mimicked him, changing the name. "Yes, Matt."

Silence, silence that stretched at her already taut nerves. Had he thought better of it? Changed his mind? The doubt was dispelled with his first word. "Good. Are you in the office?"

"No." How had she ever managed to keep her tone so cool? "I didn't go in. I'm at home."

"Stay there. I'll come for you and take you to lunch. Will one be all right?" She could read no emotion whatever in his voice.

"Yes, fine."

"Right. One o'clock, then." The line went dead. Did this man never say goodbye?

The following days would forever after be somewhat of a blur in Katherine's mind. At exactly one o'clock the big car, Matt driving himself, stopped in front of the apartment. Katherine, waiting in the small foyer, left the building quickly calling, "Don't get out," as his door swung open. She slid onto the seat next to him and without a word of greeting he pulled the car into the line of traffic, thus beginning a chain of events that left her breathless in their snow-balling swiftness.

Matt drove first to the bureau of licences where they filled out the appropriate form. From there to a small private clinic where they were given, separately, the required examinations and tests. Then, finally, he took her to lunch at a small restaurant along a route very familiar to her, as she had driven back and forth along its countless times over the years, visiting her parents.

During lunch he had taken her hand into his, slid off the broad gold band, which she had never removed, saying calmly, "If it causes you any pain not to wear it at all, I have no objections to you wearing it on your right hand." Then slowly replaced it with a jelly-bean sized marquis-cut diamond solitaire set in platinum.

Katherine sat staring at the stone, speechless, for some minutes before murmuring in an awe-hushed tone, "I can't wear this. I'd be afraid of losing it."

"Nonsense," he snapped. "I chose it for you and

you'll wear it. Besides which it's insured, so don't concern yourself about it."

She sighed her defeat. The ring remained on her finger. When they left the restaurant, the car again pointed in a direction away from Philadelphia, Matt's voice probed gently into her background. She realized the reason for his probing when, reaching Lancaster, he parked the car in front of the church that she had attended as a girl, had become Kevin's wife in, which her parents still attended.

She turned a questioning look at Matt, not at all sure of the rightness of being married in church under the circumstances.

He read the feeling correctly, face void of all expression, saying, "We'll keep it small and quiet, but I have no wish to offend either your parents or my own. I think this way is best."

Doubts lingered but Katherine had nodded her consent. Then she had been ushered from the car, along the short walk and into the Pastor's office.

To her surprise the Reverend Mr. Keller, quite old now, was waiting for them. He spoke briefly to Katherine in his soft, gentle voice before turning to Matt. Some fifteen minutes later they were back outside walking to the car when she stopped short, turning to him with the first stirring of panic. "This Saturday, Matt?"

He didn't answer until they were again seated inside the car. His tone indicating he understood her unease he explained. "I know this seems hasty and although I don't want you to feel in any way rushed, this coming weekend would be the best

time for me. I managed to clear my desk this
morning, something that doesn't happen often,
due to the holiday falling at the weekend making it
a long one. By the middle of next week it will be
covered again and there are things in the works
that will probably keep me running through the
summer and into the fall. Is there any reason you
cannot be away from your office for a few days?''

"No," she had barely managed to whisper.

"All right then," he'd stated with finality. "We'll
get it over with this Saturday."

13

"Get it over with." The words were reverberating through Katherine's mind when the jolting of the car as Matt drove in over the incline and onto the ramp leading into the underground garage, pulled her back into the present.

Sighing in self-derision at her more and more frequently wandering mind, she slanted a glance at Matt. Her sigh deepened, for the rigidly defined lines of his face told her clearly that he was still very angry. There before her, as he parked the car, sat the flame colored cause of their argument.

Leaving the car she walked quickly to the elevator, turning her head to avoid looking at the object in question, Matt at her heels. They were swept up to the top floor and had entered the apartment before Matt broke the silence. Grasping her arm firmly, he led her into the living room. "We better talk, Katherine."

"Oh, Matt, please," she cried. "I'm tired and I

don't want to start arguing all over again."

"I said talk, not argue." Katherine glanced at him apprehensively for his voice had taken on a very tough edge. After making an obvious effort at control, he went on more smoothly. "I'm going to have a drink, can I get you something?"

She started to shake her head but hesitated, deciding to be prudent, at the hard glint that sprang into his eyes.

"Yes, thank you, a martini please." The tight lines around his mouth softened as he turned and walked to the small bar across the room. Tone now mild, almost conciliatory, he said, "Arguing has gotten us absolutely nowhere but we had better damned well talk this through to some sort of agreement or the kids are going to have one uncomfortable weekend here."

His words brought her upright. He was right, of course; Janice and Tom had no idea of the true relationship between Matt and herself, but unless this strain between them was erased it would not take very long for them to get wise to it. She had also registered the fact that, for the first time since their marriage, Matt had referred to her children as the kids.

"Yes I know," she answered distractedly, taking the glass he held out to her. She sipped at the expertly mixed martini, watching him take a long drink from his usual mixture of Chivas and club soda. Emotions firmly under control again, she asked coolly, "What do you expect me to say, Matt?"

"I don't *expect* anything from you, Katherine. I

had hoped you'd use your common sense and see things as they are," he replied icily. "The car, the dinner, my sending the plane for Janice and Carlos are accomplished facts. If you remain angry about it forever, it will still be an accomplished fact. So I suggest you shake yourself out of this resentful mood and enjoy your children's pleasure in the weekend."

He polished off his drink, sat the glass down then moved to stand close to her, his body not quite touching hers. Raising his hand his fingers caught her chin, lifting her head so he could study the tight, withdrawn look on her face.

He sighed as if in extreme weariness then, his tone softening, he said, "This arrangement of ours hasn't worked out all that badly, and it would be even better if it weren't for that damned fierce independent streak of yours."

His words, though mildly condemning, were spoken in a soft drawl soothing her irritation. She shivered as one long finger was drawn slowly down her cheek. His voice, now a low rasp, murmured, "We now have the most important factor going for us, Kate. We are very good together in bed."

She went cold, stiffening under his hands. "The most important factor," she repeated incredulously. "There are more important things in marriage than sex, Matt."

"Name one," he replied sardonically, his eyes laughing at her.

"There's love and respect and consideration and the true desire to spend your life with that one person," she snapped, offended by his tone.

"I'll tell you something, sweetheart." His voice cut into her. "I know people who have all those higher feelings for one another and you know what? Their marriages are nowhere, and do you know why? Because they haven't got it in bed, and if it doesn't work there, it doesn't work at all. The ideal, of course, is to have it all, but that happens very rarely."

Not willing to begin arguing all over again, she turned away abruptly, only to be caught roughly by his hand and turned back again, into his arms. Holding her loosely without effort, his voice took on a caressing note. "I said earlier tonight that you resent everything about me. That wasn't quite true. Tell me you resent the feel of my hands on your body." He matched his words with action, moving his hands caressingly from the back of her neck to her shoulders then slowly down her back, along her hipline. "Tell me you resent the feel of my body, hard and urgent against yours." Muscles tightening, his arms drew her close to him. His lips close to hers, whispered, "Tell me you resent what my kisses do to your senses."

Without waiting for her to answer his mouth took hers in a kiss deliberately designed to arouse. Its purpose was achieved for before he lifted his mouth from hers, her hands had come up to his shoulders, clinging to him weakly. Fighting back the words of love that trembled on her lips, she whispered, "You don't fight fair."

Laughing softly, his lips close to her ear, he rasped, "I fight to win. Be reasonable, Katherine, bury your resentment this time. Relax and let the kids enjoy the benefits of my money. It's honestly earned and freely given." His mouth again covered hers in a kiss even more reason-destroying than the first.

Her voice was a barely whispered plea. "Matt, please."

He had won and he knew it. His mouth touching hers murmured, "It will give me pleasure to please you, Kate."

Bending, he slid his arm under her knees, lifting her easily into his arms. In defeat, she curled her arms around his neck tightly, turned her face into his neck, her lips pressed to the strong column of his throat. Carrying her easily, as if she weighed no more than a child, he walked slowly to their bedroom.

Katherine woke during the night filled with a growing sense of self-betrayal. He had won by default. As before, since becoming aware of her response to and growing need of his strong, physical attraction, he had used his body to bring her to heel. What made her squirm inside was the ease with which he did it. It had not always been this way. This thought sent her mind spinning once again into the past.

On leaving the church that Tuesday, they had gone to the home of his parents. Katherine had been introduced to a fairly tall woman who spoke in a no-nonsense tone that was belied by the softness around the mouth and eyes. Matt's father, thin to the point of gauntness, stood almost as tall as Matt himself with the same shock of auburn hair, liberally sprinkled with gray, and eyes as direct and piercing. He held himself ramrod straight, his face revealing the triumph over pain and disability.

She warmed to their down-to-earth attitude, answering question quietly, honestly. They accepted their son's statement that he was remarrying and his choice of partner without question, their eyes revealing their admiration if not out and out adoration of him.

They had stayed to have supper with Mr. and Mrs. Martin, then left soon after as Katherine had phoned her own parents saying she had something to tell them and would be at the house by early evening.

As she left Matt's parents' home, after a typically mouth watering Pennsylvania Dutch meal of chicken pot pie and a sour salad, Katherine thought they epitomized the character of the Pennsylvania Dutch people. Strong, self-willed, a facade of reserve covering warm, friendly hearts. Their vocabulary did not contain the words "give up."

Glancing up through her lashes at Matt's strong features, a small smile played around her mouth as she recalled her father's oft-repeated definition of his fellow Pennsylvania Dutchmen. "A bunch of bullheads, all of us, without the vaguest idea of the meaning of the word quit."

Matt, she decided, was a prime example.

Her own parents received the news as calmly as Matt's had. While her mother had gently questioned, her father had studied Matt and his answers intently, then both seemed to reach a decision simultaneously. That of approval of him, and relief that finally, their only daughter would have someone to care for her.

It was late when they arrived back at her apartment. Matt parked the car and went to the door with her then asked quietly, "Are you going into your office tomorrow?"

"Yes," she had answered wearily.

"I won't come in, you're just about beat. Can you manage a long lunch?"

She nodded, almost too tired to speak.

"All right. I'll be outside your building at twelve-thirty." His tone sharpened slightly. "I think you'd better go right to bed. You look about to cave in."

"I am tired," she admitted, not mentioning her lack of sleep the night before.

He was waiting in the back seat of the long car the following day, papers spread around him. John was standing on the sidewalk holding the door and as he handed her inside she said in surprise, "I thought you had cleared your desk!"

"Always something," came his withdrawn, pre-occupied reply.

Shrugging lightly she turned to glance out the window wondering idly where they were having lunch.

A few minutes later she turned to him questioningly as the car bumped onto the ramp and down into the garage. He closed his briefcase with a snap before glancing up. "My place. I thought you might like to see it."

"Of course," she'd murmured uneasily, her nerves beginning to tighten. She had slept well and had awakened that morning feeling refreshed and ready to face whatever new surprises Matt had in store for her, she had thought. Now she wasn't so sure.

On entering the apartment the ease with which she'd greeted the morning began to fade, for waiting for them was a woman in her early thirties and a man a few years older. She had not noticed them at first, the black and white starkness taking all her attention.

The motion of the woman's fingers tapping the arm of her chair, the man turning from the window to face the room, brought Katherine alert with an odd warning tingle at the base of her spine.

Matt's hand gripped her elbow as he led her into the room at the same time as the woman stood up abruptly and said in agitation, "Why the sudden summons, Matt? I had to break a luncheon date."

His voice revealing no trace of sympathy, Matt answered, "Sorry. I asked you here to meet Katherine. Katherine Acker, my sister Elizabeth Farrel and my brother, James."

The woman's pretty face wore a trace of suspicion and for one uncomfortable moment Katherine was afraid Beth was going to ignore the hand she'd offered as she said, "How do you do?" Then Beth touched her fingers briefly echoing her own words.

James had come across the room and as Beth's fingers fell away Katherine's hand was swallowed in a warm, firm clasp. The warmth of his hand was matched by his voice. "A pleasure to meet you, Katherine Acker."

Katherine's hand was still in his, his last word barely out of his mouth when Matt said smoothly, "Katherine has just agreed to become my wife."

Katherine's hand was given a quick squeeze before it was released. James' voice and face mirrored delight. "Wonderful, it's about time you settled down, Matt." Then his eyes dancing, he added, "Congratulations, and I think it's proper to wish the bride much happiness, which I do."

Katherine had murmured, "Thank you," her eyes moving to Beth's face, widening at her stricken expression. She had expected them to be surprised, which James obviously was, but this? Beth looked as if she had been physically struck. Her voice, when she spoke, held an almost shrill note and she spoke to Matt as if Katherine was not there or could not hear. "Your wife? But, Matt, we don't know her. Our friends don't know her."

Matt's eyes turned steely colored, his voice roughly clipped. "I know her. My friends know her."

Beth's eyes fastened on the diamond solitaire on her finger and her voice, hurried, uneven, declared, "But it will be a long time before a wedding can be arranged, there will be engagement parties and—"

Matt's voice, silky smooth, cut her off. "The arrangements have been made; the wedding is this coming Saturday in Lancaster."

Beth gasped. "This Saturday!"

Matt ignored his sister. Turning to James he went on, "I'd like you to be my best man."

"I'd be honored," James managed to get in before Beth cried, "Lancaster? Why in the world would you want to get married there?"

Patience now obviously strained, he turned back to her and snapped, "Because in case you've forgotten, that's where our parents are. Katherine's too for that matter."

There was a short, painful silence, then James put in gently, "May I ask who will be my co-witness?"

Matt glanced sharply at Katherine, who was suddenly very glad she'd had the common sense to call Carol that morning.

"Carol Bennington," she answered quietly.

Before anyone could reply Clyde's low, well modulate tones announced, "Lunch is ready, Matt."

Matt did most of the talking during lunch briefing Beth and James and, unknown to them, Katherine herself, on the arrangements he'd made. In growing wonder she learned he'd already phoned her brothers inviting them and their families to Lancaster for the long weekend, at his expense. His secretary was in the process of calling friends for the same purpose and that arrangements had been made for a small wedding luncheon in a private room at one of the bigger motels outside Lancaster.

As they were leaving the apartment after lunch James asked flippanly, "Where are you going on your honeymoon?"

"None of your business," Matt retorted dryly.

Katherine had been sitting quietly subdued on the drive back to her office when Matt said suddenly, "About a honeymoon, Katherine. There isn't time just now for a lengthy trip as I'll have to be back in the office by next Thursday. I have a house in the Poconos and I was wondering if a few days in the mountains would do for now? Maybe we can take a few weeks later in the fall if you like."

She hadn't even considered the possibility of a wedding trip and in some confusion she answered hurriedly, "The mountains will be fine, Matt, as I'll have some work to get back to in my own office."

"Good. I'll contact the people who take care of the place for me, let them know when to expect us." He slanted a considering look at her, then added, "Another thing we'd better discuss, Katherine, is where we're going to live."

His words jerked her out of the bemused state she'd been in. She hadn't considered anything past the actual wedding. Suddenly the enormity of the step she was taking crashed in on her. She still had to tell Janice and Tom and they'd both be home tomorrow. Her mind shied away from that thought uneasily.

As if he'd been able to follow her train of thought he asked quietly, "When do you expect your children home?"

"Tomorrow. Janice and Carlos are stopping over before going to Washington. Tom will probably get home some time in the late afternoon." Try as she would she couldn't keep the tension out of her voice.

"I'll come to the apartment after dinner; by then you probably will have told them."

The car slowed to a stop in front of her office building. Katherine nodded mutely in answer to Matt and moved to get out. His hand clasped her arm, holding her still. In a calm, unhurried voice, he added, "I think the best idea would be to move your things to my apartment. It will be more convenient for you to get to the office. Later we can send some of your things out to the house enabling you to spend the weekends there, if you wish. Tom may choose any room or rooms that he likes, both at the apartment and the house, there are certainly enough of them."

"And I?" Her voice was a soft whisper.

His own was a low rasp. "Will share mine. You already knew that, Katherine."

"Yes," she answered huskily. "I must go, Matt." And she had fled, both the car and him.

It had finally been over. She had become Matt's wife. Had stood with him in that lovely old church and exchanged vows that caused only momentary twinges of guilt and doubt. Had managed to get through the following two hours of congratulations and lunch with a smile glued to her lips.

The only real opposition Matt had met with had come from an unexpected quarter. Her young Tom. Janice had at once been delighted with the prospect of Matt for a step-father. Carlos, always the gentleman, had offered sincere wishes for her happiness. Tom was surprisingly hostile. Matt, being Matt, let nothing stand in his way, not even Tom. When she had wavered, at Tom's resentful objections, Matt reminded her brutally that within a short time Tom would be gone from the nest, was in fact, not there very often now, and that she had to plan for her own future. She had strengthened her resolve and Tom had managed to hide his hostility behind a mask of cool politeness throughout the day.

Finally it had been over and as they left the city limits behind, she had rested her head against the back of the seat in the rapidly cooling car with a sigh. The day was hot, the sun a merciless golden disk, scorching everything and everyone it touched. The tires hummed a different tune, as they always did in hot weather, oddly soothing Katherine's frayed nerves.

"Are you going to sleep?" Matt's soft rasp had not been an intrusion but more a blending with the tire's song.

She couldn't somehow, resist the age old response. "No, I'm just resting my eyes."

His soft laughter had flowed around and over her, adding to the feeling of relaxation slowly creeping through her.

"I haven't had the opportunity before now to tell you how lovely you look. That color suits you, deepens the color of your eyes."

The compliment, spoken in the same soft tone, startled Katherine. Turning her head she stared at him, violet eyes full of surprise, suddenly glad about the frantic flurry of shopping she and Carol had indulged in the previous afternoon. She had

finally chosen a dress in pale lilac made of silky
material which clung softly to her.

"Why thank you." Her voice was deep with feeling. "You look very fetching yourself."

A quick grin flashed at her terminology and the
sense of well being deepened in her.

Fetching was hardly the word. He looked downright shattering. A light gray suit and pale blue
raw silk shirt with which he wore a deep blue tie
blended and seemed to be reflected in his pulse-
stopping eyes.

She had lifted her head from the seat to stare at
him. Shifting his glance to her, still smiling, he
said, "Relax, take a nap if you like, we have a long
drive ahead. I'm taking a round-about route as I
want to drop off some papers at one of the
Reading plants."

She hadn't slept but had settled back quietly
allowing him to concentrate on the busy Saturday
traffic. She let her eyes absorb and appreciate
the rolling checkerboard countryside flashing by
the fields of deep green corn, buff gold wheat, the
pastures with their dotted herds of cattle
munching contently in the hot afternoon sun. This
she knew, was some of the best farm land in the
States and housed some of the best farmers. Most
of the farm buildings were painted white with
green trim and some of the barns bore the
intricately painted protective hex signs. Off to her
right, on a narrow road that ran parallel to the
highway a short distance, she caught a glimpse of
a horse drawn black buggy the likeness of which
Katherine thought was the symbol of the area. As

always the sight and smell of her birthplace filled her with a warm glow of pride.

Reading—The Outlet Capital of the World. Katherine studied the billboard sign idly as they approached the city limits, smiling as she remembered the one day shopping spree she'd had there. She'd been exhausted but happy after a day spent trooping in and out of plain factory store rooms filled with merchandise ranging from leather goods and jewelry to swim suits and jeans. The thought of the amount of money she'd spent that day still made her wince.

The stop Matt had to make took less than ten minutes, then they had left the city behind, driving toward Allentown.

As they drove close to the outskirts of Kutztown the traffic became increasingly more congested and after passing the lovely tree shaded college buildings she saw why. Drawn across the highway, above theirs heads, was a large banner which read "Kutztown Folk Festival" and underneath, the dates.

At the intersection, instead of keeping straight on the highway, Matt followed the line of cars turning left. Glancing around Katherine asked, "Where are you going?"

"To buy you dinner," came the teasingly amused reply.

He parked the car among what Katherine thought must be hundreds of others and they joined the throng converging on the festival grounds.

Matt tilted a glance down at her. "Ever been to

the festival before?"

She shook her head. "No, although I've heard
about it for years. I've somehow never found the
time."

"You'll enjoy it I think," Matt stated firmly.

14

Enjoy it she had, even with the unavoidable bumping and jostling of the immense crowd, the melting hot sunshine and fine dust in the air. She savored with deep appreciation the displays of handcraft and workmanship that were the heritage of everyone born in the region known as the Pennsylvania Dutch Country.

They moved slowly from one display to another watching with respect the varied skills demonstrated, from the blacksmith and metal workers to the candle making and the needlework displays. It was at the last that Katherine had lingered the longest, eyes caressing in particular the beautiful handmade quilts and bedspreads.

So intent had her gaze been she hardly noticed the suns rays slanting long from the west. Nor did she see that Matt had left her side until he was back again, handing her a paper bag.

Forcing her eyes from the display she'd looked up into his lean expressionless face asking, "What's this?"

"Why don't you open it and see?" he answered dryly. Then he added softly, "A small wedding gift."

"But that wasn't necessary."

"I know." Then, his voice even lower tacked on, "Even though it might be."

Completely mystified she opened the bag and peeked inside. With a gasp of pleasure and excitement, she drew out an exquisitely crocheted white shawl worked in a fine lace pattern.

"Matt, thank you," she'd whispered softly. "It's perfectly beautiful." Glancing up she saw he'd been closely watching her reaction. Apparently satisfied with it, he smiled gently, "It may prove necessary. The evenings turn cool in the mountains. Now I think we'll hunt up our dinner. Okay?"

She'd nodded absently, carefully sliding the shawl back into the bag, but her vagueness left her as they moved with the crowd toward the food pavillions. She suddenly realized she was very hungry, as she had eaten little at the wedding lunch, and the aromas that reached them on the hot, heavy air made her mouth water.

Luckily as they came up to the stand a teen-aged couple were just leaving and Matt swiftly seated first her, then himself, on the vacated stools. In unison their eyes went to the small blackboard on which the day's menu was written in chalk.

Katherine's eyes sailed down the white lines:

sauerkraut and pork, stringbeans with ham, chicken potpie, chicken corn pie, pork chops stuffed with potato filling. Matt's voice stopped her at home cured baked ham. "Intead of a platter how about ordering a la carte?"

"All right." As her eyes swung from the menu they encountered a clear-skinned smiling young girl waiting to take their order. "I'll have a bowl of potato soup, an individual chicken corn pie and a glass of iced mint tea."

"And a pon-haus sandwich?" Matt inserted, arching one eyebrow at her.

"Yes," she said laughing. Lord, she couldn't remember how many years it had been since she'd eaten a scrapple sandwich.

"Okay." He turned to their waitress. "I'll have the same."

The girl smiled and asked, "Dessert?"

"Shoofly pie and coffee, what else?" He grinned. The girl returned his grin and left to get their order.

Katherine studied the slim young form as she moved away. Her dress, very plain, was of cotton and her brown hair ws drawn back onto her head covered by a thin white cap, the cap strings dangling down the back of her neck. Shifting her eyes to the crowded walkway they came to rest on a barefoot young man, his clean shaven face proclaiming his bachelorhood. He wore a blue cotton shirt, shoulders supported dark suspenders which held up his too short, straight legged black pants. Squarely atop his shapely head sat a flat crowned broad brimmed black hat the like of which, Katherine had always felt sure, was placed onto every male head from the time they could toddle.

"I've always been fascinated by the Amish and Plain people," she murmured. "Their children are so beautiful with their fresh, clean faces. They seem to radiate health and well-being."

"Yes," Matt answered. "They work hard and hang onto their lifestyle and traditions tenaciously. I'm all for progress, obviously, and yet I feel I want to cheer every time they go into battle with the authorities to hang onto their life-style and their individuality."

The food was delicious. The soup was hot, the buttery milk broth thick with its contents of pieces of potato, onion, celery and slices of hard-cooked eggs. The pie steamed when the melt-in-the-mouth top crust was broken to reveal large chunks of chicken in milky sweet corn. The scrapple, when Katherine bit into her sandwich, was just as she liked it, fried crispy brown on the outside, creamy with just a hint of spices inside. She eyed the shoofly pie warily but managed to eat the crumby topped cake with its moist molasses bottom to the last crumb.

She sighed in satisfaction as they left the stand and Matt's voice again held that teasingly amused note. "Enjoy your dinner?"

"Completely," she answered honestly; then added, "It tasted like home."

He nodded, his expression telling her he too had experienced the sensation of certain foods, certain smells, bringing back childhood and home in a rush.

They made their way to the car and back onto the highway, the daylight now a golden glow from the western horizon. Katherine remembered very little of the rest of that drive as she dozed off and on until Matt's quiet voice roused her. "We're here, Katherine."

It was full dark and Katherine could see little except the narrow black-topped road directly in front of the car's headlights and then, as he turned on to it, the drive marked private. Then suddenly she could see the house, ablaze with lights from within, brightly lit outside from a bright light attached above the garage ceiling. No getaway for the weekend cabin this, but a large tri-level with what looked like many windows and a broad rail-fenced deck running around at least two sides.

After Matt parked the car and removed their cases from the trunk, she followed him to a door in the rear of the garage which led to a short flight of steps. At the top two doors faced each other across a wide landing and Katherine assumed, correctly, that the one on the right opened in to the apartment she'd noticed above the garage.

He held the other door for her then preceded her through a laundry room and into the brightly lit modern kitchen. At the far end of the kitchen was a dining alcove, the table placed under a large picture window, seemingly painted black so complete was the darkness outside. Where the kitchen area ended and the dining space began

was a door in the wall to the left that led onto the
wide deck. Across from the door was an archway,
through which Matt led her into the living room.

He placed the cases on the floor then stood
beside her silently while she took in the room. The
ceiling was open-beamed as were the walls, the
plaster gleaming white between the beams. The
wall on her left, which she was later to learn was
the front of the house, appeared to consist mainly
of two wide sliding glass doors that opened onto
the deck. Across the room and built into the
wall was a huge stone fireplace flanking two
large windows. At the back wall was an open
bar with four bar stools, the leather-upholstered
seats set into large barrels. On her right open
stairs, seeming to float in space, curved to the
floor above and Katherine stood, eyes wide, trying
to determine what supported it when Matt's
laughing voice broke her thoughts. "I'll never tell.
Do you like it?"

"It's fantastic," she breathed softly. In fact she
thought the entire room fantastic. There was not a
lamp or lighting fixture in sight yet the room
seemed to glow in a soft, subdued light. The
furniture consisted of several large chairs, to
accommodate Matt's big frame she was sure,
every one covered in a dark brown cushiony
pigskin. All had square matching ottomans and in
front of the fireplace a long matching sofa. The
highly polished hard wood floor was dotted with
bright orange scatter rugs, the color reflected in
the burlap weave drapes at the window and the

toss pillows on the sofa and chairs. The occasional tables were hand-made of dark walnut wood.

"I love it," Katherine whispered finally.

"I'm glad. I do, too," Matt answered in kind. Then, as he picked up the cases and started up the stairs, added briskly, "I imagine you're as ready for a shower as I am. Come along and I'll show you where to find one."

On the wide wrought-iron railed landing he stopped in front of a door that appeared to lead into the only room on that level. He opened the door, touched a switch and stepped aside to allow her to enter first.

The master bedroom. Except for the connecting bath, it was the only room on that floor. Almost as large as the living room, the ceiling was also open-beamed, the lighting indirect. The walls were paneled in white birch, a smaller fireplace built into the wall directly above the one in the living room. The floor was covered in a tawny colored carpet of fake fur. The spread which covered the large bed was rough handwoven wool, as was the one chair in the room, but in a darker gold color. The double dresser and high chest of drawers were of dark walnut. The wall facing the front of the house was covered by walnut louvered folding doors which, when Matt opened them, revealed sliding glass panels like the ones in the living room that led onto a small railed deck. Katherine stepped out onto the deck but could see very little for the darkness.

She came inside to follow Matt the length of the

room to the far wall which at first glance had
appeared solid. As she drew closer Katherine saw
the breaks in the paneling just as Matt slid one
panel open. "You can hang your things in here."

The closets were deep and ran almost the entire
length of the wall, the panels sliding behind each
other at whatever spot one wished to open. The
last panel opened into the bathroom of white and
dark brown except for the tawny rug which
continued through the bedroom.

Turning back into the bedroom Katherine saw
Matt had his case open and was piling clothes onto
his arm. He turned and giving her a brief smile
walked to the door.

"I'll grab a shower down stairs and have a drink
ready for you when you get down. What would you
like?"

"White wine?"

"Certainly. I'll put it in to chill. Take your time
and, oh, if you're going to hang your clothes,
would you do mine too?"

She nodded and he was through the door,
closing it quietly. She stared at the door a few
minutes, sighing in relief at his leaving her alone
to shower, then emptied the cases leaving out
clean undies, a lightweight jogging suit in purple
and white and flat white sandals.

A half hour later, freshly showered, face free of
make-up except a rose lip gloss, she went down the
stairs. As she reached the bottom he came around
from behind the bar carrying her wine glass and
what looked like his usual Chivas-sans-soda. He

stood at an archway in the far wall looking relaxed and attractive in dark slacks and white pullover shirt.

"Come along," he rasped softly, holding her glass out to her. "I'll show you the rest of the place."

The house was larger than she'd thought. He led her through the archway into a hallway off which were three bedrooms and two small bathrooms. Then they went down a curving stairway to the ground level which consisted of a rec or family room, a small alcove which contained the heating and airconditioning units, and a small sauna room with its own tiny dip pool.

From the rec room they went through a door and across a flag-stone patio to the steps leading up to the deck of the living room.

"It's a beautiful house, Matt. I don't see how you can ever bear to leave it." Not looking at him Katherine sipped her wine, willing some of the warm peaceful evening to seep into her, soothe the steadily mounting tension.

"Thank you, I designed it. As to leaving it, I don't very often for the simple reason I seldom get up here. Although I don't hunt, I have brought friends and business acquaintances up to hunt occasionally, including some weekends during the hottest part of the summer." She glanced up at him and he lifted his eyebrows mockingly. "Yes, I also indulge in the business-mixed-with-pleasure weekend at times."

He studied his empty glass then turned abruptly to the living room.

"Can I top your drink off?"

"No, thank you, I'm fine." She held her half full glass up for proof.

He was back in minutes, his glass three-quarters full of what Katherine was sure was all whiskey over one small ice cube. Her nervousness increasing, she gulped down her wine. Lord, this night was going to be difficult enough; she hoped he wasn't going to get drunk in the bargain. Fingers cold, nerveless, she played with the stem of her glass.

"I—I'm very tired," she murmured, wetting lips gone suddenly parched. "I think I'll go to bed."

Eyes on her face, he sipped his drink, rasping softly as he lowered his glass, "All right, you go on up. I'll be up as soon as I've finished this." Lifting his glass he gave her a small salute before again putting it to his mouth.

Katherine went into the kitchen, rinsed her glass and sat it on the draining rack, then went up the stairs to the bedroom. Fingers now like ice, she undressed quickly. She slipped into a lightweight batiste nightie, washed her face, brushed her teeth and slid into bed.

She was shivering, her arms covered with goosebumps and she drew the covers closely around herself wondering if the chill was caused by the low setting of the air-conditioner or her own fear.

Don't be ridiculous, she chided herself sharply. You're a mature woman, you've been to bed with a man before and it's probably the same with every man. But it had been so many years, almost twenty, and she was scared. Scared, hell, she was terrified.

By the time Matt entered the room she lay stiff, unmoving, fingers curling into her hands, nails digging relentlessly into her palms. He didn't bother with the lights, walking unerringly through the room and into the bathroom. The room was dark, the only light being the pale stripes of moonlight cast on the rug through the louvered doors. Katherine's eyes had adjusted to the dark room enabling her to distinguish outline and shape and she watched him, heart thumping painfully, when he came back into the room. He undressed swiftly, with a minimum of movement, tossing his clothes on the chair next to the night stand.

She watched him, unable to tear her eyes away, swallowing convulsively to ease the knot of rising panic in her throat. What was she doing here? Why had she agreed to this? This man was a stranger to her and she was more than a little afraid of him. She felt her body go even more rigid as he slid into the bed beside her. He turned to her, his head coming closer and without conscious thought she jerked her head away from him. She heard the breath catch in his throat and he became perfectly still.

Feeling frozen, barely breathing, she waited for his reaction. When it came, it plunged her into shock. He took her. He didn't try to kiss her, touching her only when absolutely necessary, he took her, coldly, unemotionally, like an

automaton, moving away immediately when it
was over.

Eyes wide, dry, she lay staring blankly into the
darkness, incapable of coherent thought, her body
shaking, cold with shock. She must have slept for
when next her eyes blinked wide, the room was
bright from the sun rays shining through the
louvered slats.

With a sigh of relief, she saw Matt was gone and
with a soft groan she left the bed. It seemed everyone of her muscles ached from the contraction of
tension and she felt tired to the bone.

Like a sleepwalker she went to the shower,
standing passively while the hot, stinging spray
worked its magic on her body. Still not allowing
herself to think just yet, she dressed in white jeans
and a hot pink pullover, grimacing wryly at the
brazen color. Ignoring the make-up case on the
dresser she brushed through her short black
curls, then slipped her feet into the sandals she'd
worn the night before.

Still moving slowly she walked across the room,
folded back the louvered doors, slid open the glass
door and stepped onto the deck. The air was still
morning sweet although the sun was hot. She
stood still, eyes closed, breathing the fresh pine
scented air deeply into her lungs, willing the rays
of heat to melt the lump of ice that had formed
inside her.

The view from the deck was breath-taking, the
mountains close and distant seeming to overlap
each other. The morning light drawing the many

shades of green into brilliance was at once a delight to the eyes, an assault on the senses. Something tugged at Katherine's memory and then she suddenly realized the scene she was gazing at was the same as the painting in Matt's apartment living room.

She didn't hear until he stepped onto the wooden floor of the desk and she jumped when his hand touched her shoulder.

Matt's voice was toneless, without inflection, although the rasp seemed more pronounced. "Mrs. Darcy has breakfast ready, Katherine. Will you come down now? I'd like you to meet her."

She nodded turning, then, "Matt, I—"

"Later, Katherine, we'll talk over breakfast." His tone brooked no argument and turning he led her through the room, down the stairs and into the kitchen where both Mr. and Mrs. Darcy waited for them.

In their fifties, they were both small and wiry with open contented faces. After Matt made the introductions and they'd offered congratulations, Mr. Darcy departed. Mrs. Darcy served breakfast on the glass topped white wrought-iron table on the deck. Placing covered serving dishes on the table, she glanced first at Katherine then Matt and, with a twinkle in her eyes, told them to help themselves and followed her husband within minutes.

"They seem very nice," Katherine said softly.

"They are. They've been with me since the house was built. They live here the year round, in the apartment over the garage."

His tone indicated that was all he'd say on that subject and she sipped nervously at her hot coffee, burning her tongue in the process. Cradling her cup in icy fingers she said abruptly. "Matt, this arrangement isn't going to work."

He was quiet long minutes, his eyes narrowed, staring out at the mountains. Then he turned his head. Cold icy gray eyes fastened on hers and held and he said slowly, deliberately, "Yes, it is, you made an agreement and you'll stick to it." The rasp ragged, his voice hardened, and Katherine's cheeks grew warm with his next words. "You're no blushing young virgin, you knew what to expect. If what happened last night is—distasteful to you, as I know it is to some women, I can only give you the consolation of assuring you it will only happen when it's absolutely necessary."

He kept her moving during their brief stay, showing her some of the attractions the mountains offered. These ranged from the modestly priced to very expensive luxury resorts with their lure of boating, fishing, golf, and practically every other activity one could think of including big name nightly entertainment.

They visited Bushkill Farms, Buck Hill Farms and Winona Falls, where the age old fascination of cascading water wove its spell around Katherine. They went on to Fred Waring's beloved Shawnee and finally ended their whirlwind tour at Camelback ski resort with its summer-time lure of water slides and breathtaking Alpine slide.

He had been true to his words and the shock, the

humiliation Katherine had suffered, slowly wore off, leaving in its wake a feeling of numbness, emptiness that not even the lure of the peaceful mountains could touch. Though she felt the enchantment of the shaded green world, her only wish was to enjoy it; alone.

15

Katherine stirred uneasily, a small shiver running through her as she came slowly out of the past.

"Couldn't you sleep?" Matt's voice was low, the rasp barely noticeable.

"No." She whispered.

"Where do you go, Katherine? What do you think about when you withdraw inside yourself like you have for the last few hours?"

She closed her eyes, feeling her throat close at the same time. Should she tell him? Try and explain that she was becoming more and more obsessed with their past in an effort to see some sort of a future? Would he understand? Would he even try? But why should he? He would, in all probability, inform her coolly and succinctly, that he had made his requirements quite clear when he'd offered her marriage and she'd accepted them. He was a business man and he'd made a business deal, simple, clear cut.

"Nothing important," she finally answered, turning her head on the pillow to look at him. His face reflected his dissatisfaction with her answer, his forehead creased with a deep frown. Sighing softly he asked, "What time does our boy usually wake up?"

Our boy! He couldn't possibly know what the sound of those words did to her emotionally. Voice husky, she murmured, "About seven."

"And Janice and Carlos won't be here before ten-thirty; it's not yet five, why don't you try to get a few hours' sleep?"

She shivered at the almost tender tone and fought back the urge to dissolve the tightness in her throat with tears.

"You cold?" His own voice had grown husky, then sliding his arms around her, he pulled her against his hard, warm body and whispered, "Sleep, Kate."

Even with her lack of sleep the day turned out to be a satisfying one for Katherine. Janice and Carlos arrived, the former glowing with good health and approaching motherhood, the latter with happiness and pride of achievement. Matt stayed home all day, his manner one of pleasant amiability, and Katherine felt the tensions of the night ebb out of her. The mildly incongruous sight of Matt striding through the apartment with Jon in his arms, laughing and teasing the baby in turn, settled on her a contentment she had not felt in a long time.

Dinner was a happy, companionable time as were the few hours they spent in the living room afterward. Plans were made for Carlos to call Katherine as soon as Janice went into labor. Matt surprised them all by suggesting Katherine, Jon and Mary fly to Washington when Carlos called and spend a week or two getting to know her first grandchild. He then added casually, "I'll have the Lear kept ready for you; that way you can be with Janice within an hour or so after Carlos calls. If I'm here, I'll go with you. If not, I'll join you as soon as possible. All right?"

"Yes, thank you." The words seemed inadequate, but Katherine was sto stunned by his thoughtfulness and consideration they were the only words she could manage. It didn't matter for she had barely finished speaking when Janice cried, "Oh Matt, how wonderful! I was hoping Mother oculd come to me then." She paused, then added, "I suppose no matter how sophisticated and independent she thinks she is, when a girl is about to have her first baby she wants her Mother with her."

"Of course," Matt replied, his tone intimating it was a foregone conclusion.

That night Katherine slept deeply, with no side trips into the past.

Saturday brought sunshine and, in the early afternoon, a smiling Tom. He laughingly suffered birthday hugs and kisses from Katherine and Janice and grinned his thank you to Carlos and Matt before asking, "Could I have a sandwich or something? I'm starving."

Lunch was served to Tom and coffee to the rest, in the living room. Tom ate his lunch with Jon on his lap, talking non-stop around his sandwich. He'd finished eating and was drinking his coffee when he looked at Matt and grinned crookedly, saying, "I'd have been here sooner but the wreck's motor is acting up and I didn't want to push it, or my luck. I was even afraid to stop to eat, afraid it wouldn't start again. Do you think Jack could have a look at it while I'm here?"

"I don't know why not. If anyone can fix it Jack can." His voice held casual interest, and the others sat avoiding each other's eyes, Janice, Carlos and Mary having seen the birthday present that morning, as he added, "As a matter of fact your Mother has a little surprise jaunt for you when you've finished there. I'll speak to Jack about it when we go down for the cars."

Toms eyes, full of delight, swung to Katherine. "A surprise trip? For my birthday? What's shakin', Mom?"

Laughing, Katherine replied, "If I told you, it would hardly be a surprise."

As soon as he'd finished they piled into the elevator, shifting about until Tom was in the very front. At the ground floor the doors slid apart. Tom took three steps and stopped dead, speechless. Then, with a mock groan, he cried, "Oh nurse, I'm worse!" With a leaping spring he was at the flame colored Trans-Am, around it and inside, touching it lovingly.

While the others stood by smiling, Katherine walked slowly to the car, Matt, Jon in his arms, at her shoulder. As if on cue they spoke at the same time, "Happy birthday, Tom."

Katherine felt her heart constrict and her eyes grow hot and prickly when Tom lifted his head to look at her. For the first time in many years her son had tears in his eyes and as he started to speak his voice broke. "Than—thank you, Mom." Swimming eyes shifted to Matt. "I don't deserve this, you know."

Matt gave a brief shake of his head, then rasped quietly, "The fact that you've said that convinces me you do."

Tom's grin flashed white and quickly brushing the back of his hand over his eyes, he said excitedly, "Can I take it for a run?"

"Is the key in the ignition?" Matt questioned dryly.

Again Tom's grin flashed as he turned back into the car calling, "Come on, Jack, let's go for a ride."

Jack hesitated, glancing at Matt. On Matt's barely perceptible nod, he slid in beside Tom and they were off.

Matt smiled, shaking his head, glanced at his watch, handed Jon to Mary and looking at Katherine said, "I have an appointment. If I'm not back by the time you're ready to leave for the restaurant go without me, I'll join you there."

"But . . ."

"I'll be there, Katherine," he snapped impatiently, striding towards the Lincoln.

Matt hadn't returned and they left without him, Jon staying with the redoubtable Clyde. When they arrived at the restaurant they were met by James and three of Tom's friends Katherine had invited to the dinner. The girl Tom had been dating fairly regularly was there, a pretty blond girl aptly named Taffy, Tom's best friend Mike and Mike's current girl, Tina, a vaguely insolent overly-sophisticated young woman.

They were seated at a large round table and had been sipping pre-dinner drinks some twenty minutes, when Katherine heard Mike whisper to Tom, "I thought your step-father would be here?"

"He will be," Tom whispered back. "I hope so." Mike said softly, "I was looking forward to finally meeting the old boy. I've heard so much about him from my father I was beginning to think the great Matthew Martin was a myth my Dad made up as an example for me."

Katherine glanced down at her drink to hide the smile pulling at her mouth. The old boy! Matt should have heard that. She looked up at the sound of Tom's laughing voice. "Well, it looks like you're about to meet the myth." Following the direction of Tom's amusement filled eyes across the large room, her gaze encountered Matt.

He had just entered the room and was speaking to the maitre d'. Then he glanced in their direction, nodded and started toward them. Heads, both male and female, turned to follow his progress. She understood why. Matt was an impressive sight at any time but fully decked out in evening dress he was something else altogether. His midnight blue Pierre Cardin suit fit his big angular frame perfectly and his pale blue dress shirt banished the gray from his eyes leaving them clear blue.

As he started around the table, heading for the

empty chair between Tom's and her own, Katherine studied the expression on the faces of the three young people. Mike's had changed quickly from curiosity to admiration. Taffy's face revealed bright expectancy. The look on Tina's face caused her to pause with a soft sigh. The only way to describe it was cool calculation. Well, Katherine thought resignedly, Tina certainly wasn't the first woman to take Matt's measure and consider her own chances, and it was doubtful she'd be the last.

Matt paused behind Katherine's chair, touched her shoulder lightly murmuring, "Sorry I'm late," then turned to Tom saying, "I don't believe I've met your friends."

Introductions were made, Matt arching one brow in speculation at the purring tone of Tina's voice. He nodded greetings around the table, said, "evening James," then turned to take the drink from the waiter who had just walked up to him. Lifting his glass he glanced round the table then turned to Tom. "I propose a birthday toast. To our Tom, may the year be as happy, as satisfying and as fulfilling as the joy you bring to your family."

"Hear, hear," Carlos and Janice chorused.

The dinner was a huge success, the food excellent, the conversation pleasant, often funny, as the four young people kept the ball rolling with amusing quips.

They had been served coffee and liqueurs when Tina purred suddenly, "Why don't we go on to a disco from here?" and a chorus of "aw right" came from Mike, Taffy and Tom.

Katherine, sipping her Amaretto, lowered her glass saying firmly, "I don't think so, Tom, it's getting late and—" She stopped speaking for Tom had turned from her to look imploringly at Matt.

The corner of Matt's mouth twitched and sliding his hand inside his jacket he removed his billfold, extracted three twenties, handed them to Tom and rasped, "This one's on me, now book."

Tom grinned widely, said, "Thanks Matt," then, "come on guys, let's go before Mom changes his mind."

Fat chance, Katherine thought irritably frowning at Matt. But for the first time she actually believed Matt honestly liked Tom and it was obvious the feeling was returned.

"Book?" she asked in confusion.

"Jargon," he answered dryly. "Means get moving, take off."

Two weeks later Katherine flew to Washington to be on hand at the arrival of her first grandchild. Matt was out of town, but, as promised, he'd left the Lear and the trip was made quickly and smoothly. She stayed at the hospital, alternately pacing and sitting restlessly with Carlos, the twelve hours Janice was in labor then stood, tears unashamedly rolling down her cheeks, gazing at her granddaughter. She went in to kiss and congratulate a tired but happy Janice, then left smiling fondly at Carlos who sat, eyes fastened reverently on his wife's face, his lips pressed to the pale fingers of her hand which he held in his.

She took a taxi to Janice and Carlos' home, peeked in at a peacefully sleeping Jon then sank gratefully onto the bed in the room Janice had prepared for her. She felt exhausted but pleasantly so. She smiled thinking of Janice's daughter who, at the advanced age of thirty minutes, had shown unmistakable signs of promised beauty.

Thinking of the baby led to thoughts of her own Jon's birth and that led her thoughts inevitably into the past.

It had seemed to Katherine at the time that she spent most of her pregnancy in bed. In truth she didn't but at the time it *did* seem that way.

Matt had meant what he'd said that first morning. He did not touch her again during the few days they stayed in the Poconos, or for two weeks after they'd returned to the city.

As he had told her he would be, he was very busy after their return and Katherine had used that time in emptying her own apartment, settling into Matt's and catching up on work in the office, being driven there in the morning, picked up at lunch, returned after lunch and picked up at quitting time, by Jack.

During the remainder of that summer Katherine's companions were Clyde, the cold empty feeling she'd awakened with that first morning and, as Tom spent most of the summer in Canada and Carol was in New England, a growing loneliness.

Although Matt only took advantage of his marriage rights on an average of every two weeks, every time was exactly like the first. No words, nor the slightest hint of caress. His possession, so

coldly, mechanically performed, left her crushed
with humiliation.

When she missed her first regular cycle two
weeks after their wedding she thought little of it,
placing the cause on her tense, nervous state.
When the second cycle passed she was almost sure
and two weeks later she was positive. She had
borne two children and all the signs were there;
she was pregnant.

Her first reaction was horror for by her calcu-
lations she must have conceived on her wedding
night. For some days she was filled with a burning
hatred for Matt until the very intensity of her
emotion shocked her. With the shock came reason.
She was as much to blame as he, if not more so.

She had been frightened, considering herself
past the age to start a family all over again. She
thought of abortion and rejected the idea at once;
she couldn't. She just could not do it.

She paced the apartment like a caged animal.
She had to see a doctor, but who? Her own
obstetrician had retired some years ago. Then she
came to an abrupt halt as a name flashed into her
mind. Mark Hunter, doctor of gynecology and
obstetrics.

She had been pleasantly surprised at her
wedding to find two of the guests Matt had invited
turned out to be Mark and his wife, the former
Marsha Drake. Marsha had laughed at Katherine's
surprise, saying, "Even though you probably don't
remember, I told you once that I intended
marrying Mark. But I must admit, I'm as much
surprised as you are. Mark and Matt have

remained close friends and we had no idea he was planning to get married. And, quite frankly, your name has never even been mentioned. Please don't misunderstand, Katherine, we're delighted. It's time, past time, that Matt got married and I think you're perfect for him. Strangely enough, I thought the same when we were still in school."

Katherine had been amazed at Marsha's statement and would have questioned her on it, but there had been no further opportunity.

She went to see Mark who, after a thorough examination, pronounced her perfectly fit and definitely pregnant. But, he added, she was much too tense. When she confided to him her fears concerning her age, he laughed gently, chiding, 'Katherine, you've been listening to old wives' tales. I assure you everything will be all right. You'd be amazed at the number of women your age today who are being safely delivered of perfectly healthy, beautiful babies.

"Now," he added briskly, "I want you to follow my instructions to the letter. Before you leave my nurse will take a blood sample. She'll also give you a diet, which I expect you to adhere to, vitamins which I'll expect you to take. And, I'd like you to quit smoking. If you can't quit altogether at least cut down drastically. I'll see you again in four weeks, and Katherine, relax. By the way, does Matt know?"

"No. I wanted to be certain before I said anything," she'd hedged.

"Understandable." He'd nodded. "Well, now go home and tell him and make him one very happy man."

But would it? She'd worried. Would it make him happy?

It had been one of the few times Matt was not away on business in the few months they'd been married, and she'd stood at the window wall, nervously twisting her rings, waiting for him to come home.

She turned quickly when he entered the room saying quietly, "Good evening, Katherine, how was your day?"

"I didn't go to the office today," she offered jerkily.

Dark eyebrows rose inquiringly. "Any particular reason?" he asked coolly, his expression of polite interest.

"Yes." She hesitated, then rushed on. "I went to see Mark Hunter."

His expression changed to taut alertness, his voice held a fine sharp edge. "Are you ill?"

"Not exactly." Again she hesitated, swallowing convulsively to moisten her suddenly dry throat. "I'm pregnant, Matt."

A breath-holding stillness seemed to grip the room and Katherine felt the tiny shiver slide along her spine. Matt's taut face lost its color, grew even more harshly drawn, a muscle jerked at the corner of the straight hard line that was his mouth. Katherine couldn't quite read his expression. Was it shock, anger? It was definitely not the happy reaction Mark had predicted.

The tiny shiver grew, expanded, and she curled her fingers into tight fists to keep from shaking.

The stillness grew and she thought if he didn't speak soon she'd scream at him.

"Mark's positive, there's no doubt at all?" He rasped, finally.

She could hardly manage the whispered. "None."

"When?"

"The beginning of April."

She could actually see the mental arithmetic he did in seconds, then, eyes narrowing, his voice rasped, more harshly, "You said you're not exactly ill. Aren't you feeling well? Does Mark expect difficulties?"

"No! No, he said everything is fine. He expects a normal, healthy baby. It was just a figure of speech." She nearly choked the words out. This was decidedly not a man overjoyed at the prospect of becoming a father.

"A figure of speech." He murmured. Then she jumped as his soft voice flicked out at her sharply. "You consider being pregnant a form of illness? Or is it the fact that it's my child you're pregnant with? I have the feeling your reaction was not quite the same with either Janice or Tom?"

Her body stiffened with anger as she spoke and when he finished she lashed out coldly, "I was little more than a girl when I carried Janice and Tom. You'll have to agree I'm no longer that." She made for the door, wanting only to get away from the condemnation of his tone.

Moving swiftly he blocked her path. "You're frightened?"

"Yes," she replied tensely.

"But there are lots of women who have babies safely at your age and even years older, aren't there?"

Was he trying to reassure her? Or was he seeking reassurance from her? She couldn't tell and by then she'd become so tense she didn't much care.

She looked squarely into unreadable gray-blue eyes and said clearly, coolly, "So Mark said. But then, he doesn't have to go through it. Nor do you, I do." Brushing past him she ran for the bedroom.

Oddly, the following weeks were the most peacefully relaxing of her marriage. Matt's business trips were curtailed drastically and he spent most evenings at home, usually ensconced on the sofa, work papers spread out on the large coffee table in front of him.

After the first few evenings of this Katherine also brought work home, making herself comfortable on the deeply carpeted floor, pinning her drawings to a large drawing board which she propped against the opposite side of the coffee table.

Conversation was limited to an occasional, "Are you comfortable?" from him, or "Would you like something to drink?" from her. After the first week the tension eased, then disappeared. They were by no means on more intimate terms, but the atmosphere of polite hostility was gone.

On a Friday in mid-November Matt startled her by walking into the apartment while she was having lunch and asked briskly, "Is there any reason why you must return to the office this afternoon?"

"No, why?"

"Richard called me this morning, Chuck and Corrine arrived last night and I've invited the four of them up to the mountains. I'd like to get packed and leave as soon as possible."

They went in separate cars as Richard and Anne were planning to drive to Boston with Chuck and Corrine on Monday morning and Matt in the lead they arrived at the house for an excellent dinner, prepared by a prewarned Mrs. Darcy.

Katherine had totally enjoyed the weekend. The men were gone most of the daylight hours as Richard and Chuck went hunting and Matt, a non-hunter, went along to, in his own words, beat the bushes. As they hunted some miles from the house, deeper into the mountains, they packed lunches.

The three women spent their time talking about babies, taking walks in the brisk fall air and generally getting to know each other better.

Katherine and Matt saw the other four off early Monday and were themselves packed and ready to leave, when he turned to her suddenly and asked, "How about a last walk before we go?"

She'd agreed eagerly as the day was bright and mild.

They had walked for perhaps half a mile from the house, Matt identifying plants and trees for her, when Matt paused to point out a tree in the distance. Suddenly a loud cracking noise cut across his words and Matt grunted deeply, then went crashing to the ground like a felled tree.

Turning quickly she cried, "Matt!" and stopped, hand flying to her mouth, eyes widening in sick horror at the rapid spreading red stain on the outside of his left thigh. "My God!" she whispered hoarsely, "you've been shot!"

Matt's grayish tinged face was a study in pained disbelief as he ground out, "If I find out who the stupid bastard is I'll kill him, ignoring the notices and hunting this close to the house."

She had dropped to her knees beside him and now cried out, "Matt, we've got to stop this bleeding. Do you have a clean handkerchief?"

He handed it to her and, as she pressed the white square against the ugly hole the shell had made in his leg, he sat up saying in a calm, if strained voice, "It went through cleanly and, by the way it's bleeding, didn't hit an artery. Hurts like hell, may have chipped the bone and I'd better not try to walk on it. Katherine, you're going to have to go for the jeep."

"Bring the jeep up here? How?"

Before she'd finished speaking he was pointing out two white birch trees, standing side by side, at some distance to his left. "There's a fairly clear, if narrow, path between here and those trees and those trees are by the side of the road. Be careful."

She was up and running before the last word was said when he called sharply, "Katherine, don't run."

Forcing herself to a brisk walk she thought irritably of course, now that he's reconciled himself to becoming a father, I must in no way endanger the heir by doing something stupid like falling, even if it cost him his life.

His life. The thought brought her up sort, almost to a stop, and it seemed everything vital and alive inside her cried out in protest. He can't die. I love him. I won't let him die. Without trying to figure out the whys or wherefores of her sudden realization she began running again. She fell down once but jumped up, gasping, to run on until she'd reached the garage.

It seemed to take a very long time but finally she'd covered the rocks, tree roots and natural earth bumps of the narrow path, and brought the jeep to a stop two feet from Matt. By the time she'd helped him to get up and into the jeep they were both wet with sweat and as he slumped back against the seat, his hand clamped against the handkerchief to stop the flow of the again freely bleeding wound, his face had a decidedly greenish tinge.

Slowly, carefully, she maneuvered the jeep around and back over the path and when she was on the road her foot pressed down on the gas pedal only to lift again, slightly, as Matt muttered. "Careful, there's a doctor about eight miles from here, stay on this road for a while, I'll tell you when to turn."

The doctor was young and of average height but solidly, strongly built. Between them they got Matt out of the jeep, into the office and onto the doctor's examining table where Matt, as if on cue, promptly passed out.

16

Katherine had paced the small hall outside the doctor's office, shaking her head at his wife's offer of coffee. Reminding herself they weren't good for her, she smoked one cigarette after the other as she tried to wear out the inlaid tile on the floor. Then she stopped in her tracks as Matt's low, rumpled laugh filtered through the door.

Feeling lightheaded she sank into the nearest chair, weak with relief. The door opened and the doctor's voice, sounding strangely distant, said, "You may come in now, Mrs. Martin, your husband is going to be fine." She stood up shakily and walked into the room wondering why it was so dimly lit. Matt's voice, sharp yet also strangely distant, rapped, "What's the matter?"

The matter? What did he mean? And why did the examining table seem so much farther away than when she'd helped bring him in?

"Katherine!"

Matt's voice was even more distant. The room seemed shadowy; had the sun gone behind a cloud? She was floating, then strong hands at her back were easing her down, down. The doctor's voice was a far away command. "Don't you dare get up. Do you want to reopen that wound?"

"But what's wrong with her?" Was that concern in that far away voice that was Matt's? "My God! She looks like death, even her lips are white."

This time there were steel teeth in the command. "I told you to stay put. Your wife has fainted, that's all. She'll be all right in a minute. Now get the hell back on that table."

The room was lighter and the command had sounded closer, not nearly so far away. Matt's growl was closer too. "You don't understand, Doctor, my wife is pregnant."

"And pregnant women often faint when under some strain. That's better, if you try to get up again I'll give you a shot and knock you out."

Katherine decided she liked this tough young man; then she realized that he was kneeling next to her. The room was bright and she blinked her eyes against the sudden glare. The two men were glaring at each other and didn't see her glance around vaguely. My heavens! She was lying on the floor. The doctor's voice, again clear, close. "Could she have fallen up there?"

Without thinking Katherine answered clearly, "Yes."

"What!" Both the men spoke at once and Katherine stammered, "I—I fell while I was going for the jeep."

"Katherine—" Matt began, but the doctor cut in. "How do you feel, Mrs. Martin?"

"A little tired."

The doctor's strong arms lifted her then cradled her against him as he rapped out, "Damn it, Martin, stay put. I'm taking your wife upstairs to examine her. I don't think there's been any damage done but when I'm through I'll have my wife put her to bed, to be on the safe side."

In next to no time she'd been stripped of her slacks and sweater, examined by the doctor who then gave her a mild sedative, assuring her it was quite safe, and tucked into bed by his wife.

She drifted into a gentle, dreamless sleep, rousing with a murmured protest when she felt herself folded into the comforter and again lifted in arms as strong, but different, than the doctor's.

"Easy, easy, Mrs. M., we'll have you home in no time." The soft crooning voice belonged to Jack, but how as that possible? Jack was in Philadelphia.

Although she was unable to lift her heavy eyelids she was aware of being carried down the stairs and out the door where she was transferred into yet another pair of arms. Hard, stronger than the other two pairs, she had never been inside their circle but she knew who they belonged to. Muscles, hard as steel, seemed to jerk convulsively as the circle closed around her and with a soft sigh she drifted back into darkness.

She was roused again at the sound of quiet voices and this time she managed to open her eyes a moment realizing with a start that they were in

the car. She was wondering why the car was
motionless when the door was opened and arms
reached in and drew her away from Matt. She
wanted to cry out in protest but all she could
manage was a low moan.

After being carried some distance she was lifted
up into yet more arms, and then placed into a sort
of narrow reclining seat. She became aware of the
fact that she was in the Lear, Matt sitting beside
her, when the scream of the jets started her into
wakefulness. She stirred restlessly and Matt
rasped softly, "Go back to sleep, we'll be home
soon."

"Your leg," she whispered.

"Is all right. Are you warm enough?"

"Hummm—" She was out of it.

The plane touching down brought her around
and by the time she was unstrapped and lifted
from her seat she was fully awake and aware that
Matt's seat was empty. This time the process was
reversed, she was handed down to waiting arms.
John's. His words drew her attention to the fading
light.

"Evening, Mrs. Martin, feeling better?"

"Yes, thank you John, what time is it?"

"Just past five," he answered coming to a stop
at the opened door of the Cadillac Matt kept at the
apartment for her use.

She was handed into Matt's arms and then they
were moving smoothly away from the airport.

"We're going to Mark's office; he's waiting for
us," he stated firmly and from his tone she knew it

was useless to argue.

After a thorough examination Mark's verdict echoed the other doctor. "I don't think there's been any harm done, but even so, stay off your feet and rest for a week or two."

The next morning Matt moved her to the house in the country and sent her to bed with an ordered, "Stay there." The move was permanent; where before they'd gone to the country for rare weekends, now the rare visits would be made to the apartment. Very rare.

The first week at the house went fairly well. Beth was civil, if not friendly and as Katherine was confined to her bed, on Matt's orders, it didn't much matter. It was a particularly satisfying time for her, so much so, she didn't even mind his orders. Matt slept in the small bedroom adjoining their bath so as not to disturb either Katherine or his leg. He had agreed to stay home from the office for one week to allow the leg to heal, but the amount of work he accomplished astounded Katherine.

Katherine woke that first morning to find him beside her in the huge bed. He was sitting up, back braced against the headboard, long legs stretched out comfortably, his briefcase alongside. When she stirred his eyes lifted from the sheaf of papers in his hand. "Morning, I didn't wake you did I?" At the brief shake of her head he explained, "I intend spending most of this week right here. If you have no objections?" He had arched his brows quizzically as he'd finished and smiled with the thought that it probably wouldn't matter in the least if she did, she again shook her head.

"Good. I'll still sleep in the other room, but I want to work in here by the phone. I'll also be able to keep an eye on you."

This time it was Katherine's eye brows that arched in indignation. He laughed softly, murmured, "I'm unimpressed," and turned to answer the phone on its first ring.

That set the precedent for the days that followed. He was there when she woke in the morning and when she fell asleep at night, no matter how late that might be. But she knew he did leave when he finally had to give into sleep for she woke once during the night and he was gone.

There was very little conversation between them, as he worked incessantly, and yet she was content. She read some of the time or made believe she did as she studied him covertly and contemplated her newly discovered love for him. She slept and ate, quite sure she could feel herself gaining weight.

Watching him through narrowed lids she'd asked herself how it had happened. Why had it happened? Except for the brief touching of lips on their wedding day he had never kissed her. In fact he'd made no advances at all, if one discounted the infrequent use he made of her body. Katherine did discount it. So then when had it happened and what was the cause?

She couldn't quite pin-point the exact cause, knowing only it was all part and parcel of the enormous respect she had felt growing inside her. It seemed that whatever task or problem this man turned his mind to was dealt with with deceptive effortlessness.

As to when it had happened, she thought it must have began growing during those weeks they had worked together in the apartment. True they had exchanged few words on those evenings and yet she had felt a closeness of sorts with him.

On the evening before Matt went back to the office he issued another order. "You are not to go into the office any longer. The drive back and forth would be too tiring. If you feel you must continue to work you will do it at home."

She didn't argue for the simple reason she had already reached the same decision. She didn't particularly like the idea that he'd made it an order instead of a request but that she let slide by her. The last few weeks she'd been to the office she had become increasingly aware of the sly looks cast in the direction of her growing body. Although her co-workers had refrained from comment, she now felt reluctant at the thought of facing those looks again.

She settled into the routine of the house. Beth left her no illusions as to who was and intended to remain mistress of the manse, so to speak. She drifted through the days eagerly awaiting the evenings, for Matt continued to bring work home from the office and on the first evening invited her to join him in his study if she had work of her own to do. She made sure she did.

The evenings together came to an abrupt end the week before Christmas for Katherine fell again. She had gone into town with Matt on Monday intending to spend the week at the apartment, finish her Christmas shopping and return to the house with him on Friday. She had luck with her shopping, finding what she wanted without effort, and by Thursday had only two items left on her list.

Jack drove her to a small specialty shop on Thursday morning where she was sure she'd find what she wanted. As she browsed around the shop she'd been unaware of the fine rain that had begun falling, freezing as soon as it touched the sidewalk. She made her purchases and as she left the store noticed that Jack was waiting for her, doubled parked. She started across the pavement at a brisk pace, her feet went out from under her and she went down with a jarring thud. With a loud exclamation Jack was out of the car and kneeling beside her in seconds. Hot with embarrassment she insisted he help her up and into the car at once, ignoring his protests that she wait a few minutes before trying to move.

Inside the car she rested her head against the seat, eyes closed, one thought uppermost in her mind. Matt would be furious. He was, at least that was how he seemed to her, for he was tight lipped and strangely silent throughout the following few hours. She was again thoroughly examined by Mark who repeated his words of little more than a month previously, with one difference. She was to rest for at least two weeks and call him immediately if any abnormality developed. After they were back at the house, and she was back in her bed, Matt finally broke his odd silence saying tersely, "I want you to stay at the house until the child is born. And I'm not listening to any arguments on the subject."

Katherine had bristled at his words but his tone had held a warning. Never before had he used that tone with her and she thought it wiser not to challenge him.

Christmas was a depressing time for her. Tom came to the house on his school holidays but, even though he dashed in and out of her room half a dozen times a day, it was not the same as before. For the first time in years she did not get to visit her parents over the holidays and they did not come to her as Dave and Dan and their families were with them. Katherine missed the fun and laughter that had always filled her parents' home when they had all gathered over Christmas. She even missed her brothers' teasing.

The one thing she hadn't minded missing was Beth's New Years Eve bash. She had been dreading it for weeks as she had not met any of the invited guests and didn't look forward t o the curious glances, and possible remarks, concerning her pregnancy. Katherine found it impossible to keep from comparing this New Years Eve in Matt's house with the previous one in Richard and Anne's. Matt's ran a bad second. She had not been lonely as Matt and James paid her periodic visits at different intervals, both bearing glasses of champagne.

Confined to the house, the weeks seemed to drag by after the holidays and Katherine was at her wits end trying to keep occupied. Matt was away four days in January, his parting words to her being, "be careful." She wondered vaguely how she could possibly be anything else and missed him terribly even though she saw little of him even when he was home. He had not touched her, in fact had not slept in the same bed with her, since her fall and she was unbelievably lonely.

Toward the end of February he told her he'd have to be away again for a few days. The morning after he left she woke with a mild cramp that quickly passed. She thought little of it until she had another some thirty-five minutes later. By lunch time the cramps were a little more severe and only twenty minutes apart. Still unconcerned, convinced she was having false labor pains, she thought it best to call Mark. Mark agreed that it probably was false labor, as it was still some five or six weeks until her due date, but he thought it best to have her in the hospital where he could keep his eye on her. Her protests got her nowhere and with a sigh she finally agreed thinking at least it would get her out of the house for awhile.

Beth had gone out for lunch so without saying a word to anyone, Katherine rang the garage, asked Jack to bring the car around and left the house.

"Feel the need of some air, Mrs. M?" Jack grinned as he helped her into the car, the grin quickly vanishing when she asked him to drive her to the hospital. On reaching the hospital she stared at him blankly when he asked, "Is Dad meeting Matt's plane?"

"I suppose so," she answered in confusion. "Doesn't he always?"

"Well sure, normally!" Jack answered concernedly. "But didn't the boss say definitely when you called him?"

"Called him?" Katherine repeated. Then she laughed in understanding. "I didn't call Matt, Jack, as I understand this is a very important conference Matt's attending and as I'm perfectly sure this is a false alarm, I didn't want to alarm him unnecessarily."

Jack stared at her in disbelief but before he could voice a protest she said softly, "Don't worry, Jack. There's no need for you to go along in as I'm sure Dr. Hunter is waiting for me. Stay close to the phone as I'll probably be calling you to take me home again in a few hours."

She had been right on one count: Mark had been waiting for her. No sooner had she been settled comfortably in bed than her contractions became harder, the intervals closer. By late afternoon she was in hard labor and she was scared. For all of Mark's earlier assurances of "Not to worry, everything's fine" two thoughts kept her mind frozen with fear; it's too soon, something must be wrong and I'm going to lose Matt's baby.

The nurse was blotting her forehead after a particularly severe contraction when, on a sigh of part relief part fear, she heard Matt's voice outside her room. He was speaking to Mark and they talked for some minutes before they both entered the room. She had only time to notice the cold, brittle look in Matt's eyes, the tight, angry lines of his face, before she was again gripped by a contraction, this one more severe than the last. She clamped her teeth together hearing the moan, that she refused to allow to become an outcry, escape her throat.

"They're very close now, Doctor," the nurse said softly. Then Mark was beside the bed, the fingers of one hand on her wrist, the other hand spread flat against her hard, distorted abdomen.

"Get out of here Matt," Mark said easily. "Go pace up and down or something. You're going to be a father before too long."

"Mark?" That surely couldn't be uncertainty in Matt's voice? The pain was easing and blinking her eyes against tears of concentration, she looked at him. Through the blur his face appeared pale and as he turned to leave on Mark's firm, "Everything will be alright, Matt. Now go," she could see a nerve dance along his hard, clenched jaw.

Within thirty minutes she had been delivered of their son and within minutes after she had been moved to a private room in the maternity ward where he came striding into her room accompanied by Mark.

His words stunned her, left her speechless, so softly, gently spoken.

"Thank you, Katherine, he is beautiful."

She stared at him, blinking at the hot, stinging at her eyes, then finally she managed a soft, hoarse, "Yes, he is."

His long fingers touched her hand lightly, then were quickly lifted as he rasped, "You're tired, I'll leave now. Get some rest, you've earned it."

He was gone and she no longer fought the tears but let them run down her cheeks unchecked. What had she expected? To have him put his arms around her and hold her close as he whispered "Thank you"? No, she hadn't expected that. But, damn it, that was what she'd wanted.

How often had she thanked whatever angel it was that sent Mary to her? At least a thousand times, for without Mary she would have taken Jon and bolted a dozen times during the following months. Having Tom at the house with her during the summer hadn't helped much as it was at this time he and Matt were circling each other warily, each taking the other's measure. When it finally came, near the end of summer, Tom's complete capitulation was almost anti-climatic.

Katherine lost weight slowly, but steadily, her nerves becoming more tautly drawn. Matt treated her with polite consideration, as befitted the mother of his child, she mused irritably. Jon was twelve weeks old before he claimed his connubial rights. He had not come near her, in that way, since her fall in November and if it had been humiliating before, now it was worse, much worse.

She had not been able to control the shudder

that had shaken her body and he had moved away
from her in disgust. She had lain awake the rest of
that night, her face wet with tears as she cried,
silently. She had been able to tolerate his cold,
mechanical possession before admitting to herself
that she loved him, but now, it was unendurable.

The summer wore on and Katherine built a wall
of cool composure around herself. Only when
alone with Tom and Mary did she relax her guard.
Although Beth seemed genuinely fond of Jon,
without words, she had made it clear her fondness
did not extend to his mother. And James' subtly
changing attitude toward her was beginning to
concern Katherine. Just the thought of Matt
frightened her. For some reason she could not
even begin to understand why her love for him had
deepened, grown almost to the point of adoration.

She had gazed at his look alike son with tears of
graditude in her eyes. Unable to reveal her love for
the father, she felt doubly thankful for the son.
And reveal her love she would not. Matt had told
her bluntly, at the outset, that he had no time to
indulge that particular emotion and she knew she
could not face his mocking derision should he find
out how she felt.

So as the summer wore on so did she, growing
thinner, more withdrawn, her one consolation in
Matt's obvious reluctance to be alone with her.
For she felt sure that had he come to her once
more with his dehumanizing, unemotional
physical demands she would start screaming and
never stop.

By the time summer was over she was fighting

one consuming urge; to run for her life. She felt she could not stay with him while at the same time acknowledging that life without him would be torture. Nerves frayed, her emotions in upheaval, she vacillated between staying and going. In mid September circumstances forced a decision. That was to go.

17

Katherine murmured a soft, sleepy protest, her hand brushing ineffectually at the warm tickling sensation running along her cheek. The tickling sensation was repeated and coming awake, she identified it as warm breath at the same instant his soft raspy laugh caressed her ears. Matt; just to think his name caused her to go all melty inside.

She opened her eyes to stare into gray blue ones, alive with amusement. He was beside her on the top of the covers fully dressed and wide awake, his face inches from he own. Again his warm breath fluttered over her cheek as he teased, "Was becoming a grandmother so exhausting you must sleep past noon?"

Her sojourn into the past until well into the early hours of the morning was momentarily forgotten and she responded to his teasing without her usual reserve.

"Oh Matt, you should see her. She is just perfect."

His soft laughter tantalized her cheek once more, the soft rasp held a note of indulgence. "There speaks the proud Grandma. But you're right, for I have seen her and she is perfect."

"You've seen her?" she asked incredulously. "When did you see her?"

"Right after I got here this morning. In fact, I went to the hospital from the airport."

"But visiting hours don't begin until one o'clock. How—?"

Her voice trailed away as his smile became a grin. She should know better, she chided herself. Would she never learn? This man went just about where he pleased, when he pleased.

"Did you see Janice?" she asked, trying to ignore the gently mocking gleam in his eyes.

"Yes, of course I saw her." His tone edged with impatience, he added, "Do you think I'd go there and not see her? She is fine, all dewy-eyed with motherhood. Come to think of it, Carlos looked a little dewy-eyed himself."

"You've seen Carlos, too?" she asked, then decided she really wasn't too bright this morning as the edge sharpened his tone. "Yes, Carlos too. Also Jon and Mary. Perhaps you weren't fully awake when I told you it was past noon. Carlos told me he'd left orders not to disturb you as you waited with him at the hospital until very late last night."

Katherine bit her lip at the sound of exasperation in his voice. When she didn't speak for a few seconds he signed and, lifting his head, began to move away from her. Impulsively she put her hand on his shoulder halting his movement and pleaded softly. "Don't be angry with me, Matt, please."

"I'm not angry, Katherine." His eyes had flicked strangely when she'd placed her hand on his shoulder and now they stared into hers intensely as he added hoarsely, "A little disappointed maybe, but not angry."

Bracing his weight on his right arm, his left hand covered hers a moment then slid down the length of her arm as he slowly lowered his head. His lips a whisper from hers, he groaned, "Katherine," then his mouth crushed hers fiercely, driving all thoughts from her mind.

She stayed with Janice and Carlos two weeks, fully enjoying her new role of grandmother. To her surprise Matt stayed with her, telling her he had business to look to in Washington. The two weeks passed much too quickly in the love that seemed to surround everyone in her daughter's home. She noted, with satisfaction, the way Janice was maturing, becoming a lovely young woman, and knew it was Carlos' gentle but firm guidance that had brought about this bloom.

Matt played to perfection his role of husband and father. There were many guests and well-wishers paying calls and Katherine felt sure that, to the last man and woman, they would have stared in disbelief if some one would have suddenly appeared and informed them of the true situation between Matt and herself.

She went back to the house reluctantly,

allowing Matt to think she hated leaving her daughter and granddaughter. She did, of course, but even more so, she hated going back to that house. As if on cue, Matt switched roles, exchanging the ones of contented husband for the more natural one of over-busy industrialist.

Except for their bitter argument resulting from the purchase of Tom's car, the six weeks she'd been away from the house had done wonders for Katherine. She felt good and looked it. But, as always before, the spontaneity and warmth seemed to drain out of her during the drive from the road to the house. Tension once more tightening her nerves, the wall of withdrawn composure was erected.

From the beginning Beth had treated Katherine with civil politeness, and DeDe had assumed the same attitude. Matt seemed not to notice. In fact, he seemed not to notice anything but DeDe.

A mask of cool unconcern hiding her feelings, Katherine, in seething fury, watched as Matt lavished attention on her. He was charming and urbane, teasing her cruelly about her ex-lovers one minutes, granting her every whim the next. DeDe lapped it up like a starving cat, purring all the while.

Consumed with jealousy, hating herself for it, she was lost to the realization that the type of attention Matt gave to DeDe was exactly like he gave to Beth. The ability to make a comparison in behavior was beyond Katherine at this point. She saw a strikingly beautiful woman flirting with an excitingly attractive man. She was sure she saw response in kind from that man. The fact that that man was Matt made her blind to objective observation.

With her almost audible sign of relief Matt left to attend a business conference in mid-November and Katherine stayed out of Beth's and DeDe's way as much as possible.

As if the six weeks away had not occurred, Katherine found herself pacing her room at night asking the same questions. Frustrated by her feeling of uselessness and her ambiguous position in the house she grew more and more restless.

Tired of her own thoughts, the endless circle her mind seemed to revolve in, she sought out Mary much of the time. A few days after Matt had left for the conference Mary came into the sitting room to find Katherine staring out the window, shaking with fury.

"You've just had lunch with the butterfly sisters," Mary remarked dryly.

Katherine turned from the window, face pale with anger, lips quivering in agitation. Not trusting herself to speak, she nodded her head. She had spent the last hour, in the dining room, as the target of saccharin sweet poisoned barbs aimed at her from Beth and DeDe. Interspersed between the barbs, the two women had gaily made plans for when Matt came home, omitting Katherine from them as if she were not there. I must be out of my mind, she thought furiously. How long do I think I can put up with this? Falling in love with that beast has scrambled my brain, for heaven's sake.

She had been staring at the carpet broodingly and now, glancing up, she found Mary's concerned eyes on her face.

"You don't look too good, Kate, you know that?" Mary asked quietly.

A small bitter smile twisting her soft mouth, Katherine murmured, "I could hardly help but know, could I? There are times during the course of one's day when one has no choice but to look in the mirror."

Mary's eyes sharpened. Katherine's cynical tone was completely out of character.

"Is there some physical cause?" The nurse in Mary had to ask, although she was sure the answer would be negative.

"No. No, Mary, I'm not ill. At least not physically. There are times, though, when I'm sure I'm about to go round the bend, as Tom would say." She forced a small, brittle laugh that didn't come off too well, and Mary snapped, "Kate! What the hell are those two she-dragons doing to you? And why the hell are you letting them? Oh, I know," Mary went on quickly at Katherine's raised brows. "But no man, not even the fantastic Matt, is worth the kind of mental agony you've been going through. I wonder if you do really realize how drawn and tense you look? You're in worse shape now then you were in September."

Katherine swung back to the window, tears smarting her eyes. "I know, I know," she whispered in an odd, faraway tone. Mary subsided onto a chair and picked up the sweater she was knitting for Jon, glancing apprehensively every few minutes at the slim, taut figure at the window.

September. That one word spun her into the past, the recent past. Was it only two months ago?

By the end of summer Katherine had become as tight as a miser's purse strings, and the one thing she had not needed was one of Matt's old girl friends. Needed or not, that was exactly what she got in the form of a thirty-five year old pale skinned, raven-haired beauty Beth had invited to the house, along with several other young women, for lunch and bridge.

Katherine had agreed to join them for lunch but when, lunch over, they had moved into the family room, where card tables were permenantly set up, she excused herself and strolled into the garden.

The garden was a riot of late summer color and Katherine breathed deeply the heady scent of roses. She had not heard the dark haired woman, who had been introduced to her as Rosalie Marella, until she spoke softly at Katherine's shoulder. "The garden is lovely, Matt must be pleased with it." Just Matt? Katherine wondered and then thought cynically, I doubt if he's even noticed it. But aloud she replied, "Yes," turning to examine the woman more closely than she had earlier. Rosalie was a truly beautiful woman, with fine dark brows, a small straight nose and perfectly shaped lips on an oval face of clear, pale matte. The paleness of her skin was relieved by the dusky rose color in her high cheek bones and her flashing black eyes.

In the few short seconds Katherine studied the other woman she felt an instinctive twinge of apprehension and with Rosalie's next words her twinge was proven accurate.

"I've been wanting to meet you ever since I heard that Matt had finally married. Curious to see the woman who had managed to draw the nuptial noose around his neck." Rosalie's voice, though soft and well modulated, had a fine edge which sent an alarmed tingle slithering along Katherine's spine.

They had been strolling along the graveled path, bordered by rose trees, and a mask of cool composure firmly in place Katherine stopped, turned slowly and calmly asked, "Why should you be curious about me?"

Rosalie returned stare for stare, before asking, in a strained voice. "You don't know who I am, do you?"

"Should I?" Katherine countered.

"I thought you might, Beth being Beth, you know," Rosalie replied thoughtfully. Then, giving a small shrug, she added ruefully, "Just like Beth to invite me here this way, when Matt's not home." Black eyes snapping, she said bluntly, "I am one of Matt's ex-mistresses. The only one, I think, that he might have married. I was too smart to become pregnant. Considered it much too old-hat a gambit which probably wouldn't work. It seems I out-smarted myself on that angle."

The words hit Katherine like a blow and she felt sick to her stomach. She had known, of course, of a few sneering remarks made when she'd delivered Jon not eight full months after their wedding, but she'd thought these remarks had been very few. Now she wondered although, in truth, she didn't really care. What had sickened her had been the boldness of Rosalie's first statement. The sick feeling spread as Rosalie continued calmly, "We were together for over two and a half years and I think I know him better than anyone else, including his ex-wife. Matt is incapable of feeling the emotion of love. Deep, romantic love, I mean. Oh, I'm sure he loves his son, the child being an extention of himself. And he loves women. Oh my, yes, he does love women. But in a purely physical, animal way, nothing deep or binding."

Katherine stood staring at her mutely, unsure which was worse, the actual words or the calm, detached tone in which they were delivered. For Rosalie was obviously carrying a flaming torch for Matt.

How does one respond to statements such as this, Katherine wondered wildly. This woman was speaking of Matt as if he were some casual acquaintance they both knew and, good Lord, they had both shared his bed. It was true, she unwillingly acknowledged, but that was hardly the point.

Nausea gripping her throat, her face grown frozen, Katherine spun on her heels, bit out icily, "If you'll excuse me," and forced herself to walk slowly into the house and up the stairs, one thought pounding inside her head—I have to get out of here.

She paused long enough to snap at Mary, "Don't ask questions, just throw some clothes for Jon and yourself into a bag as quickly as possible. I want to be out of here in ten minutes."

It was closer to fifteen minutes later when they left the house quietly and went to the garage, Katherine thinking that if Jack tried to stop her she'd fire him on the spot. Matt had replaced the black Cadillac he had put at her disposal after their marriage with a new silver-gray one as a gift to her when Jon was born. She knew the title was in her name and standing beside the gleaming machine she demanded the keys from Jack.

"But, Mrs. M., I have my orders. I'm to drive you anywhere you wish to go." Jack sounded more than a little confused, but adamant.

"Is this legally my car?" she bit out.

"Yes, ma'am, but—" Jack began, then his eyes widened at the unaccustomed sharpness of her tone as she cut him off.

"Then give me the keys at once or I'll call the police and report it as stolen."

He eyed her reproachfully but dug into his pocket for the keys. Placing them into her outstretched palm, he made his last try, "The boss is going to be very angry about this, Mrs. M."

Katherine's smile was over-sweet, her voice acid. "The boss can go to hell."

She felt a momentary regret for the position she'd placed Jack in as she backed the Cadillac out of the garage, but with a mental shrug dismissed it. She had enough problems of her own without taking on Jack's. She drove the car sedately down the driveway then out onto the road and freedom.

"Do you have any idea of where we're going?"

Mary asked softly, settling the sleeping Jon more comfortably on her lap.

"Yes, of course I do." Katherine laughed in sheer relief at getting away. Then, sobering, she added, "We're going to the house in the Poconos. I need a few days to make some plans and I can't think of any please else to go."

"And what about Matt?" Mary asked.

"What about him?" Katherine's voice had grown tight again. Then shaking her head ruefully, she added more normally, "I'm sorry, Mary, of course I intend to let him know where I am. But I need a few days alone first. I really need them, Mary."

She was not to have those few days. They stopped for an early dinner and arrived at the house in the mountains shortly after five o'clock. A few minutes after their arrival Mr. and Mrs. Darcy rushed in, all flustered and put out because they hadn't been notified as to Katherine's coming. Katherine soothed their ruffled feathers, declared the house spotless, which it was, then finally managed to assure them they would not be needed until morning.

Two hours later Katherine and Mary sat staring at the small fire Mary had built in the huge fireplace, sipping at the coffee Katherine had brewed, when Matt strode into the room, following by a worried looking John.

Katherine looked up in astonishment, a shaft of fear stabbing at her chest. Matt's face was set in cold, harsh lines of anger and his eyes made Katherine shudder. She wanted to move, jump up

and run, but two icy chips of pure rage pinned her
to the chair. She had thought his eyes could be
riveting, now she knew they could also be terrifying.

She moistened her lips, but before she could
speak, he rasped coldly, "Where is Jon?"

"In . . . in his crip, asleep." She hated the tremor
in her voice, but did not seem able to control it.

His eyes locked on hers, he snapped, "Mary, get
Jon and your things together. John will take you
home."

"Now? Tonight?" Katherine cried.

"Now. Tonight. This minute, Mary." His voice
flicked at Mary, although his eyes held hard on
Katherine.

Mary jumped off her chair and ran from the
room with the agility of a teenager. One didn't
argue with Matt when he gave an order in that
tone of voice.

Matt's eyes finally released their hold on
Katherine as he turned sharply and strode into the
kitchen, where she could hear him get coffee for
John and himself.

Days later, Katherine would wonder exactly
how long she had sat frozen to her chair. For when
she finally did move it was too late. She dashed up
the stairs, softly cursing the fact that she had
already showered and changed into nightgown,
robe and slippers, flung open the bedroom door
and ran across the room to the closet, one thought
in mind: To dress and go with Jon and Mary.

She was fumbling in the closet for something to
pull on when she heard the soft click of the door

closing. The dress dropped to the floor from nerveless fingers as she turned slowly to face him, saying softly, "Mary and Jon?"

Matt leaned back against the door as if barring her way. He had removed his coat and suit jacket and his white shirt outlined his broad shoulders against the dark wood of the door. Eyes narrowing, he rasped, "Just leaving." Then cocking his head in a listening attitude he added, "There goes the car now. Incidentally, I told John to take the Caddy. I truly hope you won't call the police and report it as stolen."

Katherine felt her face go hot at the sarcasm that laced his words and she shot back defensively, "It was the only way I could think of to get the keys from Jack."

Matt shook his head slowly, his fingers working at the knot in his tie. Undoing the two top buttons of his shirt he sauntered into the room sliding the tie from around his neck and dropping it onto the dresser.

Katherine watched him warily as she slowly stooped, picked up the dress she'd dropped and rehung it in the closet. He stopped in the middle of the room, placed his fisted hands on his hips and asked quietly, "What is all this about, Katherine?"

Katherine shivered thinking his quieter tone more intimidating than his earlier, sharper one. Forcing a calmness she didn't feel into her own voice, she answered. "I'm leaving you, Matt." She managed a light shrug before adding, "I thought I already had."

"Why?" His voice was a hair less quiet. "What is

it you want, Katherine? It's not money, because you obviously couldn't care less about mine. So what is it?"

"I want a divorce, Matt."

"No." Flat, final, the way he spoke the one word should have warned her, but in her agitation she ignored it. "Why not?" Unable to stand still any longer she walked jerkily around the room, unaware that her hands tugged nervously at the ends of her knotted robe belt.

"No divorce, Katherine."

This time the warning note reached her and spinning around to face him, she fought for control, before saying more calmly, "All right, no divorce. But you asked me what I want. I want to take Jon and go. Get my own apartment, come and go as I please. I don't expect you to support me, in fact, I don't want you to. I don't want anything from you."

"Except my son." The three words were spoken coldly, slowly, each one measured.

"Yes, your son," Katherine retorted. "Who is almost seven months old and you've hardly even looked at him."

"I've looked," he drawled.

Growing frustrated, Katherine pleaded reasonably. "Matt, I have no wish to deprive you of your son. I know I couldn't do that if I wanted to. But I do not want to. You may see your son at any time. All I'm asking of you is to let us go."

Less than two feet of carpeted floor separated them and her eyes studied him, trying to read his thoughts. Impossible scrutiny, for his face was closed to her, his eyes shuttered.

Seconds stretched into long minutes before he answered her. "All right, Katherine, if that's what you want."

Slowly she exhaled the breath she hadn't even been aware she'd been holding and murmuring, "Thank you," she walked to the door, only to stop, hand on the knob when he asked, "Do you mind if I wait until morning to leave?"

The subtle change in his voice should have alerted her. For the second time in less than an hour she'd missed the danger signal.

"No, of course not, this is your house, Matt, I wouldn't think of asking you to leave it tonight."

Hand still on the knob she made a half turn to look at him as she spoke, watching as he walked across the room to her.

"That's right, this is my house." His voice was a silky rasp and Katherine felt the first flickerings of alarm. "And that is my bed. And you are my wife. And tonight you will sleep in my house, in my bed . . . with me."

Katherine's eyes widened in fear. She should have known he wouldn't let her off that easily. Shaking her head firmly she whispered hoarsely, "No, Matt." If she tried she couldn't imagine a worse punishment than being subjected to his brand of mechanical possession. Her hand twisted the knob and pulled the door open as she turned away from him repeating her refusal. "No, Matt."

His hands clasped her shoulders painfully, spinning her back around to face him again. Holding her firmly still he rasped, "Yes,

Katherine, and this time it will be my way."

His way? What did he mean, his way? She stood rigid under his hands, her racing thoughts paralyzing her. She had heard, read about men who brutalized their wives at times, but surely not Matt! Her fear grew, closing her throat, setting her heart pounding at a terrifying rate.

Eyes darkening, his hands dropped to her knotted belt, tugging it open and none too gently.

"Matt, please."

Shaking his head he growled, "Be quiet," as his hands moved up and under the lapels of her robe. He began sliding the robe off, paused long enough to slip his thumbs under the narrow straps of her night gown, then slid both garments off her shoulders. One long arm reached past her head, his fingers touched a button, and the room was plunged into darkness. The next instant she was swept into his hard arms and tossed onto the bed. Fingers gripping the textured material of the bed spread, she lay still, her body frozen with panic.

Silvery strips of moonlight gleaming through the louvered doors gave a pale glow to the room and as her eyes adjusted to the dimness Katherine could see Matt's large outline as he undressed. When he slid onto the bed she felt her spine lift as it tightened even more stiffly.

Life came rushing back into her limbs when his hand slid over her flat tummy to her hip. With a sudden lurch she swung her legs off the bed but she just wasn't fast enough. His arm shot out, caught her legs midthigh and swung them back again. Then with slow deliberation his hand moved caressingly down the length of her leg and back up again, over her hip, to her waist, coming to a stop cupping her breast.

"You have beautiful long legs, you know that, Katherine? Even when you were a kid you were a leggy dame." His voice was a soft, raspy caress at her ear and the trembling that had begun at the touch of his hand intensified. The upper part of his body shifted, moved over her and as he lowered his head she turned her face away, as she always did. The next second his hand had left her breast and he was gripping her chin, forcing her head around.

"Not this time, Kate," he murmured, his hard mouth covering hers in a fierce, passionate kiss. Moments later he raised his head and growled, "Damn you, open your mouth." As he spoke he caught her chin between his thumb and forefinger and giving a short, firm, downward tug forced her lips apart.

"Ma—" The protest was lost inside his mouth. He kissed her roughly at first, almost brutally, then with deepening sensuality. The trembling that had shaken her body changed to a quiver and her fingers uncurled. His hands seemed to set off tiny explosions under her skin wherever he touched her. She felt desolate when his mouth left hers, then an exquisite sensation as his lips slid along her cheek to her neck. His teeth nipped sharply at her ear lobe, bringing a gasp of pain intertwined with pleasure.

"Let go, Kate," he whispered, his breath warm against her neck. "Touch me. Let me love you.

Love me back."

His words broke through the last of her weakening defenses. Her body felt consumed with heat and she wanted to touch him more than she'd ever wanted anything before. A soft moan escaping through her parted lips, her hands went to his waist, then slowly up his back. She felt a small shudder ripple through his body, then his mouth crushed hers in a kiss so demanding, so possessive, it left her breathless. Her fingers curled over his shoulders, back to front, nails digging into his skin, as she clung in surrender.

The room had changed from dim black to pearl gray before he bullied her into getting up long enough to straighten then crawl under the covers. Then drawing her tightly against his hard body he tucked the blankets around them both, saying softly, "I want no more talk about your own apartment. You're going home with me. Now go to sleep."

18

"Kate, are you all right?"

Eyes refocusing, automatically straightening her shoulders, Katherine turned away from the window at the sharp note of anxiety in Mary's voice. Dredging up a small smile she answered, "Yes, I'm fine."

"You're so pale and you stood there so long, so still. Honey, you are really starting to worry me."

"Don't go all professional nurse on me, Mary, I assure you I'm alright. I'm just being a silly female." The utter weariness of her own voice dismayed Katherine. God, she had to shake herself out of this depression.

"You are not a silly female," Mary stated emphatically. "In fact, you are one of the least silly females I've ever met. And I've met my share in my job. No, Kate, you have yourself tied up in tiny little knots over a man. An exceptional man,

I'll grant you, but is he worth the price you'r paying?"

Katherine shrugged helplessly. "Probably no but what else can I do? He won't let me leave him You know that. My mind goes in circles trying t find a solution, reach a decision." She hesitate briefly, then went on more softly, "You know Mary, I've found myself lately, at odd moments going over the past." She gave Mary a wry loo then went on. "It started in September and cam full cycle with September, just now. That's why was so still at the window. It concerns me a little this slipping back in time so to speak."

She paused to moisten suddenly dry lips an Mary, slowly shaking her head, said firmly "Nothing to worry about, Kate. You were lookin for answers?"

"Yes." The word was breathed with a sigh c relief. "But I didn't find any and I still don't kno what to do."

"There is one thing you could do."

"What?"

"Give in." Mary answered decisively. "Sto fighting him, Kate. You are his wife, the mother c his son. So far you've refused to take advantage c that position. Assume the role. Even though yo haven't said anything, I get the impression tha he's willing, too. Am I right?"

Katherine's nod was barely perceptible.

"Well then, as I said, take on the role, making absolutely clear to everyone that you are doing s And the place to begin is in this house. For you own sake, Kate, submit before you tear yourself to shreds."

"I can't," Katherine whispered.

"Why not?"

"He does not love me." Katherine had never said the words aloud before and the sound shocked her. It had been a cry of pure pain. Much, much more softly she repeated, "Mary, Matt does not love me."

"And there's the rub," Mary said in a flat, yet sympathetic tone. "I don't know how to advise you on this, Kate. I loved my husband very much. And yet, at no time, even when he died, did I feel the anguish you've just revealed to me in your face and voice. I can't say I'm sorry I was denied that, either or, heaven or hell, kind of love."

"Oh, Mary, I feel so foolish at times. The way I feel about Matt almost frightens me, it's so intense. I always thought this kind of all-consuming love existed only in movies and novels. And now, to find myself so desperately in love, at my age, scares the hell out of me."

"I can see how it might be scary," Mary smiled wryly in understanding. "What I don't see is what age has to do with it. Oh, I know I know," she hurried on before Katherine could interrupt. "We grow up believing that passionate, romantic love is for the young. That we reach a point in our lives when, if we love at all, it is by necessity a warm, companionable sort of relationship. What dribble, I simply don't believe it. I never have. Good grief, it's like asking me to believe we have a switch in our minds that automatically turns off after reaching x number of years. In my opinion we fall in love first with our mind and all the lovely, exciting responses naturally follow. So as far as I'm concerned, unless one stops growing intellectually, the impact of falling deeply in love after ones reached maturity would be greater rather than lesser." She laughed self-consciously, adding, " Thus endeth the lesson for the day. All of which doesn't help your immediate problem any way. I'm sorry, honey, but I can't help you. No one can."

Katherine stared at her unaware that her eyes mirrored her torment. With some effort she managed a slight smile, saying softly, "Yes, I know."

Thanksgiving, and once again Matt amazed Katherine with his ability to slip into the role of husband and father so effortlessly. After receiving the call from her mother, inviting them for the day, Katherine had hesitated briefly before relaying the invitation to Matt. She had not been informed as to any plans Beth might have made, yet she felt sure that if there was a conflict of plans, Matt would opt for joining in on Beth's. When he was at home, every attention, every teasing word, no matter how insignificant, he gave to DeDe cut into Katherine like a fine-edged blade. If it had not been for James' comforting presence at those times, she didn't know how she would have withstood it.

Determination gripped her. She would not spend Thanksgiving Day in the company of that woman. She was going to her parents, with or without Matt. She accepted her mother's invitation, then waited for an opportunity to speak to Matt alone before telling him of it. Her opportunity came four days before the holiday. Matt was, as usual, away on a business trip, but was expected back some time that day. Katherine had just finished dressing for dinner and was trying to bring some order to her now shoulder-length hair, while at the same time trying to avoid looking at her own reflection. She didn't care for the face in her mirror. It was too pale, the skin too tautly drawn with an almost transparent look. Worst of all were the fine lines at the corners of her eyes. She had dressed in high collared, long sleeved, soft wool dress in an effort to hide her too prominent shoulder and collar bones, but it hadn't worked. The dress clung to her slender figure giving the appearance of fragility.

With a sigh she drew the brush through her hair, pausing mid-stroke when Matt walked into the room. His eyes found hers in the mirror and he stood just inside the door for what seemed a long time, without speaking.

Completely unaware that the picture reflected to Matt in the mirror was one of delicate loveliness, Katherine grew tense at his silence, her hand clenching the brush handle moist with perspiration. Tension made her arm suddenly tired and she slowly lowered the brush to the dressing table. The movement broke the strange stillness. Matt, shrugging out of his jacket, walked into the room, his voice sounding harsh after the intense quiet. "Hello, Katherine, you look tired. What have you been up to while I've been away?"

Lowering her eyes from the glittering gaze of his, she murmured, "I haven't been up to anything. It's been very quiet around here." Why was it, she wondered, that he could put her on the defensive with the most innocuous question?

One auburn brow cocked sardonically at her tone. Voice smooth as warm satin he asked, "Bored, Katherine?"

Bored? Was he kidding? She was slowly going out of her mind with inactivity and he asks if she's bored. Irritation drove out her hesitation concerning the holiday. "Mother called a few days ago to invite us for Thanksgiving dinner. If you haven't already made other plans I'd like to go. She hasn't seen Jon in weeks."

"Neither have my parents," came the dry reply.

Hands clenching in her lap, Katherine's eyes flew back to his. "That is not my fault."

Eyes narrowing, his tone became even drier. "I don't believe I said it was." He paused a moment and his eyes grew sharp, piercing. "I'm not accusing you of anything, Katherine. Why do you react to everything I say lately as if I were?"

Katherine shrugged; had she missed something? Were they speaking about the same thing? Confused, wary under this new watchful attitude of his, she snapped, "Well, should I accept mother's inviation, or not?" Omitting to add that, for herself and Jon, she already had.

He turned away, tugging at his tie, as if suddenly uninterested in the conversation. "By all means, accept it. And if you will, call mother and dad and tell them we'll stop by sometime during the day.''

The visit was made, both sets of grandparents were delighted with their grandson. Katherine hated to leave the warmth and love of her parents' home when the day was over. Matt played his role to perfection, being easy and relaxed with her parents, showing interest and concern with Tom. During the course of the day plans were made for the coming Christmas holidays, Matt completely surprising Katherine by suggesting they go to Lancaster after lunch on Christmas Day and stay over a day or two, thereby giving, he'd added with a grin, both her parents and his the opportunity to spoil Jon to their hearts' content.

The glow that had warmed Katherine in her parents' home was quickly extinguished in the barely concealed unfriendly atmosphere of Matt's house. Katherine withdrew further into herself, becoming more coolly remote than ever. Although Matt did not go away for several weeks, he made no attempt to touch her. Katherine felt sure he was keeping another woman somewhere. The thought brought unwanted pictures to her mind which caused searing pain.

The pain settled to a permanent ache inside, generating anger and resentment. She may have taken on a life sentence with Matt, but she'd be damned if she'd suffer every day of it in the house where she felt she had no more substance than a shadow. In this frame of mind, she followed him to his study one evening, two weeks after Thanksgiving. Without bothering to knock, she walked into the room just as he was lifting the telephone receiver. Glancing at her sharply, he slowly replaced the receiver before asking calmly, "Something wrong, Katherine?"

Was something wrong? Everything was wrong and who the hell was he going to call? His girlfriend? Katherine had to bite her lip to keep from shouting the words at him. A feeling of self-disgust washed over her. What was happening to her? What was she turning into?

"Kate?" Matt prompted quietly.

Katherine glanced up quickly, suddenly realizing she'd been standing just inside the door, unseeing eyes on the carpet. He was watching her narrow-eyed, something he seemed to be doing a lot lately, and taking a deep breath, she managed to meet and hold his gaze.

"I'd like to go into the apartment for a few days, if you don't mind. See Carol, do my Christmas shopping."

"You're asking my permission?"

Katherine couldn't quite decide if his tone held disbelief or sarcasm. Feeling her spine go stiff, she lifted her chin and gave him a brief nod. "I thought I'd better, as you seemed so put out about it in September."

One eyebrow arched sharply and he drawled, "I've never suggested you need my permission for anything. But don't you think, as your husband, I have the right to be informed of your plans?"

"I did try—" she began.

"I know," he cut in, his voice suddenly weary. "And there is no point in going over it again. When were you planning to go into town?"

"Tomorrow morning."

"All right, I'll wait for you and we'll go in together."

By lunch time the following day they were once again settled into the apartment. Matt had lunch with them, alternately teasing Mary and Jon, and being coolly polite to Katherine; then he left for the office informing Clyde he would definitely be in for dinner by six.

During the following week Katherine indulged in a wild orgy of shopping, some days with Carol, some days with Mary, finding a perverse sort of satisfaction in buying outrageously expensive gifts and charging them to Matt. Carol had dinner with them most evenings as Paul was on a business trip and she was lonely and, as she put it, suffering from pre-holiday depression.

A week before Christmas, her shopping finished, Katherine was feeling some depression of her own as she thought about returning to the house. Late in the afternoon she was called to the phone.

"Katherine, you can't go back to the country yet," cried an almost incoherently happy Carol. "You and Matt have to stay in town and help us celebrate."

"Carol," Katherine couldn't help laughing. "Will you calm down and explain what you're talking about?"

"Okay," Carol's voice was almost normal. "Paul got home a few hours ago and found a message to contact his lawyer. When he finally got him he told Paul the master hearing is set for the end of this week. Katherine, do you know what that means? Paul's divorce will be final soon. We'll be able to get married." She paused to take a deep breath, then went on exuberantly. "So, Paul told me to call you. He wants to celebrate and he would like you and Matt to come with us tomorrow night. You will won't you?"

It was the first time in a week Katherine had heard the old vibrancy in Carol's voice, and some of it was transmitted over the wire to her. Her voice alive and warm, she replied, "I wouldn't miss it and I'm sure Matt will feel the same. I'll talk to him as soon as he gets home and call you back, so hang by the phone. Bye for now."

As she replaced the receiver Matt's quiet voice asked, "What will you talk to Matt about as soon as he gets home?"

She hadn't heard him come in and startled, she spun around. "Oh, Matt," she began, then stopped on seeing James with him. James grinned and said, "Hi," but before she could return the greeting, Matt persisted, "Exactly what is it you're sure I'll feel the same about?"

"That was Carol on the phone. It looks like Paul's divorce will be final soon and they'd like us to join them for a night on the town in celebration. We will go with them won't we, Matt?" Though she'd started speaking happily, Katherine's last words ended on an anxious note as she saw Matt's face settle into grim lines.

"I'm sorry, Katherine," he said flatly. "I'm leaving tomorrow morning to attend a textile conference. By tomorrow night I'll be in Scotland."

"Scotland!" she cried and for the first time in their married life she questioned him on his business. "But, must you go yourself? Surely there is someone else you could send this time? Matt, this is for Carol, she adores you and she wants the two of us to be with them, share their happiness."

"Couldn't I go in your place, Matt?" James inserted softly.

Matt's face had become even more grim. He was shaking his head before James finished speaking. "No, not this time. If it was just the conference yes but, I've been trying, for some time, to buy a woolen mill in Scotland. It has been owned by the same family since it was built and though they can't keep it going, they dug their heels in." He smiled wryly, then added, "Stubborn bunch. Well, anyway, it seems they have finally read the handwriting on the wall and are ready to talk price, with me, personally." Again he paused to smile wryly, this time at the look of astonishment on James' face, for it was obvious from his expression, he had known nothing of what Matt had planned.

"I am sorry, Katherine," Matt repeated after a few seconds. "But you go with them, if you like."

"Unescorted?" Katherine felt more disappointed than the occasion called for and she knew inside that it wasn't so much their missing the night out as the simple fact that for the first time she'd asked Matt for something for herself and he had refused.

"I'll be happy to escort you," James said smoothly, then added bitingly, "I may not be considered capable enough to be let in on a deal as important as the purchase of a small mill in Scotland, but I'm sure my capabilities run to holding a lady's chair and picking up a bar tab."

"Don't be an ass," Matt snapped. "Damn it, James, I don't have to make explanations to anyone, not even you. But I will tell you this. The only reason I haven't said anything about this is I really thought they would find a way to hold on to the business. As a matter of fact, I kind of hoped they would. Now stop your stupid sulking, you know better. As for escorting Katherine, that is entirely up to her."

Katherine's first inclination, on hearing James' offer, had been to refuse, but as Matt lashed out at his brother she felt anger and resentment burn through her. Without pausing to consider her words she said, "Thank you, James, I'd love to spend the evening with you."

Dinner was an ordeal for Katherine. James stayed, as an invitation to dinner was the reason he'd been with Matt in the first place. The two men talked business throughout the meal. Although Matt didn't mention it again, she was convinced he was angry at her decision to go out with James.

As soon as she'd finished her coffee she excused herself and went to the bedroom, there to pace in frustrated anger. Not thirty minutes later, Matt followed her, saying dryly as he closed the door, "James said to tell you goodnight, and he'll call you tomorrow afternoon to find out what time to pick you up."

She had been having second thoughts about going out with James but, at Matt's tone of voice, her resolve strengthened and she answered off-handedly, "All right, do you want me to pack for you?"

"You're angry." A statement, not a question and for some reason his calm acceptance of it angered her even more. She was standing at the window, back to him, and keeping a tight rein on her composure, she turned to face him. "Not at all. I'm sure Carol will be disappointed but, as she knows you so well, I'm equally sure she will not be surprised to hear that business comes first. For myself, I couldn't care less one way or the other." How on earth had she managed to infuse that total lack of interest in her tone? She saw him stiffen as the barb went home and, unable to stop herself, she twisted it a little. "Would it be impertinent of me to ask if you plan to be back in time to share your son's first Christmas with him?"

"Yes, of course I'll be home in time." Lids narrowing over eyes beginning to blaze gave the only indication of his own growing anger. With a few strides he was across the room. As she turned to move way his arm shot out, encircling her waist, catching her close against him. "Katherine," he murmured softly, "the conference ends on the afternoon of the twenty-third; I will be home no later than lunch time on the twenty-fourth. Don't worry, there will be no interference with our plans for the holidays." His hands moved over her back caressingly, molding her against the hard length of him. His lips slid across her cheek, planted a tiny, fiery kiss on the corner of her mouth.

Katherine felt the anger and disappointment begin to melt away and was on the point of sliding her arms around his waist, when his next softly suggestive words refired her resentment.

"To answer your first question, no I don't require you to pack for me. My requirements are of a much more basic nature." His lips brushed hers, then he paused, as he felt her withdraw. "Katherine," he whispered, "I've said I'm sorry about tomorrow night, and you'll have to admit the celebration is a bit premature anyway. When you talk to Carol, why don't you suggest we wait and make a definite date for the date the decree is handed down? On me."

Katherine went rigid. Of all the arrogant . . . even in her mind she couldn't find words strong enough to describe him. He'd almost done it again. Almost lulled her with his lovemaking. But to treat Carol's happiness so carelessly, that was too much. She looked him squarely in the eyes and said icily, "I will relay your suggestion to both Carol and Paul when I see them tomorrow night. Now, if you will excuse me, I did tell her I'd call back tonight and I imagine she is beginning to wonder why I haven't done so."

"Then you still intend going with them

tomorrow night?" His arms still held her tight, although his voice matched hers for coldness.

"Yes, of course, you also suggested that, remember?"

His arms dropped from her as if she'd suddenly become repulsive to him and, as he turned away, he grated between clenched teeth, "Do what the hell you like, I don't care if you go out every night for the next week. Just make damned sure you're back at the house by the twenty-fourth."

Carol was disappointed that Matt couldn't make it, but she assured James he made a delightful stand-in. They laughed and enjoyed themselves so much the first night that they stretched the celebration to two and then three nights. Katherine told herself repeatedly that she was only taking Matt at his word and was having a wonderful time without him. However, she didn't do a very good job of convincing herself and at the end of the third night, when Carol and Paul suggested they at least have dinner together the following night, Katherine found herself lying outrageously to get out of it. "I'm sorry, I must go back to the house tomorrow morning. I have so much to do to get ready for Christmas, I don't know how I'll finish everything on time as it is." In truth, she had nothing to do at the house, and dreaded the thought of going back.

James came back to the apartment with her, as he had the two previous evenings, but when she asked if she should have Clyde make coffee as before, he answered, "No coffee, thank you. If you don't mind I'll make myself a drink."

"Help yourself," she smiled, then went in search of Clyde to tell him she wouldn't want anything else. Then she added chidingly, "Go to bed, Clyde, and stop fussing over me like a mother hen." In wonder, she saw him smile somewhat sadly at her before saying gently, "Whatever you say, Mrs. Martin. Goodnight."

Shaking her head at his strange attitude, she went back to the living room, joining James, who was standing at the window wall.

Katherine stood in silence, savoring the panoramic view spread out before her. The lights, some of them the decorative colored ones of the season, gave the city the look of a scene dreamed of in fairy stories. When James said her name softly, she had to force her way back to reality. The words that followed her softly spoken name jerked her fully alert.

"How long do you intend living like this before you do something about it?"

Confused, feeling she must have missed something he'd said, she asked, "What are you talking about?"

"I'm talking about the fact that I'm in love with you. Divorce Matt, marry me, let me take care of you." As he was speaking he set his drink down and on the last word he drew her into his arms and kissed her lingeringly. She felt nothing. James was handsome, charming, and fun to be with, but his kiss brought not a spark of response. She pulled herself from his arms as gently as she could, saying equally gently, "I'm six years older than you are."

He drew her back into his arms, his hold, like his voice, more forceful this time. "What does age have to do with it? Katherine, leave him before he gets back from Scotland. Come with me somewhere, anywhere. I promise you I won't let him hurt you."

Completely shocked, she cried, "James, Matt is your brother!" His hold loosened, but he did not let her go, and his voice held very real pain. "I know that." Then more softly, in a tone that revealed the pain more openly, he went on, "Oh, God, don't I know it. I love him, Katherine, very much. He has always been my idol, I never outgrew it. I have never met another man I could respect as much. As far as I was concerned he could do no wrong. He has always been tough, but he has always been fair. Until lately, with you. Katherine, I can't stand by and watch him destroy you. And he is. He might try to stop any other man, but I don't think he will put up a fight with me. Come with me, please, before he gets back."

"I can't," she whispered.

"Why?" he asked angrily. "He has no hold on you."

Simply, clearly, without inflection she said, "I love him."

His arms dropped to his sides and he stared at her in disbelief. "I don't believe you. If ever a woman seemed less in love with her husband, I'm damned if I can bring her to mind. And he sure as hell doesn't act like he's in love with you." She winced at his last words and he added quickly, "I'm sorry, Katherine. It's true? You really are in love with him?"

"Yes, I really am." Her voice broke on a sob, as she added. "Oh Lord, James, do you think I could stay with him, put up with Beth and DeDe, if I wasn't?" She was crying openly before she'd finished and once again he drew her into his arms. But this time in a different way. Gone was the tight hold of the longing to possess, replaced with comforting compassion. "I'm sorry, Katherine. Sorry for you and sorry for myself. Hell, I'm even sorry for Matt, for the fool doesn't know what he's missing. I wish there was some way I could help you, but there isn't is there?"

Words muffled against his chest, she whispered, "Oh, James, you have helped me from the very first time Matt brought me here. By acting as a buffer. Not only between Beth, and then DeDe and me, but between Matt and me as well. I almost wish it could be you. But it can't be, ever. I belong to him, completely and absolutely. I always will."

19

Mid-morning the day before Christmas, the phone rang with an overseas call from Matt. It was a bad connection and Katherine had trouble understanding everything he said, but one thing was clear. The weather was bad, there was some doubt about when they could take off, he didn't know when he'd get home. His last words were as clear as if he was standing next to her. "Don't worry."

Don't worry. How does one not worry? Katherine wondered, as she stared out the window at the bright, sunlit Pennsylvania countryside. How does a woman who lost one husband in a storm, turn off the worry process, when what she wants to do is scream in fear? She doesn't scream, of course, she told herself firmly. She goes about doing her daily thing, whatever that may happen to be, presenting to the world a calm, composed exterior, while all the while she's slowly falling apart inside, piece by piece.

The hands on the clock slowly made their way around its face. In late afternoon, Tom breezed in, full of holiday cheer, love and gifts from Janice and Carlos, whom he just that morning saw off on a plane to Argentina. He had made the round-about trip to Washington to see his sister before coming home, as Janice and Carlos were taking their daughter for her first visit with Carlos' parents.

Some of his high spirits were dimmed when he learned of Matt's being stranded and, on observing the look of strain on Katherine's face, offered smoothly, with a hug, "Come on, Mom. Matt's a smart man. He hires nothing but the best. I know the man who pilots the Lear, he knows his business. He won't take any risks. If Matt doesn't make it home by tomorrow, we'll wait and have Christmas the next day. Big deal, Jon's too young to know the difference anyway."

Some of Tom's optimism, his unshakable belief in Matt's judgement, rubbed off on Katherine, and with determination she pushed her fears to the very back of her mind. She remained downstairs that evening until she could no longer bear the sound of Christmas carols mingled with Beth and DeDe's obvious and vocal concern. With a hasty goodnight, she fled to her room, to lie wide-eyed with fright until she fell asleep from pure exhaustion.

Christmas morning passed with all the gifts unopened under the tree. Late in the morning, Katherine was getting dressed, in the walk-in closet dressing-room, when she thought she heard the phone ring. Leaving her blouse hanging open, she grabbed up her shoes and ran into the bedroom, dived across the bed, and snatched up the receiver, only to hear the dull, monotonous sound of the dial tone. Scrambling off the bed she quickly buttoned her shirt, stuffed it into the waist band of her skirt, and slid on her shoes as she hopped to the door. Finally dressed, she hurried down the stairs, coming to a dead stop when she heard Beth say her name with a laugh. Not wanting to eavesdrop, yet unable to move, she listened as Beth went on.

"He will have no trouble at all divorcing her now. Or getting full custody of Jon. Will you mind, very much, raising another woman's child, DeDe?"

"No, I don't think so," DeDe answered, after a moment's consideration. "He does look like Matt, and he is a little darling. Still, I think I'd like at least one of my own. Oh, Beth, I hope Matt can hurry the legal process along; I'd like a spring wedding."

Badly shaken, Katherine spun on her heel. Violet eyes, wide with shock, stared into another pair of eyes, the exact color of her own, blazing with fury. All traces of the boy were gone. The face that stared back at her belonged to a very angry man. He stood at the bottom of the stairs and moving jerkily she walked to him, hand outstretched, as if for support.

He walked toward her quickly, clasping her hand in his while he slid his other arm around her waist. "Mother." The anger on his face now mingled with concern as he studied her wide eyes, white face.

Swallowing convulsively, she choked, "Not here, please." And breaking from him she ran up the stairs and into the bedroom, to glance around, frantically thinking, I suspected there was another woman, somewhere. But never, never would I have believed he'd do this. Not in his own home. What in the world am I going to do? The sound of the door closing with a soft click broke her thoughts. For the first time ever Tom's voice had an ugly sound. "That S.O.B. We sit here worrying about him while he's planning a divorce, and his birdbrained tramp sits in your home planning a lousy spring wedding."

The nasty-hurt sound of Tom's voice brought a measure of calm to Katherine. Taking a deep breath, she said quietly, "Tom, that's enough, name-calling will solve nothing. You have to help me, now."

They were so very alike and as the day before some of his confidence had been transmitted to her, now some of her calm stole into him. Sighing deeply, he said, "Okay, Mom, what do you want me to do?"

She was quiet a long time, planning furiously, then she answered dully. "I have got to get out of this house. We'll get ready and go to grandma's as planned. We'll take your car. I don't want Jack along to report to Matt when he gets back. But I can't stay at grandma's. Grandma and Grandpa would be wise in next to no time. Let me see—I've got it. I'll tell them Matt's called and asked me to meet him somewhere for a short holiday in private." At his sour look she pleaded, "Tom, please, I've got to make it convincing for them and you're going to have to carry the ball once you're there. I won't have mother and dad's Christmas spoiled. Oh, good grief, Dan and Dave will be there, I'd forgotten that. Oh, honey, can you pull it off?"

"In that pandemonium? It's a breeze. But where will you go? Janice is in Argentina so you can't go there. Can you go to Carol for a few days?"

"No," Katherine stated flatly. "Carol is spending the holidays with Richard and Anne and they were Matt's friends first. I don't want to put them in the position of having to choose sides."

Tom pushed his hand through his hair. "Well, can you go with Mary when she leaves?"

Katherine had insisted Mary spend the holidays with her own children and she knew Mary was at that minute getting ready to leave.

Shaking her head slowly, Katherine answered, "I probably could, but I won't. No, Tom, I'm not about to ruin anyone else's holiday. There is only one place I can go. I'll go up to the house in the Poconos."

Tom stared at her incredulously. "You're going to drive to Lancaster, make your excuse, then drive all the way up there today? Mom, you can't."

"Tom," her voice soothed, "I've been taking care of myself a long time. I will be all right. Now, come on, we've got to throw some clothes in a suitcase, get Jon and get out of here. Please hurry."

"But—"

"Tom, please."

A few hours later, driving north in Tom's Trans-Am, Katherine was amazed at the ease with which they'd pulled it off. Her parents had believed her story completely, even going as far as saying it would do both Katherine and Matt good to get away together. She had stayed at her parents' home long enough to greet and exchange gifts with her brothers, their wives and assorted offspring, have a bite to eat and be assured and reassured that Tom and Jon would be well looked after. Then she had left, feeling for the first time in her life like a deceitful daughter.

It was dark long before Katherine drove the car into the garage in the mountains and she was thinking that all she wanted was to fall into bed and sleep the clock around as she madeher way up the stairs to the kitchen door.

As she fumbled in her bag for her door key the door of the Darcy's apartment over the garage was flung open and a very surprised Mr. Darcy exclaimed, "Mrs. Martin, why didn't you let us know you were coming? Where's the boss?"

Katherine sighed wearily. Was there no getting away from the boss and his spies? Didn't these people have family or something to visit on Christmas?

He voice thinning with impatience she said, "It was a spur of the moment decision. Mr. Martin—" damned if she'd call him the boss—"will be here in a—ah—day or so. I don't want to be disturbed before noon tomorrow. Good night and Merry Christmas." With that she had opened the door

lipped inside and closed it firmly behind her. Mr.
Darcy's "Merry Christmas" echoed inside her
ead. Oh, you bet, Merry Christmas indeed.

Katherine's eyes opened and she lay staring into
he pale dimness of the moonlit room. Something
ad wakened her, but what? Turning her head she
lanced at the digital clock on the night stand.
Eleven-ten, she'd only been in bed a few hours. At
noise on the stairs she felt her blood ran cold.
omeone was in the house! Had someone
nanaged to force the sliding glass doors at the
round level or the living room? The sound of soft
ootsteps stopping on the other side of the
edroom door brought her head swiveling on the
illow. Eyes wide with fright she stared at the
oor, panic gripped her throat, closing off any
cream or sound she may have made. Eyes
astened on the door, body taut with fear, she
vatched as the door opened and a man stepped
nside. A soft sigh of relief whispered past her lips
or even in the shadowy room the large outline of
Matt's frame was unmistakable. Katherine's voice
vas not much more than a strangled whisper.
'Oh, Matt, you frightened me."

His head jerked sharply to the sound of her
oice. His voice was gruff, sounding more tired
han she'd ever heard.

"I'm sorry, Katherine, I tried not to waken you."

Automatically, without thinking she moved to
et up. "Are you hungry? Can I get you some
offee or something to—"

"Stay where you are," he ordered gruffly. "I
on't want anything but the feel of that bed. I'm

tired and I'm cold. The damned car heater quit halfway up here and the night turned bitter."

"I'm sorry," she murmured, feeling vaguely responsible somehow.

"Yeah." The reply wasn't much more than a grunt and she glanced at him quickly noting with surprise that he was already undressed and moving to the bed. Apprehension stirred inside her as he slid under the covers, then calmed when he lay still, exhaling a long, weary sigh. He lay, unmoving, for some time then, as if he suddenly reached a decision, his long arms grabbed her dragged her across the small distance separating them, held her tightly against him. The chilled skin of his body sent a shiver through her warm one. He was cold. The raspy stubble of a day's growth of beard scratched her cheek when his face brushed hers. His lips found hers and clung. What am I doing? Katherine thought wildly pulling her mouth away. "Matt—" she began, only to be cut off by his raggedly whispered "Katherine, shut up. My God, woman, can't you see I'm starving?"

"But you said—" she started, then the real meaning of his words registered. "You said you were tired," she went on, lamely.

"I said I was tired, not dead." His mouth caught hers again in a hungry, devouring kiss, his arms tightened convulsively, molding her to him.

Again she tore her mouth from his. "Matt, stop." What she had meant to be a firm order, came out as a feeble plea. Her reeling senses, urgent for the feel of him, the touch of him, pushed away the memory of the outrage and hurt that had cut into her the day before.

"Katherine," he groaned. "I'm cold, warm me. I'm so tired, help me rest." His hands moving slowly, caressingly over her set her skin on fire wherever he touched. Her body, of its own volition, arched eagerly against his hard one.

"Oh, Matt." The whisper was lost against the mouth that crushed hers, the words swirling around his probing tongue. In sweet surrender, her arms crept around his neck, fingers sliding into his hair to grasp and hold his head more tightly to her own.

The room was bright when she opened her eyes and she blinked several times to adjust her eyes to the early morning sunlight. Shifting her gaze her eyes came to rest on Matt's broad back framed between the partially opened folding doors, where he stood staring out the windows, smoking a cigarette. In hungry desperation, she allowed her eyes to roam slowly over him, imprinting the look of him on her mind. His big frame was clad in a mid thigh length dark brown and white kimono-like robe, which concealed little of his long, muscular, straight legs. The sash was belted tightly, outlining his narrow waist, the robe's material lay smooth and taut against his back and over his shoulders. The bell-like sleeves fell to his elbows revealing forearms, strong wrists and broad, long fingered, sensitive hands. As her eyes stopped on his hands she felt a shiver slide down her spine in memory of their touch. The events of last night, the day before, washed over her, devastating in the hard light of reality. Her thoughts a chaotic jumble, she thought, he had no right, I had no right. She did not feel well or rested, in fact, she felt on the edge of exhaustion, defeated.

As if he felt her eyes on him, he made a half turn, his cool calculating eyes pinning hers. He was freshly showered and shaved and the alert, watchful look of him made her feel rumpled, foggy.

Before he could speak, without a word of her own, she jumped from the bed, caught up her robe and dashed for the bathroom.

She had hoped the stinging spray of the shower would banish some of her weariness but it hadn't worked. In a deepening depression she walked back into the bedroom, drawing the belt to her robe into a firm knot around her too slender waist.

Matt still stood at the window drawing deeply on a fresh cigarette. But he had moved during the intervening minutes for he now held a steaming mug in his hand.

"There's fresh coffee," he said quietly, nodding his head at the pot resting on the low table in front of the fireplace.

His eyes followed her relentlessly as she moved to the table. In her growing nervousness she spilled the milk she was adding to her coffee. He waited until she straightened, cradling the mug in her hands, before he questioned too softly, "So you're on the run again. What is it you want this time, besides a divorce, that is?"

His soft, sarcastic tone flicked her on the raw

and she retaliated in quick anger. "That would be perfect for your plans, wouldn't it? Save you the bother of all the pretense."

"What are you talking about?" he snapped.

"Oh, stop it Matt, I know all about you and DeDe."

"Me and DeDe?" His voice held unmistakable incredulity. "Explain that remark, Katherine." Her anger had dissipated into deep weariness, she was just not up to fencing with him. "I overheard Beth and DeDe yesterday." At his raised eyebrows, she inserted, "I did not mean to eavesdrop."

"I didn't think you did." He emphasized his words with a sharp shake of his head. "Go on."

"They were discussing your plans to divorce me, take Jon from me." Trying to hide the sudden catch in her voice, she added bitingly, "You'd better get cracking, Matt, DeDe wants a spring wedding." His eyes narrowed on her face, his voice took on an edge. "I haven't the vaguest idea what you're talking about. I don't know what you think you overheard and I'll say this one time. I have never thought of DeDe in any way other than Beth's friend."

"I don't *think* I heard anything. I *know* what I heard." She brought her cup to her lips with a jerk, anger again aroused.

"Or are you laying a smoke screen?"

"What do you mean?" she mumbled around her cup. He turned away to snub out his cigarette. His casual tone and seeming change of subject threw her into confusion. "So you went out with James to help Carol and Paul celebrate, hummm?"

"Yes, I told you I would," she replied unsteadily.

"And I understand the celebration lasted a few nights?" he went on smoothly.

His attitude, at variance with the watchfulness of his eyes, started a crawly sensation up her arms.

"Yes, we were out three nights."

"I see," he murmured. "You enjoy James' company?" Small signals of alarm gave her the first inkling of what he was getting at. "What are you trying to say, Matt?"

"I wasn't sure I'd find you alone up here."

Eyes beginning to widen with the instinct of coming shock, she cried, "What are you accusing me of?"

Cold, hard, sharp as the tip of a whip, his words lashed her. "Are you sleeping with my brother?"

The expected shock struck, leaving her rigid, eyes filled with horror. Unable to move, barely able to breathe she stood as if carved from stone while his words echoed and re-echoed in her mind. Slowly, then with increasing speed, the echo set off a spark of anger that swiftly flared into a red hot flame. She actually saw red. Never in her life had she felt such fury. Suddenly she moved as if propelled across the room by an explosion, at the same instant one word was expelled through her stiff lips. "No." Her sudden movement, coming after her total stillness, caught him off guard. And caught off guard he took the full force of her blow, palm to one cheek, back hand to the other.

Ignoring the pain that shot into her hand and up

her arm, she spat, "How dare you accuse me? You, with your tramp installed under the same roof as your wife." Then, with a small gasp, she stepped back, the red haze evaporating under the icy glitter of blue gray. Vision clear, she saw the muscle jumping spasmodically along his clenched jawline, the two white lines of fury etching his hard, compressed mouth. In cold fear she backed away from him until she felt the side of the bed against the back of her legs. His arms hung stiffly at his sides, his hands clenched into tight fists, the knuckles hard and white. Terrified at the savage look of him, Katherine watched Matt fight for control. After endless minutes the struggle was won. His ragged breathing became more normal, the muscle calmed along his tension-eased jawline. She exhaled slowly, then winced as he made a sudden move, bringing his hand up to draw the back of it across his mouth. He hadn't missed her wince, however, and his voice rasped, "You came very close to getting raped, Katherine. I wouldn't advise you to try that again."

She had had it. If she was close to the edge before, the tension of the last half hour gave the final nudge over. Her shoulders began shaking moments before the racking sob was torn from her throat. Her hands flew up to cover her face as she sank slowly to the edge of the bed. "Oh, God, I can't bear any more of this." In crushing defeat she felt sure Matt's plan was to charge her with adultery and gain custody of Jon. Crying openly, she begged, "Matt, please, please don't take Jon from me. I'll do anything you ask, I won't try and fight you. I'll agree to any conditions you want, but please don't take him from me."

"Katherine, what in the hell is this?" His voice was laced with sharp concern and glancing up quickly she was sure her tear blurred eyes misread his expression, for his face seemed pale, his eyes filled with an unfamiliar look not unlike fear.

Her attempt to read his face was cut short as he moved across the room toward her with purpose. When his hands grasped her shoulders she cringed, crying out, "Matt, please."

"Jesus H. Christ, you're damned near hysterical. Kate, I'm not going to hurt you." He was standing beside her on one foot, his other knee bent, rested on the bed. When he'd finished speaking in that strange panicky tone, he thrust his body up and across the bed, dragging her with him. She cried out again sobbing uncontrollably now and his hands released her, leaving her lie where she was, her head level with his chest.

He lay beside her quietly, not touching her, not even moving except to reach across the bed to her night stand, remove the box of tissues from the drawer and place it next to her. The storm of weeping finally abated leaving her weak, drained of all emotion. Still he waited several minutes before speaking and when he did, although his voice was gentle, he sounded as tired as she felt. "All right, Katherine, you can have your divorce. No strings this time."

"Jon?" she asked tremulously.

"Damn it, I have never even considered taking

im from you. You're his mother, for heaven's
ake, he belongs with you."

"But I heard Beth and DeDe—"

"Katherine," he cut in exasperatedly, "I told
ou I'm not interested in DeDe. Christ, if I'd
anted her I could have had her ten years ago. I
idn't want her then and I sure as hell don't want
er now. She's been too well used."

Before she could think of a reply to that, he went
n in a much harder tone. "James—do you love
im?"

"Yes, of course I love him." He grunted as if
e'd struck him. "I see."

"No, Matt," she said tiredly. "You don't. I love
ames in the same way I love Dan and Dave. I am
ot in love with him. There is a world of difference
etween the two as I tried to make him see when
e asked me to go away with him."

"He what?" Matt asked very softly.

"He asked me to divorce you." She sighed. "Go
way with him before you came home from
cotland."

"That rotten bastard," he snarled viciously.
When I get through with him he'll consider
imself lucky to get a job as day-laborer. That
eaky—"

Katherine lay listening to Matt curse his brother
bscenely until she couldn't stand the sound of his
oice any longer and she almost screamed, "Matt,
op it. James is your brother and he loves you."

"Yeah, sure he does."

"He does, more than you could imagine. He told
e he respects you more than anyone he'd ever

met, but he couldn't stand by and watch—" She
stopped, appalled at herself. What was she saying?
What in the world had she started here?

"Well, finish it," he ordered. "He wouldn't
watch me do what?"

She hesitated, then whispered, "Destroy me."

"Destroy you? Is that what he thinks? Is that
what you think? Kate, I give you my word, I never
meant to harm you in any way."

Beyond the point of thinking or caring about
what she said, she murmured, "When a woman
falls in love, she places the weapon of her own
destruction in the man's hands. She has very little
control over what he does with it."

It was some seconds before she realized he had
gone absolutely still, not even seeming to breathe.
Then the content of her words struck her. Good
Lord, she had just made him aware of the fact that
he held that weapon. Wildly, she cast about in her
mind for words to negate what she'd said.
Suddenly he jackknifed to a sitting position,
grasped her shoulders, turned and drew her up
along his chest as he slowly lowered his head to
the bed. His upper arms resting on the bed, he
held her effortlessly over him, her face inches
above his own.

"You love me?" he demanded. "You are *in* love
with me?" She nodded mutely.

"I didn't hear you."

She shivered, but answered honestly. "Yes."

Wild triumph vied with pure male supremacy in
his gleaming eyes. In a tone of purring satisfaction
he rasped softly, "All deals off. No divorce.

Katherine. Not ever. You may run away, retreat as often as you like but I'll find you and bring you back, believe it. You are mine and you will remain mine for the rest of your life."

He lowered her gently to his chest, then his hands left her shoulders to cup her head. Fingers digging into her mass of black, unruly curls he drew her mouth to his in a hard, demanding, totally posessive kiss.

20

Sometime later, sated, at least for the moment, he lay on his side facing her, his arms loose around her. His mouth was at her forehead and he was amusing himself by softly blowing at an errant curl. She shivered, murmured, "I don't know why, but I feel at peace here. At home."

As Katherine surfaced from the effects of love-making she had decided to make at least a small bid for a measure of independence, now she said softly, "I'd like to go back to work." She waited for the blast of his anger and was startled when he laughed softly. "Okay. Do you want to go back to the office?"

"No," she answered in confusion for his lips had brushed lightly along her hairlilne. "I'd rather work at home to be close to Jon."

"Will you work in my study again?" A small shiver danced through her as his fingers made an outline of her ear.

"Yes."

"You love your work, don't you?" The words were barely audible, murmured as they were, through lips that slid along her temple.

"Yes." She sighed, her breathing growing shallow. Her hand had been resting lightly on his chest and without being conscious of it her fingers began sliding through the tightly curled auburn mat.

"Does it pay well?" he began, his lips making the slow run from her temple to the corner of her mouth. Then, "Ouch." Her little finger had tangled in the thick hair, but as she started to slide it away he murmured "No," his big hand covering hers, moving it sensuously over his chest. "Does it pay well?" he repeated, against the corner of her mouth.

"Yes," she moaned, her body alive and aching for him.

His tongue outlined the inside of her upper lip. Once. Twice. When he felt her shudder, digging her nails into his skin, he whispered, "You want me again, Kate?"

"Yes. Oh, Matt, yes."

Bliss. It was the only word Katherine could think of to describe the two days they'd been together in the mountains. And now, on the third morning, she stretched and purred like a contented, well-fed house cat. Matt was already up and out of the bedroom and she flung out her arms luxuriously, wrigglng her body back under the warmth of the covers. She felt well, relaxed, all tension gone and drowsily she thought over the last two days.

Matt had told the Darcys, that first day, to take a vacation and they had happily left to visit their daughter in Allentown. She cooked for him and picked up after him and, yesterday afternoon, had brought him sandwiches and a drink when he lay sprawled lazily in the huge arm chair watching a football game on TV. At the start of the second half she had passed too closely to his chair with a carelessly asked, "Who's winning?" Moving faster than she would have believed possible, he caught her around the waist and pulled her down beside him, growling, "Who the hell cares?" He had made violent love to her on that chair, in broad daylight and instead of being embarrassed, she had loved every minute of it.

She had called Tom, telling him without going into lengthy explanation that she was all right. Then Matt had talked to him. Forcefully at first. "I know she's your mother, Tom. But she is also my wife, and damn it, I'm your brother's father." Then more reassuringly, "Tom, I give you my word, there was not a word of truth in what you and your mother overheard. And I promise you those two half-witted cats will not hurt your mother again."

He had carried her, protesting loudly, into the shower, soaping her body caressingly, ordering her to return the compliment.

Katherine's cheeks went pink at that thought and her body tingled with remembered pleasure.

Just then Matt strode into the room saying cheerfully, "Coffee's ready if you're—" he paused, a slow smile curving his mouth at the sight of her pink cheeks and heavy lidded sleepy eyes. "Pleasant thoughts?"

The slow smile did crazy things to her heart beats and her cheeks went a deeper pink. She held her arms out to him invitingly, for the first time obeying an impulse in regard to him.

His eyes flicked, then in three strides he covered the distance between them, dropping full length on top of her, pinning her under the covers. His arms closed around her as he kissed her lightly, then lingeringly on the mouth. "You better be careful, my Kate. Or you'll be spending the better part of our last day here right where you are."

Katherine's arms loosened around his neck, the thought of going back to the house a chilling one. Matt lifted his head to stare at her. "Don't withdraw from me again, Katherine. Not here, not when we get home."

She moved her head agitatedly back and forth on the pillow. "Matt, I don't want to go back just yet, must we?"

"You know we must. We have to spend some time with the parents, both yours and mine. And then there's Beth's funny little New Year's Eve party."

"I hate Beth's parties," she cried almost childishly. "I'd rather go to Richard and Anne's."

"So would I," he murmured soothingly. "But I told Beth we'd be there, and we will. I think it's time Beth and I had a heart to heart. I've spoiled her, Kate, now I have to try and straighten her out." He paused, then added, "I've also got a few words for James."

Katherine felt a twinge of anxiety. "Matt, about James—"

"It's all right, Kate. I'm not going to banish him from the earth or anything. I'm just going to lay a few facts on him. We'll work it out, so don't worry about him."

He nuzzled the side of her neck and suddenly, even at the risk of ruining this new, more intimate relationship between them, Katherine had to have some answers. "Matt, will you answer a question for me?"

"Yes. If I can." His breath was a cool caress on her skin and she was almost sorry she'd said anything.

"Why?"

"What?"

"Why? I've been tormented for months by that word. Why? Why?"

His head came up with a jerk, slanting a sharp glance at her, he said quietly, "Go on."

She took a deep breath and plunged. "Why did you ask me to marry you? Why not a younger woman? Why me? Oh, your reasons at the time were perfectly logical but there's one catch. Except for that one short weekend here, I've never been asked to play hostess. I've never been asked to play the companion. And the way I shared your bed, up until September, doesn't bear thinking about."

Matt rolled away from her, sitting up on the

edge of the bed to light a cigarette, draw deeply on it. He was quiet so long Katherine grew nervous thinking, Oh, Lord, I have spoiled it. Sitting up in the middle of the bed, she drew her legs back and under herself, shaking fingers pleating then smoothing the sheer material of her nightgown. Her eyes followed him as he leaned to the night stand, snubbed out his cigarette and immediately lit another. When he turned to her, his face was remote, devoid of expression. Reaching across the bed, he placed the cigarette between her lips, then trailed one long finger down her now paled cheek. Voice as flat and expressionless as his face, he said, "I'm going to tell you a story, Kate. I hope you're comfortable for it's a very long story." Without waiting for a reply, he asked. "Do you remember when I asked you to be my date for the prom?"

The question threw her. What in the world could that possibly have to do with this? "Yes, but—"

"No buts. Do you want to know what I did after I walked away from you that day. Don't bother to answer, I'm going to tell you anyway. I went out into our small field of corn, lay down between two of the rows and cried."

Katherine's eyes widened in astonishment.

"Yes, for the first time in many years, I cried." A small, crooked smile of self-mockery twisted his lips as standing up, he picked up the ashtray, handed it to her, lit another cigarette, then went on. "I cried like a little kid whose favorite toy had been taken away." He paused to laugh harshly. "In a way that is what happened. I wanted you for a toy. At any rate I sure as hell wanted to play. And Kevin had taken you away. I knew, I had known almost from the first time I saw you, that you were for me. Why, I asked myself, didn't you know it? That was the last time I ever cried."

"Matt," Katherine's voice was tremulous, her thoughts disbelieving. Surely he hadn't married her simply because he couldn't have her for a playmate all those years ago.

His hand sliced through the air in a silencing motion. "I decided that whatever you and Kevin had going would eventually wear itself out. I'd bide my time, see what happened. I had things to do and I set about doing them. For two years, I worked and studied and worked and when I had a few free minutes I thought of you. Just before I started my third year in college, I had a day off at Labor Day, an unusual happening, I assure you. Mom sent me the papers regularly and I had a stack of them in my room. I settled down with them to catch up on the news from home and was just about halfway through the pile when I saw the write-up on your wedding. I never did finish those papers. I went out and got drunk. If I missed a few of the bars in that town it was not for lack of trying. At the last place I went in there was a dark-haired girl a few stools down the bar. I gave her the sign, she gave me the nod. She was with a man and when he left her to go to the men's room, I moved in. We were making our way out of the joint when he came back. He wasn't overjoyed with the idea of his girl taking off with me. He threw a punch, I threw a punch, a brawl started, spilled onto the sidewalk. At the first sign of sirens she dragged me away from the place. I was the cause of the damned thing and I was probably the only guy involved who didn't spend the night in the city lockup. She took me to her place and she took care of me. In every way. She cleaned up my cuts and bruises, she slept with me, then she mopped up the bathroom after I was sick all over it. I never got drunk again."

He had been pacing the room restlessly as he talked and now he stopped, rubbed the back of his neck, and said abruptly, "Christ, I'm thirsty. Sit tight, I'll go get the pot of coffee."

He was back in minutes carrying a tray which held the coffee pot, a jug of cream and two mugs. He set the tray on the night stand, plugged the pot's cord into a socket in the wall and filled the two mugs, a small smile on his lips. As he handed her one of the mugs he murmured, "She was a nice girl. Bright but uneducated, with a lousy paying job. She still is nice."

"You still see her?" Katherine's voice betrayed her feelings. Matt cocked a mocking brow at her. "Very often. But for business reasons only. She works for me, has, since I bought my first mill. Makes a good salary. Worth every penny of it, too." He lit a cigarette and sipped his coffee then mused. "Where was I? Oh, yeah, you married him. A fact of life that had to be faced. I did so, make up my mind to forget you and go back to work. I soon found that forgetting was not only hard, it was impossible. I lived with it. I managed. And as the years slid by it got easier. I could go weeks, without thinking of you."

"But you got married," she protested.

"Yes, I got married," he repeated, once again pacing, cup in hand. "I have to explain about Sherry. She was engaged to a friend of mine. We were together in Viet Nam, advisory personal. He got killed. I went to see her when I got home. She'd gone to pieces, literally fell apart. She needed someone. I was handy. Neither of us was under any illusions. She didn't love me. I didn't love her. But I liked her and she needed someone. Anyway, we got married. It couldn't last of course." He stopped to study the look on her face, then he grinned wryly. "Oh, it was a normal marriage in every way, including sex, but we were growing in different directions. When we split, after two years, she was stable, ready to face living again. I still see her too. She's married again, has two kids, a happy, contented woman."

"But you got nothing from the marriage," she cried.

"Wrong. For two years I was kept so busy either working or with Sherry; there was very little time left to torment myself with thoughts about you."

Katherine's throat went dry and she gulped down what remained of her coffee, grimacing, for it had grown cold. Without asking, he took the mug from her hands, refilled it and handed it back. He started talking again as he refilled his own mug. "You see, Kate, I was never free of the thoughts for long. Whether I was alone or with—ah—someone."

"Like Rosalie?"

He shot her a glittering look. "How do you know about Rosalie?"

"I met her."

"Where? When?"

"Beth invited her to the house for lunch. In September."

His eyes and mouth went hard with anger. "The bitch," he said softly, then added, "Beth, not Rosalie." He studied her thoughtfully, then added, "Rosalie's the reason you came up here in September?" She nodded.

"What did she say to you?" he demanded.

"That of *all* your mistresses she was probably the only one you considered marrying—"

"Wrong," he interrupted. "I never considered it with any of them. What else?"

She hesitated, then said quickly, "If she'd been a little smarter she'd have become pregnant, and then you would have married her."

"On that point she's right. I would have."

"How many others were there, Matt?" she asked in a small voice. He laughed easily. "Not nearly as many as you've been led to believe there were. Actually there were four. That's really not many over a twenty-three year span. But understand this, Katherine, whether it was during the periods I was with one of them or whether I was alone, there always came the nights when I could no longer keep the thoughts at bay. On those nights I was usually overworked or overtired or both. Lord, Kate, I probably could have been arrested for the things I did to you in my mind on those nights. I tormented myself until I could have cut my throat with wanting you."

"Oh, Matt."

"I'm not finished. As I said before, those nights happened less often as the years passed. It got easier, until I walked into Richard's house that New Year's Day, then it started all over again. You wouldn't believe how close you came to being kidnapped when I drove you into town the next day. When you told me Kevin was dead I decided then and there, by using fair means or foul, I was going to have you. I knew you didn't particularly like me or approve of me, but I wasn't about to let that stop me. I bided my time, waiting for the right moment. That moment came the night I proposed. You see, I knew the mental state you were in. I had lunch with Carol that day. She told me she was worried about you, the depression you were in. That's why I was waiting outside your office for you, insisted we have dinner together. That's why I proposed that night. And that's why I wanted a quick wedding. I knew you'd shake yourself out of that depression before long and when you did, probably tell me to get lost. Do you understand what I'm saying, Katherine? Have I answered your question?"

Katherine's eyes felt gritty, her throat hurt and her head ached. "Yes, I understand." Her voice was hoarse, uneven. "While you were still little more than a boy you wanted a girl. Not being able to have that girl made you want her more. As you grew older you brooded about it and as the years passed the brooding became an obsession. Finally, as a mature man you decided the only way to end that obsession was to have the girl, now a free woman. Have you succeeded in ending your obsession, Matt?"

His voice raw, he answered, "Have I been acting like a man who's ended his obsession?"

Bowing her head, she closed her eyes against the hot stinging tears that overflowed her lids, burning like acid as they ran down her face. He was beside her in an instant, his hand lifting her head to face him. His voice was an agonized rasp. "Kate, baby. Don't cry. Good Christ, I wait twenty-five years for the chance to tell you I love you and when I get it, I blow it. I love you. I always have loved you. Will you stop crying? You scared me enough the other night with your tears, you know that don't you?"

Uncertain if he was teasing or not she stared at him wide eyed, shaking her head. "Well you did. Almost as much as when you had Jon."

"What do you mean?" She gulped.

"I mean I was afraid, that's what I mean. Why do you think I wasn't too enthusiastic when you told me you were pregnant?"

"I thought you didn't want our baby."

"Not want him? My sweet love, I've always wanted our baby. But I thought it was too late, and I lived with fear the whole time you carried him. When Jack called and told me you were in the hospital, I thought I'd go out of my mind. You had fallen twice, you weren't due. The fact that you didn't care enough for me to call me yourself didn't help much. I kept thinking, she hates me and she's going to die having my child."

Instead of stopping, the flow of tears increased and leaning forward she rested her forehead against his chest sobbing, "I wanted you with me so badly and I thought you didn't care."

Dipping his head he caught her mouth with his, lifting her head as he raised his own, pressing her gently back against the bed. Moving his mouth off hers he slid his parted lips slowly up one cheek and down the other, drinking her tears. In between short, hard, salty kisses, he whispered, "Not care? Not care? I wonder if I dare tell you how much I care? I lied to you a little while ago when I said I never cried or got drunk again. I did both the night you had Jon. I didn't cry like a kid or get falling down drunk. No, I wept in sheer relief that it was over, you were safe, then I got quietly stoned. Dare I tell you that since our wedding night I've been ragingly jealous of a man that's been dead for twenty years? I was the first man since Kevin, wasn't I?"

"Yes."

"I knew it. I wanted you so badly, love. And when you turned your head away I was sure it was because you couldn't bear the thought of any other man touching you. I tried to stop myself, but I had waited so long, wanted so long. God, I felt like an animal and yet I could only go so long without coming to you again. The jealousy of Kevin started that first night. I had never felt it before. Tell me Kate. Were you still mourning him or was it that you just couldn't stand me?"

"It was neither." She answered truthfully. "I was simply afraid. It had been so long and I felt so inadequate. For some time after Kevin died I really couldn't bear the thought of another man touching me. And then later I couldn't bear the thought of going to bed with a man, just to go to bed with a man. Do you understand?"

"Yes. You felt you had to be in love with a man before you could give yourself to him."

She nodded. "That's why I was so frightened that first night. I wasn't in love with you then. At least I don't think I was."

"And you are now? You're sure?" His voice held an odd fearful note.

Her hands went to his face, holding it firmly as she stared steadily into his eyes. "Matt, I loved Kevin. But it was a very young love. An immature love. Never, never with him did I feel the terrible pain I've felt thinking you didn't love me. Or the unbelievable joy that's filled me since you told me you do. Yes, darling, I'm absolutely sure."

Her hands still held his head and now she drew it down to her. Her lips moved in small, soft kisses over his face then sought his mouth. She heard the breath catch in his throat as she slid her tongue into his mouth then his arms crushed her to him, the muscles taut and hard.

When at last his mouth released hers, she was breathless and still her mouth caught his again. All the sweet passion singing through her veins, the aching need of him, the overwhelming love she felt for him, was transmitted to him from her mouth into his. She tore her mouth from his, and her lips found the rapidly beating pulse at his throat.

Drawing his head back he stared at her, eyes blazing with love. Grinning wickedly, he teased. "You're a beautifully bad woman, my love, the effect you have on me is almost indecent, and I crave it like a narcotic." He kissed her hard, fast, then whispered against her lips, "I love you, my Kate. If you ever run away from home again, take me with you."

JOAN HOHL

WINDOW ON YESTERDAY

Author Of More Than 5 Million Books In Print!

"Exciting...the sparks really sizzle!"
—Romantic Times

Her mind ablaze with thoughts of handsome historian Sean Halloran, Alycia Matlock can think of nothing besides their shared interest in history, their uncanny sense of being kindred souls, and their desire to spend their lives together. Oblivious to the furious rainstorm around her as she drives to Williamsburg, Alycia doesn't notice a truck veering toward her—until it is too late.

When Alycia comes to, she is still in Virginia, but the year is 1777! Although Alycia can't tell if she is caught in a time warp or some incredible dream, her situation heats up considerably when she meets Major Patrick Halloran—a virtual double of her beloved Sean. And while Alycia gives herself freely to Patrick, she can't forget her love from another time and place....

_3620-7   ·$3.99 US/$4.99 CAN

JOAN HOHL WINDOW ON TODAY

Author Of More Than 5 Million Books In Print!

"Ms. Hohl creates a lot of sizzle and spark!"
—*Romantic Times*

With her new art gallery a hit and her two best friends in town to celebrate, Karla Janowitz couldn't be happier. The absolute last thing she needs in her life is a man to complicate it. Then accomplished artist Jared Cradowg shows up—gorgeous, determined, and certain that he and Karla are fated to be together. Karla finds him almost impossible to resist.

Though rumors of his womanizing abound, Karla accepts his invitation to an art-inspired tour of Arizona. Against the magnificent background of Arizona's deserts and glorious canyons, they discover their passion for art is far surpassed by the passion they have for each other.

_3653-3 $3.99 US/$4.99 CAN

DANCE of the FLAME

ELAINE BARBIERI

Elaine Barbieri's romances are "powerful...fascinating...storytelling at its best!"
—*Romantic Times*

Exiled to a barren wasteland, Sera will do anything to regain the kingdom that is her birthright. But the hard-eyed warrior she saves from death is the last companion she wants for the long journey to her homeland.

To the world he is known as Death's Shadow—as much a beast of battle as the mighty warhorse he rides. But to the flame-haired healer, his forceful arms offer a warm haven, and he swears his throbbing strength will bring her nothing but pleasure.

Sera and Tolin hold in their hands the fate of two feuding houses with an ancient history of bloodshed and betrayal. But no matter what the age-old prophecy foretells, the sparks between them will not be denied, even if their fiery union consumes them both.

_3793-9 $5.99 US/$6.99 CAN

An Angel's Touch

Time Heals
SUSAN COLLIER

Tired of her nagging relatives, Maeve Fredrickson asks for the impossible: to be a thousand miles and a hundred years away from them. Then a heavenly being grants her wish, and she awakes in frontier Montana.

Saved from the wilderness by a handsome widower, Maeve loses her heart to her rescuer—and her temper over the antics of his three less-than-angelic children. As her angel prods her to fight for Seth, Maeve can only pray for the strength to claim a love made in paradise.

_52030-3 $4.99 US/$5.99 CAN

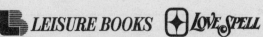